Praise for *Swimming for Beginners*

'*Swimming for Beginners* is the perfect summer read. It's funny, smart and will break your heart a little (and put it back together again). The characters jump off the page and the dialogue fizzes with humour, as control-freak Loretta finds herself making room for six-year-old Phoebe in her life. A compelling page-turner that shows you what happens when you think your life is all mapped then fate intervenes. Funny, poignant, romantic and uplifting – this book has everything. I loved it!'
**Eleni Kyriacou, author of *She Came to Stay* and
*The Unspeakable Acts of Zina Pavlou***

'Please meet my new favourite book. I roared with laughter and wept buckets for Phoebe and Loretta. So much heart on each beautifully written page and one to read again and again.'
'Touched me so deeply. Loretta and Phoebe are incredibly well portrayed and sharply observed and I already miss them!'
Jessica Ryn, author of *The Extraordinary Hope of Dawn Brightside*

'A heartfelt tale of love, loss and coming back to life.'
'Moving, insightful and evocative.'
'Brilliantly observed – a touching story about finding love in the most unlikely of places.'
Gillian Harvey, author of *Perfect on Paper*

'From the moment we met Phoebe in her fairy wings and sparkly boots, this book swam away with my heart. Poignant and uplifting, it addresses loss, sadness and the horrible feeling of never quite fitting in, but with a lightness of touch and humour that makes it a pleasure to read.'
Eleanor Ray, author of *Everything is Beautiful*

'I loved spending time in Loretta and Phoebe's world. Brilliantly funny, incredibly touching and so relatable. Another fabulous book from Nicola Gill.'
Louise Hare, author of *This Lovely C───*

'Heart breaking and life affirm───
'As a parent, this book ab──
comp──
'Gill's writing is funny, punchy ───── ─up.'
**Tim Ewins, aut───

'I love, love, LOVED this book! A massive great hug of a story: warm, funny and big-hearted. Uplifting fiction at its very best!'
Louise Mumford, author of *Sleepless*

'I ADORED it. It's original, refreshing and full of soul. A truly unforgettable read that's heartbreaking and spirit lifting in equal measure, with characters and life lessons that will stay with me forever.'
Helly Acton, author of *The Shelf* and *Begin Again*

'This story was so compelling and easy to read, it was hard to put down. The witty writing and pacing keep the story moving and I devoured it in two sittings.'
Sharon M. Peterson, author of *The Do-Over*

'I loved this book which made me both laugh and cry, often at the same time. Little Phoebe and the wonderfully quirky Loretta captured my heart from the very beginning with all their imperfections, social awkwardness and complex emotions. Nicola Gill has expertly crafted a page-turning, emotional and relatable novel which will warm every heart. The perfect book to curl up with. I absolutely adored it.'
Louise Fein, author of *People Like Us*

'A Nicola Gill book is always a treat and I loved this so much – laugh out loud funny, warm-hearted and feelgood, with characters that jump off the page. Loretta and Phoebe are the kind of characters you miss as soon as you turn the last page.'
Frances Quinn, author of *The Smallest Man*

'I adored *Swimming for Beginners*. It's both laugh-out-loud funny and incredibly touching in equal measure. Nicola Gill has created such fabulous characters in Loretta and Phoebe, and I shall be thinking about them for a long time to come. Wonderful.'
Charlotte Levin, author of *If I Can't Have You*

'Nicola Gill never disappoints: funny, pithy and always satisfying.'
Anstey Harris, author of *Where We Belong*

'A beautiful read full of heart and depth.'
Nina Pottell, *Prima Magazine*

Also by Nicola Gill

We Are Family
The Neighbours

NICOLA GILL

SWIMMING FOR BEGINNERS

Bedford
Square
Publishers

First published in the UK in 2023 by
Bedford Square Publishers Ltd, London, UK
bedfordsquarepublishers.co.uk
@bedsqpublishers

ISBN
978-1-915798-70-1 (Paperback)
978-1-915798-71-8 (eBook)

4 6 8 10 9 7 5 3

Typeset in Garamond MT Pro by Palimpsest Book Production Limited,
Falkirk, Stirlingshire

Printed in Great Britain by CPI Group (UK) Ltd, Croydon CR0 4YY

MIX
Paper | Supporting
responsible forestry
FSC
www.fsc.org   FSC® C171272

For Mum. Love you always.

Chapter One

Big social gatherings are like running – I know they're good for me but, God, they're painful.

I had to take deep breaths before walking in here tonight, tell myself five times that it would be okay and I wasn't going to bolt home. So tempting to get in my pyjamas and lose myself in a book, though. I could even pick up a takeaway.

Samira only invited me tonight because she had to. We're part of a team of three at work and, as she's genuinely friendly with Zoe, she had little choice but to include me. I got the pity invite, in other words.

Normally, I would have pretended I was busy, but Samira happened to catch me in a rare 'I should make more of an effort' moment of weakness. This wasn't unrelated to the fact I'd just had a call with my mother, the main purpose of which seemed to be telling me how she worries I'm 'all work, work, work' and 'never seem to have any fun'.

So, here I am gulping metallic-tasting Prosecco out of a penis straw, trying not to mind that the two people I know said cheery 'hellos' when I arrived but then went back to the conversations they were having. This left me to make small talk with strangers which is very much not my forte. I never see the point. I don't

1

need to know what someone does for a living, I'm perfectly well aware that it's warm for this time of year and I don't have a funny story about how I know Samira.

I've done okay so far, though. I negotiated the introductions (wondering why so many of the women have absurdly puffy lips and eyebrows that look as if they've been daubed on with felt tip), put on my pink 'hen' sash and tiara without complaint and managed to be very discreet about sanitising my hands under the table. (Why do people insist on shaking hands? Nice to meet you, let me transfer microbes all over you.)

Harriet, a small loud thing who organised tonight, tells me I'm lucky because even though I'm late, there's still time for me to have my tarot cards read.

'Oh, no reading for me, thanks.'

'*Everyone* has had one,' Harriet barks. 'That side room over there.'

I rise from my seat. There's no point making a fuss. Or thinking about how I could be halfway through a lamb pasanda right now.

Anne the tarot reader has a doughy face and tiny dark eyes like currants. She is dressed like an estate agent and exudes very little in the way of psychic powers (not that I believe in such things).

'Do you have a specific question about your future?'

There is one question about my future I'm obsessed with right now and that's whether I'm going to get this big promotion I'm chasing. There's no way I'm opening my heart to a complete stranger, though. 'No thanks.'

Anne starts moving the cards around and spouting nonsense. 'Blah, blah, blah aura… blah, blah, blah energy… blah, blah, blah you've experienced pain in the past…' (Who hasn't?) 'Ah

2

ha,' she says, turning over the final card. 'I see a child in your future.'

It's all I can do not to laugh in her face. She must have thought she was on to a safe bet saying that to a woman in her thirties who's wearing an engagement ring, but if there is one thing I'm 100 per cent certain of, it's that I don't want kids. Why on earth would I take a blowtorch to my life like that? 'Err, I don't think so.'

'It's the Empress card,' Anne says sullenly, rapping her fore-finger on it.

I glance down at the card which depicts a woman in what looks like a winceyette nightie with a crown and sceptre. 'Riiiight.'

Anne's eyes flash and she draws in a deep breath before sweeping up the cards.

'Bye then,' I say.

I go back to the group.

'What did she say?' Jenna asks.

'That I was going to have a baby. Which is absolutely ridiculous—'

'Aww, lovely,' Jenna says. She whips out her phone and starts showing me pictures of her baby. He looks like a potato.

'He's gorgeous.'

It's the correct response and Jenna's eyes light up. I feel like I'm on a gameshow and the buzzer has just sounded: Score!

Jenna starts telling me about the potato's nappy rash. The 'poor little mite' has a bottom that's red raw; she's been to the doctor three times now but none of the creams they have given her have made a jot of difference.

And people find *me* dull.

My mind drifts to the meeting I have in New York next week with a prospective client. I am very excited about it, especially as Greg, my boss, made no secret of the fact this could be the clincher in terms of my promotion. I picture myself in the conference room. The world is neat and ordered, I am giving the presentation of my life, I am surrounded by people who don't talk about nappy rash.

A hyena-ish laugh from further down the table snaps me back into the present.

Jenna is *still* talking about the nappy rash. She feels so responsible because, if she hadn't tried towelling nappies, none of this would have happened. It's all very well worrying about the environment but what about poor little Zack?

It strikes me, not for the first time, that I have no idea why our society venerates motherhood so much. Why everything, from newspaper articles to TV commercials, peddles the idea that a halo appears somewhere around the third trimester, turning hitherto normal women into the epitome of selflessness.

In my experience, mothers are just as shitty as the rest of us and I'm pretty sure Jenna would shoot a polar bear in the face if the trade-off was Zack's bottom being restored to its former levels of health.

I don't say this, of course. I've learned it's almost always a good idea to keep my thoughts to myself. She's a quiet one, people say, or she likes to keep herself to herself.

I've had to work on this skill. I changed school often as a child and every time I made myself the solemn promise that I'd learn from previous experiences. I'd be more like my oh-so popular sister. I would edit between brain and mouth. This would always work for a few days and then something (me) would slip out.

I tried to look like everyone else too. You'd think that wouldn't be hard in school uniform but, somehow, I always managed to get it wrong. My hemline was too long, my bunches too babyish, my shoes too 'sad'.

I tune back into the conversation to see we have reached the obligatory oversharing part of the evening.

Harriet blurts out that her husband never goes down on her.

Jenna says she isn't sure if having a baby wasn't a massive mistake.

Kate admits she hates her 'dream job' in TV production.

Christ, it isn't even 10 o'clock! I sit back on the red velvet banquette, sip my Prosecco and try to smile.

Why is this emotional incontinence considered a good thing? I don't want to open my heart here any more than I do on Instagram. I don't believe a 'good cry' ever makes people feel better, think a problem shared is often a problem doubled and know the world would be a far nicer place if people learned to control their anger.

'You're very quiet, Loretta.' Harriet's eyes are locked on me.

'Oh, y'know.'

Harriet cocks her head to the side in the manner of a small dog. I squash down a wave of irritation. I don't have some big secret I want to discuss and if I did, I wouldn't pick to share it with Harriet who I barely know (even if I do now know that she always showers before sex and keeps everything very tidy down there).

'When are we going dancing?' Farida says. 'It's not a proper hen party if we don't have a boogie.'

I murmur my approval. At least if we go dancing people will stop behaving as if they are on *The Jeremy Kyle Show*.

'Maybe we could try that new place in Frith Street?' Harriet says.

Maybe? Has Harriet not decided where we're going? If I'd been in charge of tonight, every part of the itinerary would have been planned to within an inch of its life. Not that I would ever be in charge of anyone's hen night. I have friends (sort of) but I'm certainly not anyone's best friend.

Hmm, that's not strictly true – I may be Robert's best friend but only in a de facto sense because he generally 'doesn't have time for friendships'. Robert is my fiancé, a statement that, four months after his proposal, still seems improbable. I say proposal but there was no going down on one knee or single moment. We just started talking about how we'd been together a few years and it made sense to think about pooling expenses. Plus, there are considerable tax breaks when you're married.

'Let's have another round here, first,' Harriet says.

I excuse myself to go to the toilet, not so much because I have to pee but because I need a few minutes locked in the cubicle in blissful solitude. Does anybody actually enjoy events like this? They're just so exhausting.

I sit on the toilet long after I've finished my wee, savouring the silence. They have extremely unusual wallpaper in here: lots of illustrations of people in different sexual positions. Perhaps that would be a good thing to talk about when I return to the hens? Something funny and light and suitably risqué. I know I'd find a way to make it uncomfortable, though.

When I come out of the cubicle, Zoe is outside brushing her hair. Zoe is the closest thing I have to an actual friend at work. I like her and she seems not to mind me. She sees me in the mirror and smiles. 'Hey you.'

'Hey. You having a good night?'

'I really am. What about you?'

'Yeah, great.'

Zoe is staring at me, and I realise she probably thinks I'm washing my hands for too long. What she doesn't realise is that most people don't wash their hands for nearly long enough. It needs to be a minimum of forty seconds with lots of hot water and soap and you need to wash between all your fingers and right up your wrists.

'Did you look at the client feedback on the creative work?' I say, over the sound of the hand dryer.

'Let's not talk work,' Zoe says.

Her tone is light but I feel rebuked. I got it wrong. As usual.

'You're not going to try to sneak away early tonight, are you?' Zoe says.

'Of course not.'

We go back to the table, and I see Jenna has moved seats. Despite myself, I feel a little pang of hurt, especially as I made such an effort to look interested as she droned on about potato-baby. I am now sitting next to Farida who smiles awkwardly and asks me how I know Samira.

'We work together.'

'At the *ad agency*?' Farida sounds incredulous. I'm used to this. Farida, like many others, can't envisage me in a job that screams 'people person'. They don't realise that work me is a very different creature. I interact well with clients and, to a lesser extent, colleagues – it's life's unscripted moments I find hard.

'Cool,' Farida says, eventually managing to close her mouth.

I squash the urge to tell her I'm actually very successful at work. That I was in AdTalk's *Thirty To Watch Under Thirty*.

Harriet taps the side of her glass with a spoon and rises to her feet. 'Samira, as your maid of honour, I wanted to say a few words. I first met Samira three years ago, although I feel like I've known her my whole life.'

There is a chorus of 'awws'.

'When we first met, neither of us was in a good place. We'd both been dumped.'

A series of boos.

'We were at rock bottom.'

Rock bottom? Really?

'We have shared a journey to wellness.'

A 'journey to wellness'? Who does this woman think she is? Gwyneth sodding Paltrow? She does seem like the sort to steam her vagina, although if earlier revelations are anything to go on, steam is the only thing blowing up there.

'I quickly discovered you were one of the kindest, most loving and most generous people I've ever had the privilege to know.'

Lots of the women have tears in their eyes.

'And one of the strongest.'

That just goes to show that Harriet doesn't really know Samira that well at all because, while I'm the first to say that she is kind and big-hearted (look at her inviting me this evening), I would not describe her as particularly strong. The only person at work I've seen cry more than her is Maddie, and she'd win gold in the weeping Olympics.

'Not a day goes by when I don't think how lucky I am to have you in my life.' Harriet's voice cracks. 'When I don't thank the universe for bringing me this awesome, inspirational, wonderful woman.'

Jeez, maybe they ought to get married?

'Tom is the luckiest man in the world.'

Everyone breaks into applause which I join in with a beat too late.

'We love you, Samira!' Harriet raises her glass aloft.

Lucky I'm never going to be anyone's maid of honour. I definitely couldn't do that kind of speech. It was hard enough listening to it.

Drinks are poured and conversations started. Suddenly, I become aware I have zoned out and haven't been contributing at all. This is against the rules and a wave of panic churns in my stomach. It's okay to let other people do most of the heavy lifting when it comes to conversation, indeed most are only too happy to talk about themselves, but you have to appear engaged by throwing in the odd 'umm' and 'yeah' and laughing in the right places. Sometimes, you have to initiate a conversation too – at least once in an evening.

My mind goes horribly blank. Shall I talk about the unfolding crisis in Afghanistan? No, wrong vibe. Shall I talk about the book I'm reading? None of them look like readers. Maybe I should tell a joke? Urghh, what am I, six?

I turn to Farida. 'So, you like your eyebrows very pronounced then?'

Chapter Two

I'm standing in the airport check-in queue when a suitcase is wheeled over my foot. I look up to see a slightly feral-looking child dragging a bright orange suitcase and trotting along next to a woman who is an older version of her.

The pair of them are chattering away, oblivious to the fact I've lost what feels like a layer of skin off the top of my foot.

Irritation fizzes through my veins as I watch them walk away. I was already grouchy. Not only am I nervous about this crunch meeting in New York, but I'm still smarting about the performance appraisal I had on Tuesday. I'd been looking forward to it, and I realise that makes me sound weird, but I know I give the agency everything I have. So, I was pretty chipper as Greg ushered me into his office. It's not called his office because officially Burnett White is an open-plan agency. However, Greg commandeered that meeting room about four years ago to 'make a few calls' and it's been his ever since. This has always made me deeply envious. I want walls, to be able to shut everyone out. All that inane chatter about what they did the night before or whether they fancy sushi or burritos for lunch (a conversation that usually starts while they are shovelling their toast or porridge into their mouths).

I reach the front of the check-in queue, where an uninterested-looking woman with lipstick on her teeth takes my passport and asks if I packed my own bags.

Greg started the appraisal by talking about my strengths and successes. Then he steepled his fingers and said it was time to discuss my weaknesses.

I knew exactly what he was going to say: I work too hard; I need to be better at delegating.

'In a smallish agency like ours, it's important you really mesh with your team.'

What?

What the fucking what?

Greg was talking again. I watched his fleshy lips move but I could barely take in the words. I caught phrases like 'seamlessly working with your colleagues', 'cohesiveness' and 'morale'.

And that's when it hit me like a punch to the solar plexus. Greg was saying people don't like me.

Suddenly, I was fourteen again and my mum was telling me she worries I 'don't seem to have many friends'. She can't understand it, she tells me. She is such a social person and so are my dad and my sister. Why am I so... so... She pauses, seemingly unable to find the word. She wishes I could make a 'little more effort'. I bite back the urge to scream she has no idea of the effort it takes to get through every single school day.

Greg's comments last Tuesday stung every bit as much. Work is my safe place. The thing I'm good at.

I walk through the busy airport, the memories making sweat prickle my armpits and nausea start to rise.

Greg started spouting some nonsense about how dolphins like to swim with dolphins and how it's important to be part of

11

the pod. Then he wrapped up the meeting all smiles, as if he hadn't just casually hurled a grenade into my world. Fury coursed through my veins. My previous boss Paul would never have given me an appraisal like this. He didn't require me to be a sodding dolphin.

Now, I could picture Greg taking this promotion away from me. See him giving it to Maddie instead.

Maddie meshes with the team; swims with the pod. They don't appear to mind that she frequently lets her personal life affect her work. She seems to lurch from one relationship drama to the next and is often to be found crying in the toilets. Just the other day, I walked in to find her weeping as she applied the M&S grapefruit hand cream that HR had placed in there as 'a little morale booster'. I had no choice but to ask if she was okay and was rewarded by a blow-by-blow account of how her fledgling relationship seemed to be going wrong. How she'd told the guy she loved him the night before, but he hadn't said it back. And I soothed and cajoled and fetched more loo roll, but inside my head there was a voice screaming: YOU NEVER SAY 'I LOVE YOU' FIRST!

The queue to go through security is long and snaking. The child who wheeled her suitcase over my foot is just ahead of me. My foot is still sore, and I feel a flash of annoyance, although I guess I am partly to blame for wearing flip-flops. Robert did point out they weren't a very practical choice. 'What happens if the plane crashes and you need to escape quickly?'

Robert is someone who considers all eventualities. That's why he'd never travel to India or try to park in the West End on a Saturday night.

The child is chattering away non-stop to her mother and appears to be unable to stand still. Her outfit is as loud as she is. She is wearing a bright green dungaree dress, a yellow top, hot pink tights and, just in case this ensemble might be a little understated, silver boots and glittery fairy wings.

A headache starts to pulse behind my eyes. Strangely enough, I have always loved airports, drinking in the sense of excitement and possibility, but this bit, while undeniably important, is never fun. The staff whose piercing stares make you feel guilty even though you've done nothing wrong, the chugging down water you don't want because it's time to dump your liquids, everything from your tampons to your breath freshener being caught on camera for all the world to see.

The queue is moving particularly slowly today and I squash down a wave of impatience. At least I'm not in a hurry. I always leave plenty of time – just watching a stranger have to run towards a departure gate gives me palpitations.

Robert is exactly the same. He often jokes he knew I was a keeper the minute he realised I was the only person in the world who likes to arrive at the airport as early as he does. We both think you need to eliminate the possibility of being derailed by something unexpected.

Like my appraisal has derailed my life.

The hours directly after leaving Greg's office are blurry in my mind, but I do know that evening I bolted home the second I could, grateful that Robert was out and not there to witness the shuddering, snotty mess that was curled in a foetal position on the bed.

When I was eight years old, I started at my third new school in as many years. I was frenziedly pursuing Martha Baker and her posse. This caused nausea to churn in my belly and my eczema to bleed and weep. Suddenly, it dawned on me that it would be infinitely less painful to just stop trying. This wasn't a conscious thing – I was only eight – but more of an instinctive reflex. I was a warthog hiding from the lions.

My new way of existing in the world calcified as I grew older. I would always prefer people thought me standoffish rather than desperate. I had occasional moments when I broke cover, of course. At uni, I managed to make a few friends, mainly other 'peripherals'. Dating was also surprisingly okay, since many men seemed happy to put up with you being a bit 'weird' as long as you'd sleep with them. In my working life, there have definitely been times when I've felt like one of the gang, especially if there was a particularly intense project to force me and my coworkers together. Zoe, Samira and I have definitely bonded a little since working on the Kitkins account together, for example. I do have an almost uncanny ability to say the wrong thing or misread social cues, though. I guess lack of practice makes very far from perfect.

By the morning after the appraisal, I was done licking my wounds and ready to fight back. As I sat on the tube, I opened my Moleskine notebook, turned to that day's to-do list and made some additions:

Sign up for agency softball
Listen to Pete's boring stories (no noise-cancelling headphones!)
Have lunch with someone
Ask Maddie how it's going with her boyfriend

To mix metaphors, it was time to stop being a warthog and be a dolphin instead.

I would treat this like any other work assignment. I would set goals and, every day, I would assign myself tasks to help me to achieve those goals. Operation Mesh With The Team was underway.

Orange suitcase kid has broken into a loud tuneless song. It isn't doing a great deal for my headache – or presumably the sanity of anyone in the vicinity – and I wait for the mother to tell the girl to be quiet. She does no such thing, however, instead staring at her offspring with unabashed delight. Dear God, people can be so blind when it comes to their kids. It's like that woman at the hen do being convinced her potato-baby was beautiful.

'Hi,' the child says, catching me looking at her. 'I'm Phoebe and I'm going to Spain to meet my mum's friend who has a little girl who is just a bit older than me and called Skye and it's the first time ever I've been on an aeroplane.'

'That's nice.'

The child nods earnestly, her fairy wings jiggling. 'Where are you going?'

'New York. America.'

Her eyes widen. 'That's very far, Sophie P in my class at school went there once and she told me that, and she also said they have cheese that comes in a tube – like toothpaste but cheese!'

The mum, who has huge, tired eyes and spectacularly messy hair, smiles at me before turning to put her bags into the plastic crates. All the while, the child keeps talking at her. Can she have a new sticker book for the plane? She's very hungry now. Sophie P has been to Spain once and she said it was hot.

No wonder the mother looks so tired. I can't imagine ever having a child. Of dealing with all the mess and chaos they bring.

When it's my turn, I place my laptop, phone, and bag in a crate. I walk through the scanner, my mind drifting to the task ahead of me when I reach New York. The client owns an upmarket group of private members' clubs. The sort of places you might describe as bougie if you weren't of the opinion that people who use that word are punchable. They are just about to open their first London outpost. Officially, they are happy with their existing ad agency. Unofficially, they have agreed to talk to

Burnett White. Not a proper full-on meeting, they said, that would be disloyal to their current agency, just a 'chat'. They stipulated they didn't want a whole team turning up in New York, just one person. Something I'm sure will be hugely comforting to the incumbent agency when they discover an account worth millions has walked out of the door.

I scoop my belongings out of the plastic crate. I *have* to ace this meeting. As the thought registers, another immediately collides with it: the middle section of my presentation is flabby. It can be fixed, of course, but I feel a rush of self-hatred at having had it wrong in the first place, especially as I have already shown it to Greg. No point learning to be a dolphin who swims with the pod if I can't even get my job right. I don't have time to dwell on this thought, though, as I turn and suddenly find myself flying through the air, before landing flat on my face on the filthy floor.

'Whoopsie,' comes a small voice. 'You fell over Timmy the tiger.'

From my new vantage point, I can see that the small orange case has black stripes and eyes.

'Are you okay?' the child's mother says.

'I'm fine.' First my foot and now this. I need to get as far away from this child and her case as possible. I stand up and dust myself off. I feel embarrassed somehow, although I can't think why.

'Are you sure? You went down pretty hard.'

'Absolutely fine,' I say, rubbing my throbbing wrist.

'Oh look, your lovely white shirt is all dirty now.' The woman turns to her daughter. 'Phoebe, sweetheart, you really are a hazard with that thing. You need to be a bit more careful.'

'It's fine,' I say quickly. 'Honestly, I should have been looking where I was going.'

16

The woman rakes her hand through her messy hair. 'Can I at least buy you a cup of coffee or something to say sorry?'

I can't think of anything worse than having to make awkward small talk with the woman and her child. 'That's very kind of you—'

'I don't drink coffee but Mummy does and she says most grown-ups do as well which I think is weird because I tried some once and it was very yucky.'

The child seems to speak without full stops or even discernible pauses to breathe.

'I've a few things I need to buy from the shops,' I say.

'We're going to have our lunch at the airport,' Phoebe says. 'Even though it won't really be lunchtime, but we'll be hungry you see so we're going to have some, and Mummy says I can have whatever I want but I must have one healthy thing too. Are you going to have some lunch before you go on your aeroplane to go to America?'

'Umm, probably.'

'I need to do a wee first before anything else because I really need one quite badly so we have to go now and if I don't go quite soon, I might even do a wee on the floor even though I'm not a baby at all 'cos I'm six.'

'TMI, Phoebe,' her mum says, laughing. She turns to me. 'Sorry about tripping you up. Have a good time in New York.'

Chapter Three

My first priority was to get as far away as possible from the girl, her mother and their offers of coffee. Once I'd done that, I immediately found a café and started to fix that middle section of my presentation.

I am slightly put off by a couple at the next table who are sucking each other's faces. Why do people do that in public? Robert and I have never been like that. I think back to our date night last Wednesday evening. I may not be that socially aware, but I did clock the waiter's look of pity when he brought our wine: you're one of *those* couples.

Robert and I were both glued to our phones at the time. Which isn't de rigueur when you're dining in somewhere a review described as 'London's most romantic restaurant'. When there's a soft colour palette, flickering candlelight and cosy nooks, you're supposed to have your eyes and hands fixed adoringly on each other and not your inbox.

They say opposites attract but the two of us are the same person. At the hen do, Samira went on a drunken ramble about Tom and said that one of the things she loved most about him was that he constantly surprises her. I don't get that at all. What

I love about Robert is that he doesn't surprise me. I know exactly where I am with him.

We both hate big parties, musicals and people who go travelling and then bore the hell out of you talking about how they found themselves, when really all they did was put off grown-up life for a year to be off their faces on magic mushrooms on a Thai beach.

The couple at the next table are really ramping things up now. I'll say one thing for the pair of them, which is they're extremely bendy. That said, they're quite putting me off my superfood salad. I have a well-calibrated airport routine that always involves a light meal. This means not only am I able to avoid soul-crushing airline food, but I can use the whole flight to work without interruption.

After scarfing down the last of my rather tasteless quinoa (if indeed there is any other sort), I head for duty-free.

Robert and I are both driven and ambitious. When Greg asked me to go to this client meeting in New York, I realised it would mean bailing on a longstanding plan Robert and I had to go to the Cotswolds for the weekend. But I also knew Robert would be completely sanguine about that. 'That should help the promotion effort along nicely,' he said. 'And we can go to the Cotswolds another time.'

We often talk about how all the sacrifices we're making now are for future Loretta and Robert. Very occasionally, I question this in my head. Shouldn't we be prioritising a bit more fun together now? Will there even be a future Loretta and Robert without that?

Should we be more like the couple who put me off my salad?

I push these thoughts away. Robert and I do have fun together, especially on holiday. We want the same things from life, we always have loads to talk about and he isn't going to suddenly break my heart. I don't think I've ever had my heart truly broken and, from seeing it happen to friends, who have had to take time off work because they couldn't do anything but lie on the sofa and sob while they forensically dissected every conversation they and their ex had ever had, I know I don't want to. That's why I can't understand anyone being reckless with their heart, giving it away willy-nilly so some undeserving person can do as they please with it. Generally, I have been the one to do the dumping, not least of all because if I sensed even the slightest hint of it, I'd be in there first. I was upset after my break-up with my first serious boyfriend Mark but not 'can't go into work upset'. I can't really imagine being like that, and I certainly don't understand the 'can't live if living is without you' vibe which is surely nothing but a mawkish song lyric.

A man is buying a neck pillow. Does he not realise how much more expensive they are here – not to mention the fact they've been groped by the germ-laden fingers of multiple passengers? You couldn't pay me a thousand pounds to put one near my face.

I glance at my watch and see I still have a full three hours until my flight takes off. Which is great because, while I still have internet, I want to research all the people who will be attending the meeting. I already know quite a lot about the senior client, Remy, of course, but it would be a huge mistake to underestimate the other people in the room. I know for a fact there are normally at least seven decision-makers involved in a company changing ad agencies. I have already studied everyone's LinkedIn profiles, poring over where they worked before, where they studied, and checking if we have any shared contacts. My biggest worry is a woman called Maxine because her sister works at the incumbent ad agency.

I leave duty-free and join the long queue for the coffee shop.

When Robert asked me how my appraisal had gone, I couldn't bring myself to tell him about the negative stuff. He knew I was expecting it to be nothing but a praise-fest, and it felt kind of shaming to admit that wasn't what had happened. Especially as the thing I was pulled up on was effectively not being likeable enough. I don't want Robert thinking I'm not likeable.

This queue is taking forever. I drum my foot impatiently, wishing I didn't have an overriding need for caffeine.

I wonder now if I should have told Robert the truth? But everyone wants their partner to see the best of them, don't they? That's why you close the bathroom door when you're shaving your legs or bleaching your moustache or doing a poo.

Anyway, there's no need for me to tell Robert the truth because I have my 'weakness' in hand now and am not going to let it stand in the way of this promotion. Operation Mesh With The Team will fix things. The morning after the appraisal, I didn't put in my noise-cancelling headphones, instead making actual eye contact with people as I asked them if they had had a nice evening. I made Samira a cup of tea and suggested Zoe and I grab lunch together. I listened as Pete regaled me with a tale about a dream he'd had. (Side note: did anyone ever open with the words 'I had a strange dream last night' and then go on to thrill their audience?) The story – and I use that word in its loosest possible sense – went on for nearly four minutes and I kept thinking about all the work I could be doing in the time.

I also asked Maddie how things were going with her and Alex. Admittedly, that interaction took a turn for the worse when she said I sounded surprised that it was going well.

'It's just, normally, if you say you love someone and they don't say it back, it's not a great sign, is it?'

Maddie's face looked as if it was melting.

'I mean not usually. There are always exceptions.'

'Some people are just slow burners,' Maddie said emphatically. 'It takes them a while to voice their feelings.'

'Right. Or they don't have them. I mean, he probably does. He's probably not a douchebag.'

Maddie said she had to go to a meeting.

No wonder this queue is so slow. People keep insisting on talking to the poor barista. As if he gives a damn where they're going or if they've treated themselves to Premium Economy because you only live once. The woman at the front is telling him she is going to Milan to see her son. He is working out there, a very good job in IT. He married an Italian girl who is nice but a bit fat. She is quite worried about her husband because he is a very nervous flyer. He is sitting quietly in the lounge now, trying to do some breathing exercises.

Why do people feel the need to share their life stories with strangers? I open my email and see the subject line: *Agency Family Fun Day!!!* There is nothing guaranteed to be less fun than a day with 'fun' in its title. Normally, I would decline the invitation in a heartbeat but, with the need to mesh with my colleagues uppermost in my mind, I'll have to go. I message Robert.

Loretta

Fancy coming to the agency summer fun day with me? BBQ, rounders etc. Sunday 19 June.

Robert

Can't think of anything worse than a day spent playing team sports with a bunch of advertising tossers. ☹

I am tempted to remind Robert he is marrying an 'advertising tosser' in a few months' time but I can't be too annoyed as I wholeheartedly share his lack of enthusiasm for the event and, to an extent, people in advertising.

Loretta
It's at Greg's house. Think it will help my promotion efforts...

Robert
Oh, go on then.

Finally, I reach the front of the queue and, coffee in hand, I scan the room for somewhere to sit. The airport seems particularly packed – maybe a flight or two have been cancelled. I spot a free seat and am making my way towards it when a man with a large blue rucksack catches sight of me out of the corner of his eye and races towards it.

I scan the room again. There is an empty seat over in the corner near the windows. I head towards it, giving blue rucksack man a dirty look as I pass.

It isn't until I am nearly there that I spot the orange suitcase and silver boots. I am about to turn around when the child sees me.

'Hello! I bought a new book to read on the aeroplane and some sweeties and a sparkly pink butterfly hair clip and Mummy bought some boring things like shampoo and medicine for grown-ups and wipes because you can never have too many.'

I stand rooted to the spot. I do not want to sit next to these two. However, I can only see one other free seat and that looks as if it's wet.

'I didn't even have time to have my lunch yet even though I was quite hungry but that's okay because we're going to have it right now, isn't that right, Mummy? I've got an egg sandwich in

French bread, it's called that because it comes from France and it's really crunchy, in France they don't call it French bread though they call it bag... bag...'

'Baguette?' I say, as I sit.

'Yes!' the little girl says, clapping her hands together delightedly.

'I have a bit of work to do,' I say, pulling my laptop from my bag.

'I do work for school, spellings and maths and sometimes stories which is what I like best because I'm good at them.'

There is something strangely adult about this child. You wouldn't be surprised if her conversation suddenly turned to house prices or pension plans, or if she said 'oof' when she sat down.

I pull up Maxine's Facebook profile and scroll through her about-info, photos and recent posts. It suddenly occurs to me that, although I have been looking forward to a few days' break from Operation MWTT, there is never any real respite from trying to make myself likeable. I feel as if it's a mission I've been failing at since I was six and no one wanted to come to my birthday party. 'I don't understand it,' my mother hissed to my father. 'I thought the ice skating would swing it.'

I shake my head as if to dislodge the negative thoughts. I'm not completely socially inept. I think some of my clients even quite like me.

I see that Maxine is getting married in September. Excellent – I can slip in a casual mention of my own wedding and within seconds she'll be talking about dresses and cake designs and flowers.

The little girl is swinging her legs backwards and forwards. I have to admit the silver boots are pretty fabulous. Although I don't want kids, if I was ever to change my mind, I'd definitely want to buy them cool clothes and not dress them in those horrible frumpy old-fashioned things that involve loads of smocking.

My nostrils are suddenly assaulted by the sulphuric smell of egg and I look up to see the child chomping a baguette as big as her head. Crumbs rain down all over her but neither she nor her mother seems to care.

'Why are you going to New York?' she says.

'Phoebe,' her mother says. 'Let the lady do her work.'

I smile and go back to my Facebook stalking. I can feel the child's eyes boring into me, though, and start to feel guilty I didn't answer her question. 'I'm going to New York for work.'

Chapter Four

Of course, it was a grave error. By answering that one question, I opened the floodgates and Phoebe started chattering away, her words tumbling over each other in their hurry to get out. And it isn't just her either. It turns out the mother, who introduced herself as Kate, is just as loquacious. It's as if the two of them are taking part in that radio gameshow where you're not allowed to pause.

Neither of them waits for the other to finish before speaking themselves, merely turning up the volume to be heard. Sometimes, they conduct two entirely separate conversations and sometimes, as if by happy accident, they intersect.

I look across the departure lounge where blue rucksack man is sitting peacefully reading a book, entirely undisturbed by any of the people around him. Lucky, seat-stealing bastard.

Kate is wittering on about the blister the size of a walnut on her left heel, while Phoebe is talking about how Sophie P doesn't like Sophie G and neither of them like Olivia or Zara.

The headache I thought I'd nipped in the bud with extra-strength tablets starts to pulse behind my eyes. I really want to go back to looking at Maxine's Facebook profile. 'I should prob—'

'Zara had a party where you got to paint plates or mugs or

things,' Phoebe says. 'But she didn't invite Sophie P or Sophie G.'

'I haven't seen Janey since she moved to Spain,' Kate says. 'Although we message each other about a million times a day. She's renting a gorgeous little finca in Murcia. Do you know it? It's in the south-east. Looks absolutely to die for in the photos...'

My mind drifts away from the chatter coming in my direction. I'm not sure my lunch with Zoe went that well. She kept firing questions at me about me and Robert which made me uncomfortable and then she said, 'You don't give very much away, do you?' and it was kind of jokey but kind of not.

The child's high-pitched voice snaps me back into the present. 'My mummy is thirty-one.'

'Oh, okay. Me too, actually.'

'It's a great age to be!' Kate says, beaming.

A nonsense comment if ever there was one. There is nothing inherently good or bad about being thirty-one.

'Janey has got a little girl who's just a bit older than me,' Phoebe says.

Kate squeezes her arm. 'She has, and I bet you two are going to get on great.'

'And Janey has a new boyfriend,' Phoebe says. She adjusts her fairy wings. 'Which is lovely because it's a bit lonely when you're in a new country and you don't really know anyone except your child.'

This clearly parroted observation tells me Kate must discuss things like this with Phoebe. This seems bizarre and yet, in a way, totally unsurprising. In the short time I have spent with them, I have noticed they speak to each other more like a couple of girlfriends than mother and daughter.

'It was a real coup de foudre,' Kate says.

'What's a coup de fool-re?' Phoebe asks.

Kate scrapes her hair back into a messy bun and laughs delightedly. 'Coup de foudre. It means love at first sight.' She turns to me. 'Do you believe in such things?'

Well, of course I don't. 'Coup de fool-re' pretty much sums it up. Attraction at first sight is one thing, but love, come off it. Robert and I didn't fall in love the day we met; that came later when we realised we ticked most of each other's boxes and neither of us had voted Brexit. 'Umm—' Kate has moved on to talking about how Janey's new man has already moved in with her. It seems fast but sometimes you just know, don't you?

I glance at Phoebe, wondering how her six-year-old brain processes such topics, but she seems wholly unconcerned and has launched into talking about Olivia's superior lunchboxes. Ham sandwiches made with *white* bread, *three* biscuits, fruit made into *kebabs*.

My mind drifts back to work. I shouldn't feel too down about Operation Mesh With The Team. I have only just started it and, anyway, if I really ace this meeting in New York, then surely Greg might even be prepared to overlook my lack of meshing? I picture him telling me the promotion is mine, having new business cards with Board Account Director printed on them, telling my mum.

Okay, I'm not sure where that last little bit of the daydream came from. My mum might have been born in Genoa, but she rather smashes any stereotypes. She has never been known to smother with love or pasta. She can definitely act the Italian mamma – big hand gestures, expansive, public displays of affection – but it never feels as if it goes below the surface. The last time I was promoted I phoned home immediately. 'That's great,' Mum said. There was a small pause. 'Although I'm still not sure why you chose to go into advertising.'

When I tell her about this promotion, it will be different, though. Everyone understands it's something to be on the board.

Kate appears to still be talking about her friend's new boyfriend. 'Apparently, he's brilliant with her little girl,' she says, pulling out her hairband and letting her hair tumble free.

'I'm sorry,' I say, cutting across the twin forces of Kate and her mini-me. 'It's been lovely talking to you, but I really ought to get on with my work.'

I'm not sure why I said it's been lovely. Or, for that matter, 'talking to you'. I have done no talking whatsoever.

'Of course,' Kate says. 'Of course.' She puts her hair back into a bun.

'Are you going to go in one of those yellow taxis like you always see in the TV programmes?' Phoebe says.

'Umm, probably.'

'Sophie P went in one of those when she went to America but it made her feel a bit sick and her mummy had to take a plastic bag out of the suitcase in a big hurry. Sophie P says...'

I wait for Kate to cut in and tell Phoebe that I am working and to leave me alone but no such comment is forthcoming. In fact, Kate has also started up again, embarking on some compli-cated story about an exploit she and Janey shared when they were at art college. '... God, the pair of us got into some scrapes. No wonder my mother disapproved of her so much. Mind you, my mother can be one tricky customer.' She laughs, pulling her hair back down. 'Isn't that right, Phoebs?'

Phoebe breaks off from talking about Sophie P's set of scented highlighter pens to agree that Granny can be very tricky.

She is obviously her mother's confidante, even if the subject under discussion is her grandma. Surely that can't be good? Just as it can't be right that earlier, when Phoebe announced that her teacher was a 'real poo poo head', her mother enthusiastically agreed.

Still, what on earth do I know about parenting? More to the point, what am I doing being sucked into thinking about the intricacies of their mother/daughter relationship? I should be focused on preparing for the meeting.

Phoebe is now talking about the book she bought earlier. It's about some fairies which is good because she likes fairies very much. Do I know they can do *actual* magic?

And then, in what seems like seconds after the story reaches its crescendo, Phoebe falls fast asleep. It's one of the most extraordinary things I have ever witnessed. How can someone go from on to off so quickly, as if a switch has been flipped?

'Good for her to have some rest,' Kate says. 'Although I'd rather she'd waited until we were on the plane.' She piles her hair on top of her head again. Up, down, up, down – it's exhausting to watch. 'This is all so exciting. I cannot wait to give Janey the biggest ever hug! Do you kn—'

I raise one finger in the classic teacher pose, hating myself a little in the process. 'Sorry, I really must return to my work.'

'Oh. Right.'

I resume my Facebook stalking. Then I check out the journey from the hotel to the meeting venue and see it's a twenty-minute cab ride away. I make a mental note to allow forty-five minutes because you never know, and I certainly do not want to arrive feeling rushed and sweaty. I'll wake up two hours before that, which will give me enough time to dress, have a leisurely breakfast and skim the day's news looking for an anecdote or joke to warm things up when the initial introductions are made.

My stomach flutters. My normal way of dealing with nerves is to bury them by preparing, preparing, preparing but, because this has all been a bit last-minute, I don't feel as ready as I'd like to be. I'm progressing, though, and I still have seven hours on the plane where I'll be free from the distractions of phone and email, not to mention Kate and Phoebe.

Kate's voice cuts into my thoughts. 'Do you know I think I've drunk too much coffee? Do you mind keeping an eye on Phoebe if I just nip to the loo?'

'Ummm.'

Kate unpeels Phoebe from where she is resting on her shoulder and gently lays her down across the two seats. 'I'll be back in a tick.'

Chapter Five

She's taking an awfully long time for someone just nipping to the loo. Twelve minutes to be exact. I suppose it doesn't matter. The child is asleep and I'd be sitting here working anyway. It rankles, though. The sheer nerve of the woman. Dumping her child on a complete stranger and then going AWOL. I picture her messing about with make-up or making a few calls or, probably most likely of all, boring another stranger with her life story. *We're off to see my friend Janey in Spain… the pair of us were at art college together… the scrapes we got into…* Like they care.

The child makes a sort of snuffling noise. It amazes me she can sleep wearing those fairy wings. The one on her right is crushed underneath her.

I glance at the clock on my computer screen. The woman has been gone for nearly fifteen minutes now. Talk about taking advantage.

I am at the point of waking the child up when she opens her eyes. 'Where's Mummy?' she says, sitting up.

'She has just nipped to the loo.' With 'nipped' being a word I use very loosely. Irritation fizzes in my belly. Wait until I see that woman. How dare she just dump her child on me like this? I'm on my way to one of the most important meetings of my life and I could do without playing babysitter. It's downright irresponsible of her too. I could be an axe-murderer for all she knows.

The child rubs her eyes. 'I need a wee too.' She jumps down from her seat. 'Where are the toilets?'

'I'll take you,' I say, shoving my laptop into my bag. This really is wildly inconvenient. I should be concentrating on my work right now. 'They're this way,' I say, pointing.

The child moves surprisingly quickly and I am forced to break into a jog to keep up with her, noting vaguely that Robert was right about flip-flops being a poor choice if you have to move fast.

The toilets smell of urine and artificial pine.

'Mummy,' the child calls. 'Mummy.'

Where the hell is she? I picture her wandering around duty-free, pulling her hair in and out of a bun, trying on sunglasses and spritzing herself with free perfume. Surely she wouldn't have the nerve, though, not when she has left her child with a complete stranger? I feel a prickle of anxiety. What if something has happened to her? What, though? She's hardly likely to have been mugged or kidnapped in the middle of Terminal 5.

'There she is,' the child says, running towards the end cubicle. 'I can see her shoes.' She bangs on the fake wood door of the cubicle. 'Mummy, Mummy.'

Silence. Cold fear floods my belly.

'Mummy, Mummy.' The child pounds on the door with her small fists.

I run out of the toilets and grab the first person in uniform I see.

It's only afterwards that I realise I should have got the child out of there before they opened the cubicle door. Instead, she was right there as we discovered her mother slumped on the toilet, limp and lifeless and a ghastly grey colour.

The child's screams reverberate around the toilet block. Screams of pure, naked terror.

A man appears and starts giving instructions. Call an ambulance immediately. Let's move her out of that cubicle where there's more space. He interlocks his thumbs, places both hands in the middle of her chest and pounds them up and down.

'Stop it,' the child screams, throwing herself down on the floor. 'Stop it. You're hurting her.'

'Someone take her out of here,' the man says, continuing to pound down on her mother's sternum.

My mind snaps into focus. 'Someone' is me.

'C'mon,' I say, putting my hand on the child's shoulder. 'Let's let the doctor do his work. We'll see Mummy again when she's better.' Is it okay to say this? Mummy doesn't look like she's going to be better. I push the thought away. 'C'mon.'

The child shakes off my hand. 'NO. NO, NO, NO, NO, NO. I WANT TO STAY WITH MY MUMMY.'

For a second, in my panic, I can't remember the child's name. 'Phoebe,' I say, as it clunks into my brain. 'We need to let the doctor do his work.'

'NOOOOOOO,' Phoebe wails, tears and snot rolling down her cheeks. She has clamped herself to her mother's legs.

I try to pull her away. 'Help me,' I say to the security guard.

He looks about fourteen and is rooted to the spot, his face a mask of horror and the master keys dangling from his hand.

'HELP ME.'

My shout snaps him out of his paralysis and together we manage to drag Phoebe away as she punches and kicks and screams.

Meanwhile, the doctor continues to pound her mother's chest, the sweat pouring off him and his face set with grim determination.

'Mummy is going to be okay,' I say to Phoebe.

Surely that has to be true?

Chapter Six

Phoebe is hysterical. Her fairy wings jiggle violently as she lets out big, choking sobs that make her tiny body shake. 'I want Mummy... I want Mummy... I want Mummy.'

'Shh,' I say, patting her arm and trying not to focus on the huge bubble of snot that is hanging from her nose. 'Shh.'

We have been shepherded into a nondescript beige room and offered a Styrofoam cup of stewed brown liquid that passes for tea (tea makes everything better!).

'Was Mummy feeling ill this morning?'

'N... n... nooo.'

Then how the hell did this happen? Perfectly healthy people of thirty-one don't just go off to the loo and then end up like *that*. A picture of Kate slumped on the toilet flashes into my mind. She looked... well, dead. I shake my head as if to dislodge the thought. She can't be dead. The doctor wouldn't have been doing CPR.

I have been waiting for someone in authority to take the child from me but, so far, there seems to be no such person. 'Shh, shh,' I say uselessly.

'... I want m... m... mummy.'

'Hey,' I say, squeezing her arm. 'Try not to get so upset.'

This makes her cry all the harder.

My phone rings and I see it's Robert. I called him as soon as we were brought into this room, feeling the need to tell someone what had happened, but his phone went to voicemail.

'My God,' he says now. 'How awful. Is she going to be okay?'

Phoebe's crying has become even louder.

'I hope so,' I say, biting back treacherous tears.

'What's that?' Robert says. 'I can't hear you very well.'

'I said I hope so.' I take a few steps away from Phoebe who immediately stands up and follows me.

Robert is saying something else now but I can't make it out. I take several paces away from Phoebe but, after the briefest of pauses, she follows me.

'Hold on a sec,' I say, covering the receiver. I turn to Phoebe. 'Stay right here, I'll be back in a second.'

This instruction appears to fall on deaf ears because, once again, I have a small shadow and, this time, it has turned up the volume.

'What *is* that dreadful racket?' Robert says.

'It's the child.'

'What? I can't hear you over all that noise.'

This is ridiculous. 'Stay,' I say to Phoebe.

I take a few steps away and she doesn't follow me. 'That's better,' I say to Robert. 'I was telling you it's the child. She's very upset. As she would be.'

Robert is speaking again but I can't hear what he is saying because Phoebe and her crying are suddenly back at my side.

As the two of us were led towards this room, I felt the eyes of everyone we passed upon us, and it crossed my mind I ought to find someone who was better with kids than me. There was a kindly-faced woman in a red and gold sari who looked like a grandmother; someone who had put plasters on countless grazed knees and could always whip up a batch of cakes or a brilliant bedtime story.

To be honest, I'm sure pretty much anyone in the airport would be better at this than me.

'Phoebe,' I say, my voice coming out more sharply than I intend it to. 'Sit here in this chair and don't move. I am just going over there.' I point in the direction of the corner. 'You will see me the whole time and I will be back as soon as I have finished speaking on the phone.'

Mercifully, the child nods her assent.

'That's better,' I say to Robert. 'Now I can hear you properly.'

'I'd better be going back into court, actually. Poor old you, though. All this must have been a terrible shock.'

I look across the room at Phoebe, whose small silver boots seem to be dangling unfeasibly far from the ground. She cannot be left without a mother.

'It's a bugger you're having to look after the kid,' Robert says. 'Surely there must be a police officer you could leave her with?'

'Yeah, the police are on their way. They've also called social services.'

'What time is your flight?'

'1.30.'

'Well, at least you still have lots of time. Listen, I really do have to go back into court, but I'll leave my phone switched on if you need me, okay? I hope someone takes the child off you soon. Make a fuss if you need to.'

I stand in the corner after I've ended the call. Phoebe has stopped crying now and is sitting silent and red-eyed.

Somehow this mute, catatonic version of her is even more pitiful than the hysterical one.

Chapter Seven

Phoebe has a broken wing. I have only just noticed it but I guess it must have happened as we dragged her off her mother. 'Do you want to, umm, take off your fairy wings?'

She shakes her head.

A policeman with a thick white beard and a shiny pink head comes over and sinks to his haunches. 'Hullo, I'm PC Derek Morris.'

'Where's my mummy?'

Derek massages his beard. 'She's on her way to the hospital, Polly.'

'Phoebe,' I correct him.

He nods. 'In the meantime, we thought it might be a good idea to give your daddy a call.'

'I don't know his phone number.'

'That's okay. If you just tell us Daddy's name, we can find the number.'

'Mitch.'

'Great. Mitch Harris.'

Phoebe shakes her head.

Derek rubs his beard. 'Does Daddy have a different last name?'

Phoebe nods.

'And can you tell me what it is?'

Phoebe stares at her silver boots. 'He didn't tell me… when I met him and I was three years old and he bought me a toy that was for babies and Mummy said I had to say thank you because it was still nice of him.'

My heart plummets. Of course Kate is a single parent. Which means if she is dead— I don't allow myself to finish the thought. There is still hope. They're taking her to hospital.

'What about Granny and Grandpa?' Derek says. 'Do you have a granny and grandpa?'

Phoebe's damp eyes flash. 'Yes – otherwise I wouldn't have a mummy.'

In different circumstances, this would make me laugh. Derek quizzes Phoebe for more details and I look around the room. How on earth did this happen? One minute, I was Facebook-stalking a client, the next, I was caught up in all this. Mind you, I could be Kate. I could have gone from babbling about my upcoming holiday to fighting for my life. I still don't understand how it could happen.

Derek strides away, telling us he will be back soon.

'I forgot Timmy the tiger,' Phoebe says, her eyes filling with fresh tears.

'What?'

'My suitcase.'

Of course. The one I tripped over another lifetime ago. 'It's okay.'

'It's not okay. Mummy said I mustn't lose it. It cost a lot of money but I made her buy it for me but only because I promised I'd really look after it.'

'I'll ask the security people about it,' I say. 'They've probably put it somewhere safe.' I picture the small orange and black case being blown up by the bomb disposal squad.

'Mummy will be cross.'

A lump rises in my throat. 'Your mummy won't care about your suitcase.'

Phoebe's lip wobbles. 'Yes, she will.'

I don't know what to say to this and am suddenly overcome by a tidal wave of exhaustion. It's the shock, I suppose. I told Robert I was fine but I can't ignore the fact my hands shake violently as they hold the Styrofoam cup of tea. My mind keeps playing everything I've seen on a loop, like some kind of macabre movie trailer.

'I'm cold,' Phoebe says.

I feel a rush of pity and shame. Never mind what I've seen.

'My jumper is in Timmy.'

'Here, have my cardigan.'

'It's too big for me.'

'We'll push up the sleeves.' I ease Phoebe's broken wings off and help her put on the cardigan.

It is eerily quiet in here. There's just the occasional crackle of a police radio followed by some sort of gobbledegook number-laden speak. It's hard to imagine that, outside this room, the airport is teeming with people who are blissfully unaware and going about their business: buying sun cream, deliberating between two forgettable paperbacks, posing for selfies with a glass of Prosecco held aloft, hashtag out of office.

Derek and a young policewoman are coming towards us. I have a terrible sense of foreboding and my stomach flips.

'Are you going to take me to my mummy now?'

Derek smiles tightly.

'May I have a quick word with you outside, Miss Martinelli? PC Sarah will stay here.'

'Is she dead?' I blurt, the second we are out of the room.

'No.'

Relief courses through my veins.

'But she's not in a good way.'

'Is she going to—'

Derek clears his throat. 'I don't know any more details at this stage. Look, the airport security staff assumed you were a friend of the family and that you were travelling as a group. However, I now understand the little girl was a stranger to you up until today. So, I wanted to tell you that you're free to go. The grandmother is on her way and so are social services. In the meantime, we can look after Polly.'

'Phoebe.' Later, I will wonder if I might have made a different decision if the man had got Phoebe's name right. But how can I possibly leave her with someone who can't even manage that? I will stay until the social worker arrives. 'I'll stick around for now.'

'Are you sure?'

I picture the fierce jut of Phoebe's chin when she told Derek she wouldn't have a mummy if she didn't have grandparents. 'I'm sure.'

Chapter Eight

Phoebe and I are playing Snap with the cards the security guard pressed on me, saying they might 'help to take the poor kid's mind off things for a bit'.

How on earth do people look after small children all day long? I had forgotten how boring their games are. We have only been playing Snap for about five minutes but I already fear that large parts of my brain have atrophied.

'Snap,' Phoebe says, putting her six of clubs on top of my six of hearts.

She took the news that her mum was being taken to hospital surprisingly well. 'Hospitals make people better,' she said, with a certainty that made my heart hurt. There were tears when she was told she couldn't go to the hospital yet but she has rallied since then.

'Snap,' I say, trying to sound enthusiastic.

The social worker seems to be taking her sweet time to arrive and I keep glancing at the clock. But I still have plenty of time before my flight, and I'll leave as soon as Phoebe is safely in her hands. I can't in all conscience leave her in the 'care' of Derek and Sarah, though.

I keep going over and over what happened in my head. How

could a seemingly healthy woman of thirty-one suddenly be in that state?

Less dramatically, how did I end up being the person looking after her kid? I wouldn't be in this room right now if blue rucksack man hadn't nicked that seat.

There are other, more important 'what ifs' too. What if I had gone to look for Kate more quickly? Checked she was okay rather than sat there stewing on how rude and inconsiderate she was being. How will I live with myself if my decisions cost her her life?

Stop it, I tell myself. No reasonable person goes to check on an adult because they're taking a bit too long in the toilet. And Kate is *not* going to die.

'Shall we stop playing this now?' Phoebe says.

Thank God!

'Is Mummy going to be okay?'

Well, that serves me right. Come back, Snap, all is forgiven.

'I'm sure the doctors and nurses are going to take very good care of her.'

Phoebe seems to think about this for a while, her small face dark and serious. 'I went to the hospital when Sophie P hit me in the face with a tennis racket and the doctors and nurses were very nice.' She rakes her hand through her hair. 'Will Mummy have to stay in the hospital for the night, and if she does, will I be able to go there with her? I could sleep in her bed with her because I am quite little and sometimes I do that when I have a nightmare or something.'

My head spins. Judging by how she looked earlier, I imagine Kate will need to stay in hospital for a lot longer than one night. 'I know your granny is on her way. You'll probably stay at her house tonight.'

Phoebe's eyes fill with tears. 'I don't want to stay there without Mummy.'

I force myself to smile. 'I'm sure she will take you to see Mummy.' Is it okay to say that? What if— *Don't.*

'Do you have any paper and pens?' Phoebe says.

'Umm, probably. Do you want to do a drawing?'

'I need to make a list of things I need to stay overnight at Granny's house. All my things were in my tiger suitcase so I need things like pyjamas and a toothbrush.'

I feel a tug of connection to this strange little person. I am devoted to my lists, all of which are made in the A5 navy Moleskine notebooks I batch buy. I never imagined a six-year-old would share my passion for list-making, though. I rummage in my handbag, pull a page from my notebook and hand that to Phoebe with a pen.

She pokes the tip of her tongue through her teeth as she starts to write in big but surprisingly neat handwriting.

I can't imagine having a child of my own, but if I ever change my mind, I want a little list-maker.

'I'll be able to use Granny's toothpaste, right?'

'I'm sure. Do you often make lists?'

'Hmm, quite often. Mummy always asks me to if I'm going on a trip somewhere because, otherwise, you forget things you need and then that's a bit annoying, but if you have a list then you don't forget.' She folds up the paper, puts it in the pocket of her dungaree dress and hands the pen back to me. 'Thank you. Do you think Granny will take me to see Mummy right now because I would like that and I know Mummy will too. She always says she misses me when I'm away from her for too long, even when I'm just going to school or something.'

I feel as if there is a heavy weight pressing down on my chest.

I run my fingers over the grubby tip of Phoebe's broken wing (the wings having been put straight back on after the cardigan). 'I'm sure she will take you as soon as she possibly can.'

Mercifully, this seems to satisfy Phoebe. 'I wouldn't mind going to Granny's so much if she hadn't given away Mummy's old doll's house. I used to love playing with it, but then when Granny and Grandpa were divorced, she said she didn't have much space in her new house and it had to go to the charity shop. Mummy said she thought it was funny that someone who has seven teapots was saying they didn't have much space.'

Memories flood my brain of my own beloved doll's house. I used to spend hours dreaming up stories for its tiny inhabitants, much preferring their company to that of real people. The doll's-house people knew it took a bit of time to get to know me, that I didn't always say the right thing or have anything to say at all. 'I had a doll's house.'

'What was it like?' Phoebe says, twisting her body more towards mine.

'It was yellow on the outside and it had a spiral staircase in the middle and green and pink flowery wallpaper in the living room. I used to spend all my pocket money on furniture for it, and sometimes I would make things too. I remember a light I was very pleased with that used the top of a washing-up liquid bottle.'

'I'd like a doll's house,' Phoebe says.

'You'll have to put it on your Christmas list.' I ruffle her mussed-up hair. She deserves a doll's house. And she deserves her mother to be okay.

Chapter Nine

Phoebe appears to have taken an instant and visceral dislike to the social worker. I can't say I blame her, frankly – Denise is annoying: the way she adopts a whole different voice when she speaks to Phoebe, her simpering smile, the constant repetition of 'what I'm hearing is' as if she is one of those dolls with a set number of phrases. I also can't help noticing she has terrible BO – and God, if you're going to wear Birkenstocks, maybe cut your toenails?

'Tell me more about your doll's house,' Phoebe says.

Denise cuts in before I have a chance to answer. 'Actually, Phoeeeeee-be, I think Loretta has to go now.'

'I'm okay for a bit longer,' I say, surprising myself. Just before Denise made her slow, lumpen arrival on the scene, I was counting the seconds until I could get out of here. Phoebe is sweet but her constant stream of chatter and questions is exhausting. Does her granny know her mummy is going to hospital? Will she ever actually go on an aeroplane? Why is the man always stroking his beard? Why couldn't she go in the ambulance? Is orange cheese made with different milk to yellow cheese?

'Well,' I say, 'the doll's house had real lights you could turn on and off.'

47

Phoebe nods approvingly.

'And my favourite room of all was the kitchen because I loved all the tiny plates of miniature food. Potatoes no bigger than the head of a pin...'

Why am I still here? Because Phoebe doesn't appear to like Denise? Or because I, hardly the Pied Piper myself, have somehow decided that the social worker isn't very good with the child? The idea is preposterous. Denise is trained, for goodness' sake. Not that you'd know that from her saying 'surely it's not that bad' when Phoebe started crying hysterically after tripping over and bashing her knee. That made me furious. Couldn't this doltish woman see Phoebe was crying over *everything*?

'Was there a garden?' Phoebe asks.

Denise looks up from her clipboard. 'Are you hungry, Phoeeeee-be? Would you like something to eat?'

Phoebe turns to me. 'Are you going to come with us?'

Denise speaks before I have the chance. 'No, remember Loretta has to go.'

I have never been great with being told what to do. 'Well, actually, I am a bit peckish.'

Denise's mouth forms the shape of a cat's bottom. 'I'll fetch us some sandwiches and bring them back here. What would you like, Phoeeeee-be? Cheese, tuna?'

'Ham on white bread. Just ham, no funny stuff.' Phoebe scratches at a scab on her arm. 'Please.'

Denise lumbers towards the door.

'That lady smells,' Phoebe says.

'Phoebe!' I say, biting my lip to stop myself laughing.

'Well, she does. Does Mummy's friend know we're not coming?'

'I'm not sure.'

'She's a yoga teacher like Mummy. I can do some yoga, would

you like to see it?' She adopts a downward dog before I can answer. This morphs into a series of poses, all accompanied by a stream of narration.

Denise reappears, carrying a brown paper bag. 'Come up off the floor, Phoeeeee-be.'

Phoebe stays in her bridge position.

'C'mon, Phoebe,' I say.

Phoebe sits back down.

Denise takes out a sandwich and hands it to Phoebe.

'Shall we give your hands a little clean?' I say, fishing some anti-bacterial hand gel out of my handbag.

Denise gives me a bit of a look but I can't believe she'd let a child eat when her hands have been all over this filthy floor. Like she needs an upset stomach on top of everything else.

Phoebe eyes the sandwich suspiciously. She unpeels the top slice of bread and stares at it. 'I don't like this.'

'But it's what you asked for,' Denise says, looking palpably irritated.

I'm irritated by her, though. After everything Phoebe has been through, it seems inconceivable that an adult, and a trained adult at that, might choose to go to war over a ham sandwich. 'Would you like to swap with me? I've got cheese.'

'Is it yellow cheese or orange?'

'Yellow.'

'Yes, please.'

Sandwiches are swapped and Phoebe starts eating.

'Your nana is on her way,' Denise says.

Phoebe's tiny nose crinkles.

'Your granny,' I explain. A picture of a twinkly old lady with big kind eyes and snowy hair springs to mind. I will go the minute she arrives.

I reach for my phone.

Robert picks up straightaway. 'Is there any news on the mother and have you handed over the kid yet?'

'No and not quite.'

'Oh, is there a problem?'

'No problem—' I trail off, suddenly unsure what to say. Why am I still here? I don't feel I can explain to Robert that I feel some sort of responsibility towards this child. Or that I am somehow under the impression that I am more use to her right now than Denise. I know he would tell me that's ridiculous. It *is* ridiculous.

'Did a social worker arrive?'

'Yes, she's here.'

'Then why—'

I cut him off. 'I'm going to leave any minute.' The second the snowy-haired granny arrives. 'I'll still have plenty of time.'

'Who were you on the phone to?' Phoebe says.

'Robert.'

'Your fian… fi… fi…'

'Fiancé.' Phoebe has asked a zillion questions about Robert and the wedding. What is Robert like? What is my dress like? Am I going to have lots and lots of bridesmaids? She was a bridesmaid once and it was a very important job because she had to walk into the church first and not be shy when everyone was looking at her and remember to walk nice and slowly and throw her rose petals on the floor but not all at once.

I turn to Denise. 'Did Phoebe's granny say what sort of time she thinks she'll be here?'

'About 12.30.'

12.30 is fine. I'll still be in plenty of time for my flight.

Chapter Ten

'I went to the shops and I came back with three oranges, a loaf of bread, some butter and some ham,' I say.

My sister and I used to love this game when we were kids. It kept us entertained for hours in the back of the car. I remember Dad telling Mum it was amazing how good the two of us were on long journeys. Not like those kids you hear about who squabble from the moment you pull out of the drive.

'I went to the shops and I came back with three oranges, a loaf of bread, some butter, some ham and a monkey,' Phoebe says.

'A monkey? You can't buy a monkey at the shops!'

'Well, you said I could buy whatever I wanted at the shops as long as I remembered everything.'

I laugh. I did indeed say that. Back when I explained the memory game to Phoebe about 4,000 light years ago.

I have never thought of myself as someone who is good with children and none of the ones I have come into contact with have disabused me of this notion. Babies cry the minute they are placed in my unwilling arms, my cousins' kids give the impression of only really being interested in me when I have a present, and there was that very unfortunate incident with Greg's son and the fake spider (how was I supposed to know he had a phobia? I thought I was being fun). Phoebe, however, seems to like me.

Maybe this explains why I am still here. Earlier, Denise noticed me glancing at my watch and told me, not for the first time, to feel free to leave. 'Oh, I'm not in any rush.' This wasn't strictly true. It can't be that long until my flight starts boarding.

'I went to the shops and I came back with three oranges, a loaf of bread, some butter, some ham, a monkey and a swimming pool.'

Phoebe giggles. 'You can't buy a swimming pool at the shops.'

'What are you two laughing about?' Denise says, coming back from talking to Derek.

I don't know if it's my imagination but Denise sounds slightly displeased by the laughter. Maybe she thinks it is inappropriate given the circumstances? Or maybe, not unreasonably, she just wishes I would sod off?

'We're playing "I went to the shops".'

'Oh, I like that one,' Denise says.

'Actually,' Phoebe says, rising from the hard plastic chair and tipping her head towards the floor. 'We've finished now and I'm going to do a bit more yoga.'

If Denise notices the slight, she ignores it. 'I do yoga sometimes.'

'*Really?*' Phoebe says, standing with her legs apart and her small arms outstretched towards the ceiling. 'This is mountain pose or Tad… Tad… Tadasana.'

I scroll through all the emails that have flooded into my inbox. I should have been keeping on top of them instead of trying to play babysitter. I ought to return to the meeting prep too.

Phoebe is kneeling on the floor now. 'And this is called child's pose but it's not just for childs, it's for everyone – even grown-ups.'

The narration is endearing. It's like listening to the world's tiniest yogi.

Phoebe stretches out her arms and puts her forehead on the floor. I am not particularly happy about the latter but since Denise doesn't say anything, I don't feel I can.

I chew my bottom lip as I read an email from Zoe. She just had a slightly tense conversation with one of Kitkins' clients who 'has to admit to being a little disappointed' with the latest round of creative work we showed them. Was she right in thinking Zoe was the only member of the account management team in the office over the next couple of days? That Samira and I were both otherwise engaged?

Phoebe is now doing cat/cow.

'She's pretty good, isn't she?' Denise says. 'I suppose at that age you're super bendy.'

I force a smile. I absolutely do not want to engage in small talk with Denise. I've wasted enough time already today. Maybe I should be on my way now? Okay, Phoebe doesn't seem that keen on Denise, but she must be a reasonably competent and kind individual? On the other hand, the grandmother is due any time now and given I have stayed this long, another twenty minutes or so isn't going to make much difference. Plus, I am cracking on with some work now so what is the harm?

My phone rings and I see it's an unknown number. 'Loretta Martinelli,' I say, punching the green button.

It is one of the florists I approached for a quote on the wedding flowers. Would now be a convenient time to talk she wants to know.

I push away the feeling that it seems ridiculous to talk about the finer points of one flower over another when a woman exactly the same age as me is fighting for her life. 'Yes, I can talk briefly.'

I want the wedding to be perfect – of course I do. And I have a clear idea of what I want from the tablescapes. 'I'm thinking of having huge candelabras, draped with ivy and grapes to create a sort of opulent Roman banquet theme.'

I ignore Denise giving me the side-eye, making a bitchy mental note that I don't imagine her ever having to concern herself with flowers for her wedding.

The florist says she can do a ring of flowers at the base of each candelabra. She has 60 cm ones in silver.

I swallow a wave of irritation. Didn't I just say I wanted the candelabras draped? Why then is this woman talking about a ring of flowers at the base? Also, why silver candelabras? My initial email clearly stated they must be brass. I end the call as quickly as I can, mentally crossing that florist off my list.

'This is warrior one,' Phoebe says. 'I start in mountain pose and then I take a big breath out…'

'I need to have another chat with the police,' Denise says. 'Are you okay with Phoebe for a minute?'

Of course I am okay. What exact role does Denise think she has been fulfilling sitting here on her bum making the odd asinine comment?

My mind flashes to the meeting tomorrow and how I have to be back on top of the preparations. I am the queen of preparation and believe it is the one thing you can control in tough situations. Gaining a first at uni wasn't so much about natural ability as the fact I revised, revised and then revised some more. And, yes, I had palpitations from all the caffeine pills but it was worth it. Even my mother was grudgingly impressed.

'It's all about the breathing,' Phoebe says earnestly.

I pull up the presentation and start reading through it, and it's good. If I was the client, I would be persuaded by it. But then

I spot a typo on one of the slides. A typo! How has that slipped through when I have read this so many times? How did Greg not see it when I took him through it? Or perhaps he did see it and he was waiting for me to notice it myself. He is like that. One of his favourite expressions to trot out is the old adage about teaching a man to fish rather than just giving him a fish.

Sweat starts to bead under my armpits. If I failed to notice a typo, what other mistakes might I have missed?

A voice in my head tells me it isn't the end of the world and that it hardly matters when you consider recent events.

'I'm bored,' Phoebe says, abruptly finishing her yoga session and plopping herself down next to me.

I carry on reading through the presentation.

'I'M BORED.'

'For goodness' sake, would you shush?'

Phoebe's eyes immediately fill with tears and I feel like the most horrible person in the world. I am glad Denise is on the other side of the room and not here to witness me snapping. 'Sorry. I was just trying to catch up on some work.'

Phoebe stares at her silver boots.

Why am I still here? 'Listen, I should probably go.' I stand. 'I was going to stay until your granny arrives but it's a bit late and I need to catch my plane. You'll be all right with Denise for a little bit, won't you?'

Phoebe doesn't say anything for the longest time. 'I'll be quiet,' she says, finally.

'No,' I say, feeling worse than ever.

Denise reappears. 'Are you off then?'

I look at Phoebe's small bowed head. 'Not yet.'

Denise's smile fades.

'I was just stretching my legs a little,' I say, sitting back down.

The grandma will surely be here any second and, if I have waited this long, I may as well stay until Phoebe is with someone she knows and loves. I turn to her now. 'Right, what are we going to do to keep ourselves entertained then?'

Chapter Eleven

I had imagined the arrival of her grandma would be an immediate balm to Phoebe but, instead of scooping the child into her arms and offering words of reassurance, Sylvia has brought a restless, flappy energy. She keeps firing questions at Phoebe. Was Mummy feeling okay this morning? How come Phoebe wasn't with her when this happened? Why was she asleep?

Phoebes stares at her boots as she answers and a wave of sadness washes over me. She needs someone calm and solid right now.

'What a thing to happen,' Sylvia says, flapping her batwing sleeves. 'I was on my way out for the day when I got the call.'

This strikes me as a bit of an odd thing to say. Is she suggesting this is some kind of inconvenience?

Still, who am I to say how someone should act in a situation like this? A lot of people find me weird in the most normal of circumstances.

Earlier, Denise talked to me about 'processing the trauma' I had experienced and I bit her head off. I hadn't experienced any trauma. It was Phoebe and Kate she ought to be worried about. Denise gave me an infuriating smile. 'If you don't need counselling now, you could find you need it in the days and weeks to come.'

Ridiculous.

'Whatever are you wearing those angel wings for, Phoebe?' Sylvia says, flicking her aubergine-coloured fringe out of her eyes.

'Fairy wings,' Phoebe says, almost inaudibly.

Sylvia sucks on her bottom lip. 'And do you have any bags?'

Phoebe looks tearful. 'I did have my Timmy the tiger suitcase but I left it behind when we went to find Mummy.'

'I've asked security about it,' I say.

'They might have picked it up,' Denise adds, somewhat super-fluously. Until she spoke, I'd forgotten she was here.

'What a thing to happen,' Sylvia says. She glances across at me. 'Sorry, but I didn't catch your name before.'

'Loretta Martinelli.'

'And you were the person who was with Phoebe?'

'Yes.'

'Well, you certainly got more than you bargained for.' She shakes her head. 'What a thing to happen.'

I try to imagine Sylvia comforting Phoebe when she's upset, or going to her when she wakes from a nightmare, or even reading her a bedtime story, but I can't picture it. She is probably a very different person in private, though – and she must be in shock about everything that has happened. After all, her daughter is at this moment lying in a hospital somewhere in goodness knows what state.

Sylvia has turned her attention back to Phoebe. 'Who does that cardigan belong to? I can see it's not yours.'

'Loretta. I was cold, you see, and my jumper was in my Timmy the tiger suitcase which I forgot.'

Sylvia nods. 'I see. Well, perhaps you'd like to give it back now?'

'But I'm still cold,' Phoebe says, her voice cracking.

'It's fine,' I say, jumping in. 'I'm very happy for Phoebe to keep the cardigan.'

Sylvia frowns. 'Hmm, well, it does look a little dirty. Perhaps I should give it a wash and then send it back to you. If you could give me your address.'

'It's really not nec—'

Sylvia cuts me off. 'I insist.'

I write down my address and hand it over. 'Right, I really need to go or I'm going to miss my plane.' I sink to my haunches. 'Well, Phoebe, I guess this is goodbye. What a day we've had togeth—'

I am surprised by Phoebe throwing her arms around me and squeezing me with a force that belies her tiny frame. She smells of baby shampoo and clean washing.

I am not really a hugger but I find myself putting my arms under her broken, battered wings and hugging her back.

'Come on now,' Sylvia says. 'We need to let the lady go.'

Phoebe's small shoulders start to shake.

'Hey,' I say, but fat tears have somehow started to roll down my own cheeks too. It is completely irrational but suddenly I don't want to leave her. There is something about this little girl that is not like other children. A heart-melting seriousness that makes you feel as if you are talking to a wise old woman trapped in a child's body. The way she always says 'please' and 'thank you' – even in these terrible circumstances. Her small earnest face as she listened to the rules of the shop game or performed her yoga routine. Her obvious dislike of the dreadful Denise.

'Phoebe,' Sylvia says. 'We mustn't make the lady miss her flight.'

The word 'flight' snaps my mind back into focus. I give Phoebe one last big squeeze and pull away from her. I rise to my feet, wipe away the tears and force a wobbly smile.

I have no idea why I am so upset.

But I guess it has just been a very emotional day.

Chapter Twelve

I am in a taxi taking me from JFK airport to my hotel. The taxi driver is whittling on about the High Line and the view from the Top of the Rock and I am cursing my luck to have a chatty sort in a city famed for being unfriendly. I could really do without it, especially as it took me so long to pull myself together.

I couldn't stop crying when I left Phoebe. I was surprised at myself. I'm not normally a blubber and I wasn't helping anyone by being so self-indulgent. But I couldn't erase Phoebe's face from my mind. Or stop obsessing about the fact her mother is the same age as me and woke up this morning feeling completely fine. They should have been on a plane too right now.

I managed to work once my flight took off, but my mind kept drifting.

'Forget going up the Empire State,' the driver says. 'The lines are crazy and you have a better view from the Top of the Rock.'

I stifle the urge to tell him I'm here on business and I have bigger things on my mind. I block out his chatter and take some deep breaths. I am going to forget about everything that has happened and move forward. Tomorrow, I will give the presentation of my life, smile through the post-meeting drinks and find a way to bond with Maxine by chatting about all things wedding.

The taxi pulls up outside the hotel and I go to pay, but when I look for my corporate credit card, it's nowhere to be seen.

If it was my credit card, I'd just cancel the sodding thing. But cancelling a company credit card means talking to Dana in the agency finance department and I *really* don't want to do that. Dana has a mouth the size of Texas and the last thing I need is for people at work to gain the impression that I'm careless and untrustworthy. That's hardly going to help my promotion efforts.

So, I'm on the phone to Heathrow security. It took me about eleven billion hours to find the right number for them and then another seven billion listening to infuriating automated menu options that made me jab angrily at my phone and shout: I JUST WANT TO SPEAK TO AN ACTUAL FUCKING HUMAN.

I didn't mean this actual fucking human, mind you.

'We have thousands of people coming through this airport every day,' it says to me now, the boredom dripping from every syllable.

I push my nails into my palms. 'I'm well aware of that.'

'A great many of them lose things.'

'Well, yes, but—'

'As I said before, what I would recommend is that you call the credit card company in question – cancel the card.'

'*As I said before*, I can't do that.' I stare at the ceiling of my hotel room. I want to be standing in a shower that's hot enough to turn my skin pink right now. 'Look, I'm not the sort to lose things but it wasn't a great day. I was keeping an eye on a stranger's child and the mother was taken ill.'

'The woman who died?'

I sit bolt upright on the bed. 'She didn't die.'

'She did. At the hospital. Probably shouldn't tell you that.'

I feel as if all the air has been knocked from my lungs.

'Are you still there?' says Awful Human.

'Yes,' I squeak.

'Give me your number and I'll phone you if your credit card turns up.' She is not so bored now. I have catapulted myself into being a person of interest.

'It doesn't matter,' I say, ending the call.

I sit on the edge of the bed shaking and crying. The light fades outside but I am unable to stand up to switch on a lamp.

I shouldn't be this upset. Yes, this is a tragedy but it's not my tragedy. Bad things happen every day. I didn't know Kate and I barely know Phoebe, even if I can't stop picturing her little face.

There's another face I keep seeing as well. And with it comes a whole host of memories I have fought so very hard to forget.

Chapter Thirteen

Four days later

A man on the tube thuds to the floor, making me jump. Pull yourself together, I tell myself. He has just fainted. It's hot and crowded in here. He's probably hungover.

But there is no logic to the visceral panic that engulfs me. The sight of the man's crumpled, lifeless-looking body on the floor brings back memories of discovering Kate.

I am grateful that other people step in to help. That I can stay in my seat and attempt to get my breathing under control. This will be my first day back in the office and I can't afford not to be at my best. I am already annoyed with myself for being so late in leaving the flat. Normally, I am in the office before anyone with the possible exception of Greg. The two of us have become locked in a sort of unofficial contest that neither of us openly acknowledges. Today, Greg will definitely win because, after a terrible night's sleep, I repeatedly hit snooze.

I think of Denise the social worker saying I might find the trauma hard to process.

Denise doesn't know me, though. I aced my presentation in New York and even managed to do well at the post-meeting drinks. True, when I went to bed that night I couldn't sleep, but that's just jetlag, right?

We have reached a station and the man, who is now conscious but woozy-looking, is helped onto the platform by two women.

I look back to my notebook and my to-do list. Just before the man fainted, I was adding today's tasks.

- *Ask people about their weekends (at least three people)*
- *Send all-agency email saying there are chocolates from New York to enjoy with a cuppa (use the word 'cuppa' even though it's hateful)*
- *Engage with Zoe*

This all seems so *trivial*. Am I thirteen again, for Christ's sake? It's not as if my previous attempts to 'mesh' with my co-workers have gone that well either. Maybe I should challenge Greg to give me this promotion without me having to jump through the eight million hoops to popularity? I am good at my job and people don't *hate* me.

There is a woman outside the tube station selling 'lucky' heather. She never finds a buyer in me. In my experience, 'luck' is often the label people give to hard work and determination.

It flits through my mind I want to call Robert. I'm not sure exactly what I want to say, though. Yesterday, when I returned home from New York, he met me at the door and gave me a hug. Did I want to talk about what had happened at the airport? It must have been upsetting and he expected I just wanted to forget all about it. It was exactly what I was about to say but I was slightly irritated he hadn't let me get the words out.

My mood is not helped by the fact London has turned itself into a giant pressure cooker intent on boiling its residents.

Newspaper front pages boast pictures of toddlers cavorting in water fountains or office workers spreadeagled on parched yellow grass alongside headlines like 'It's a scorcher!' or 'Feeling hot, hot, hot'.

I step into the revolving doors to the office, grateful for the vicious air conditioning and the man on reception who doesn't know my name but tells me to have a nice day.

I will have a nice day. A nice *normal* day.

When I walk in, though, things are immediately strange because, not only are there lots of people here before me, but they all crowd around me saying they heard what happened and how terrible.

I wonder how they even know about it but then the answer pops into my head: big-mouth Dana. After discovering the missing credit card hadn't been handed in to Heathrow security, I had no choice but to call her to ask her to cancel the card. God knows why I decided to tell her the full story. I guess I didn't want her to think it was normal for me to go around losing company property.

'What happened to the woman?' Pete says.

I've asked myself that question a zillion times. How could a perfectly healthy-looking woman, of exactly the same age as me, just die like that? 'I have no idea. One minute, she seemed fine, the next she went to the toilet and just didn't come back.' A stream of unwanted images flashes through my mind: Kate's limp, lifeless body slumped in the cubicle, Phoebe's terrified tear-stained face, me and the security guard having to drag her off her mother as she kicked and screamed.

'It must have been so upsetting,' Zoe says, putting her hand on my arm.

I shrug. Kate and Phoebe are the people who deserve sympathy.

'Dana said you stayed with the little girl until her grandma got there.' Maddie can't keep the surprise out of her voice. I can't say I blame her – it wasn't exactly an on-brand move.

'Yeah. For a bit.' I am sweating, despite the fridge-y air conditioning. I just want to get to my desk and get on with my work.

'That was kind of you,' Zoe says.

It's weird that Operation Mesh With The Team, so unsuccessful to this point, seems to have been given a totally unexpected boost. And I guess it's nice that people seem concerned about me. Even if I don't deserve it.

'We should catch up on Kitkins,' I say to Zoe.

'Yeah, when you feel ready.'

When I feel ready? Kitkins is a very demanding account and I know that with me and Samira both being off, Zoe must have been crazy busy.

Maddie puts her hand on my arm and asks if I'm sure I don't want her to make me a coffee. They are all here for me, whatever I need.

There are murmurs of agreement all round and I manage to mumble my thanks before sinking down at my desk. What on earth just happened?

Chapter Fourteen

I think about picking up the phone to my sister.

For some strange reason, I want to tell her about Phoebe. Growing up, Emilia was always the maternal one. I remember when our Auntie Emanuela had a baby and Emilia, who couldn't have been more than about seven herself, begged to be allowed to give him his bottle. She sat there staring at the baby the whole time. When the milk was duly guzzled, Emilia burped him (how did she even know to do that?) and then insisted on helping Auntie Emanuela to change his nappy. I glowered from a distance, struggling to comprehend my sister's interest in this red-faced noisy blob.

Emilia would be just as bemused by me now. *You stayed with the child at the airport, even when there were people in authority you could have handed her over to? It's days later and you can't get her out of your head?*

I stare at my phone, my fingers hovering.

But, of course, I don't call.

Chapter Fifteen

'So, we've got coconut and chocolate chip, banana and pecan, or double chocolate with fudge.'

The wedding cake lady reminds me a bit of a Labrador. I'm convinced there's a thumping tail somewhere under that pleated skirt.

'I'll just go and get your Prosecco,' she says. 'You can't do a wedding cake tasting without some cheeky bubbles.'

'She called Prosecco cheeky bubbles,' Robert whispers to me as soon as she's out of earshot.

I smile and take a bite of the coconut and chocolate chip cake. 'Wait until you taste this, though. You'll forgive her anything.'

Robert takes a bite. 'Oh, wow, yes, I absolutely will.' He licks a bit of buttercream off the tip of the fork. 'How was your day at work?'

'Weird. People kept wanting to talk about what happened at the airport. I understand they were trying to be nice, but I just want to forget it ever happened, to be honest.'

'Yeah, why wouldn't you?'

'I must admit I'm finding it hard to get Phoebe out of my head, though. Poor little thing.'

'Yeah, it's awful.'

I suddenly have this weird feeling I might cry. I swallow hard and force a smile. 'Shall we try the banana and pecan? Mmmm, I think this might be even better than the first one.'

'Maybe,' Robert says, taking another bite. 'But I definitely need to do more research! I am very glad you talked me into coming to this, by the way. I stand by my point that I don't understand all the fuss surrounding weddings, but cake tasting is not a bad way to spend an evening, especially when they're as good as this.' His mobile rings. 'Oh, bugger, it's that solicitor again. Listen, I'd better take it.'

He wanders outside in search of better reception, and I am left sitting at the table alone. My mind drifts back to the day we met, over three years ago. It was at the supermarket, something I'd previously believed only happened in rom coms. Robert always jokes that it was odd because I wasn't even on his list and, the truth is, it was very unlike both of us to strike up a conversation with a stranger in Tesco. I guess we owe our relationship to a preternaturally long queue.

When we first told our families we were getting married, Robert's mum joked she hoped he hadn't proposed in the spot where we first met because no one should ask someone to marry them next to the toilet cleaner. The laughter died out when we said there hadn't been an actual proposal; that we'd just mutually drifted towards the idea of marriage. I don't care, though. Like Robert, I am mystified by people who pop the question on the big screens at football games or hire a flash mob. If I'm totally honest, I guess I would have liked it to be a bit more romantic, but it hardly matters in the scheme of things.

Robert comes back. 'Sorry about that. Still no cheeky bubbles?'

'Not yet. Do you think we should write our own vows?'

Robert shrugs. 'If you want.'

'Apparently, Samira and Tom did.'

Robert raises his eyebrows. 'If we do write them, you'll remember to include the part about obeying me, won't you?'

I poke my tongue out.

'Here we are,' says cake lady, bouncing back into the room with two flutes of Prosecco. 'Sorry I took so long. I had one of my brides for this Saturday calling me to ask if the cake could be vegan after all. Bit of a problem as I baked it yesterday!'

'Your cakes are delicious,' I say.

'They really are,' Robert agrees. 'I can't stop eating them.'

Cake lady beams. 'How would you like to try a little bit of the rose and pistachio? I know I'm not supposed to have favourites, but I reckon that's mine!' She lets out a burst of high-pitched laughter and bustles away, saying she'll bring us some of the Earl Grey and cardamom cake too. She knows it sounds a bit 'out there' but trust her, it's delicious.

'You know the agency summer fun day?' Robert says. 'How would you feel if I didn't come?'

I want to say that I'd feel absolutely terrible. That big social events are hard at the best of times but they're even worse when you feel like your future depends on them (not, of course, that Robert has any idea of the truth about my appraisal). It doesn't help, of course, that I grew up being told I hadn't performed well at various social events I attended with my family. That I had 'sat in the corner all night', or 'had a face like a wet weekend' or 'said completely the wrong thing'. So, I don't think I can get through the agency summer fun day alone. And I know that's stupid and pathetic and shameful, but there it is.

Of course, I don't say any of that, though. Instead, I force a smile and try to squash down my feelings, which lodge painfully in my chest like something I can't swallow.

I realise Robert is still talking. 'It's just you know I have this big case starting the next day.'

The stem of my Prosecco glass feels fragile beneath my finger-tips, and the sweet, thick smell that hangs in the air and was so enticing a minute ago is suddenly cloying and almost nauseating. 'That's fine. No problem at all.'

Robert reaches over and grabs my hand. 'And this, Loretta, is why I love you. So many women I've been out with would have gone crazy if I hadn't been able to go to some big do. You're no drama.'

I push away the thought that I want to be loved for what I am instead of what I'm not.

Chapter Sixteen

I sit on the tube dabbing at my sweaty face with a tissue. I managed to get up the second the alarm went off today despite another fitful night's sleep. Thank goodness too because, even though it's not yet 7 o'clock, it already feels as if it's about 900 degrees on the tube.

I walk up the escalator. Robert made a comment earlier about how the jetlag still seemed to be affecting me. He'd noticed I'd been up a few times in the night. 'Yeah,' I replied. 'And I don't suppose it helped that dinner was four tonnes of cake and several glasses of Prosecco.'

Lucky-heather woman is outside the station. Today, the sight of her and her foil-capped sprigs prompts a totally irrational flash of rage within me. Does she really believe in the luck she is peddling? Does she think Kate would still be alive today if she'd been in possession of one of her mangy sprigs?

Stop it, I tell myself, as I pound along the pavement. Thinking about Phoebe and Kate doesn't help them and it certainly doesn't help me.

At the coffee shop, the woman behind the counter, who is given to chattiness, is even worse than usual. She is practically bouncing on the spot as she tells me all about her new granddaughter. It's her first one and she can't wait to 'squish' her. Her daughter is recovering well. She had to have a C-section but all that matters is a healthy mum and healthy baby, right?

I dig my nails into my palms. I am pleased for this woman (Nadia? She told me months ago but I'm not sure I am remembering correctly) but I did not wake up at 5.30 a.m. for this. Perhaps I'll have to start making my coffee at home or buying it from one of the faceless chain shops where it is easy to dodge any interaction that's more than three words long.

When I eventually manage to escape, I am conscious I have almost broken into a jog. Which is ridiculous. It doesn't matter if Greg is in the office before me. Except it sort of does.

Only me and the cleaner. Phew. I sit, wait until I'm sure she isn't looking and fish out an anti-bacterial wipe to clean the desk. Burnett Wade recently become a hot-desking agency but, because I arrive so early every morning, I always manage to land the same spot. Good job too – there aren't enough anti-bac wipes in the world to clean up after some of my colleagues. The other day, I watched in horror as one of the designers dropped ramen all over his keyboard and then used his fingers to scoop the errant noodles into his mouth. I pictured the bacteria swarming over each strand.

'Morning,' Greg says, walking in.

'Morning.'

'How are you bearing up?'

I squirm at Greg's choice of words. Normally, he uses 'how are you' as a conversational nicety and isn't really listening to the answer, but this feels different. 'Yeah, fine.'

There's a long and uncomfortable pause where I can practically see the cogs of Greg's brain whirring. Should he bring up what happened? He mentioned it yesterday so perhaps that's enough?

'I'm planning on leaving early today,' Greg says, eventually. 'It's George's school play and I wouldn't miss that for the world.'

I know full well that Greg has missed lots of his son's school events for much less than the world – a day playing golf with clients, one more beer at agency drinks, another look at that pitch document… He rarely leaves the office before nine, frequently works weekends and often jokes he would have about as much chance of scoring a goal in the World Cup as he would have of telling you what his son will and won't eat. If he was a woman, he'd probably be considered a crap parent.

'I'll be on email and Slack, of course.'

'Of course,' I say.

Greg disappears into his 'office'.

I switch on my computer and start working.

An hour or so later, more and more people are streaming in, and the place is becoming noisy. I instinctively reach for my noise-cancelling headphones but then I remember Operation Mesh With The Team and leave the headphones in my bag. Instead of just giving people a brief nod, I force myself to stop what I'm doing to talk.

'How are you bearing up?' Zoe says, as she unpacks seemingly endless lip balms and hand creams and snacks from her bag and scatters them across the desk like a fox pulling stuff out of a bin.

How are you bearing up? That's exactly the same phrase Greg used. I hope this is not how my colleagues are going to be around me now. I may be on a mission to mesh with them, but all this undeserved and unsolicited sympathy is excruciating. 'Fine, thanks.'

Zoe raises her eyebrows ever so slightly but then thankfully turns her attention to a bacon bap.

'Loretta,' Greg says, poking his head around his door and beckoning me over. 'I am just off the phone to Remy. He said they were, and I quote, "bowled over" by your presentation in New York.'

'That's great.'

'It really is, and it gets better because they have now formally invited us to pitch for their business.'

'That's terrific,' I say, wondering why I don't feel nearly as excited as I should do. This has to help my promotion efforts. It's exactly what I wanted.

'Naturally, I'll be putting you in charge of the pitch.'

'Great.'

I walk back to my desk.

I should be ecstatic.

But maybe it just hasn't sunk in yet.

Chapter Seventeen

Office kitchens tell you everything you need to know about human beings. The named food in the fridge, the comedy mugs that spark a chain of all-staff emails if they are used by the wrong person, the passive-aggressive notes.

> *The dishwasher is the white thing with buttons below the worktop.*
> ☺
> *To the person who ate my lunch, pay no attention to the cold sores, they're probably nothing.*
> *Your mother doesn't work here – clean up after yourself!*

Today, I have time to observe it all because I am making six – yes, six – cups of tea and coffee. Normally, I steer clear of participating in tea rounds, finding them way too much of a time-suck in the middle of my working day, but now I am supposed to be Meshing With The Team, there is no escaping them, particularly since I won't let anyone make me tea because I can't trust them to wash the mug properly first.

I have to make time for this then, just as I have to for all the other exhausting business of having friends at work. The having to remember that Helen is house-hunting, that Maddie has broken up with Alex *again*, and Zoe is going through IVF. I put reminders in my notebook to make sure I ask people about the right things on the right day.

Chris, one of the copywriters, appears in the doorway. 'Zoe said you were in here. I just wanted to say, I heard about what happened and I'm so sorry. It must have been incredibly upsetting. I would have reached out to you before, but this is my first day back in the office after annual leave.'

I happen to loathe the phrase 'reached out to you' but I guess he's just trying to be nice.

Chris pours himself a glass of water. 'So, how are you?'

'Fine. You?' Did Maddie say she wanted tea or coffee? Coffee, I think. The coffee maker has a label on it: **Don't forget to change my filter!** Underneath, some wag has scrawled, *Don't forget never to use Comic Sans!*

'No, I mean how are you *really*?' Chris says. 'It must take a while to get over something like that.'

'Yeah, fine. Oh, what kind of animal leaves teabags in the sink? Put them in the bin, for goodness' sake.' I glance at Chris who is looking at me expectantly. 'I'm fine. It's not me who died.'

Chris says nothing but I hate the way he is looking at me as if he can see inside my head. I'm not sure why he feels the need to check on my welfare – the two of us have a perfectly cordial working relationship but it's not like we're friends. In fact, I've always found him a bit weird (I know, pots and kettles). When I started here a few years ago, he was tipped for the top and everyone assumed he'd be made Creative Director. But, somehow, he took his foot off the pedal – started leaving every night dead on 5.30 and refusing to work weekends. Now, he's just a copywriter and people younger and a lot less talented have been promoted over his head.

'Excuse me,' I say, needing to squeeze past him.

I open the fridge carefully, as experience has taught me it's always so jam-packed, opening the door can mean a flying Tupperware hits you smack in the middle of the forehead. I reach for the milk which is nestled behind a pot of hummus called John and a salad called Carla.

I shut the fridge. Chris is still staring at me and it's making me decidedly uncomfortable.

'It's kind of a big deal when a seemingly healthy person suddenly drops dead,' he says. 'And for you to be the one looking after their child.'

A stream of unwanted images flashes into my mind. My hand shakes as I add milk to the tea and a little sloshes over the edge of one of the mugs. 'I'm fine. Really.'

Chris gives me a small sad smile that makes me want to punch him.

And then something terrible happens because hot tears prick the back of my eyes. I turn away from Chris, busy myself with wiping down the worktop and choke them back down.

'Excuse me,' I say, bustling past him with my eyes fixed on the tray I'm carrying.

Chapter Eighteen

Why the hell am I going backwards? The day after Kate's death, I coped with a high-stakes meeting and yet now, a whole seven days later, I'm struggling to return to normal. (My normal – I long since abandoned a quest for the other kind.)

The constant pressure to make an effort with my colleagues doesn't help. Tonight, I'm at agency drinks. I'd much rather be at home in my pyjamas but I had to come because I am Cinderella trying to make the most of every minute before midnight. I know my new-found popularity at work will be short-lived – that it's nothing more than a sympathy vote. Usually, I'd accept that trying to hold onto it is like trying to carry water in your hands but, with Greg's words at my appraisal never far from my mind, I am driven to at least try.

We are out on the roof terrace. It's a beautiful summer's evening. The fierceness of the day's heat has subsided but it's still warm enough not to need a cardigan. I have a cold drink in my hand. It could even be described as nice, but anxiety gnaws at my insides. However hard I try, I can't stop obsessing over Phoebe and Kate.

For other people, I imagine an event like this might serve as a good distraction. For me, it's an added stress. My mother says

I have always been 'shy to the point of awkwardness' and that if I do speak I 'often say the wrong thing'.

This means things other people seem to find enjoyable feel, to me, like some awful game to which no one has taught me the rules. I spent the whole of my freshers' week crying in my bedroom and, by the time I found the courage to emerge, it seemed I had missed the friendship bus.

Zoe's voice cuts into my thoughts. 'You're very quiet tonight, Loretta. Are you okay? I expect you're still upset.'

Is that true? Nothing actually happened to me. 'I'm just tired.'

Maddie puts her hand on my arm. 'We're here for you if you need to talk.'

'I'm just tired.'

There's a pause and then Zoe says it's impossible to sleep in this heat. Have I tried freezing a hot water bottle? She knows it sounds bonkers, but it makes all the difference.

I tell her I'll give it a try.

Zoe shovels a handful of crisps into her mouth, licks her fingers and then goes back for more. She catches me looking at her and holds the bowl towards me. 'Want some?'

'No.' This comes out more emphatically than I meant it to. 'No, thank you.'

The conversation swirls around me and I try to listen, but my mind keeps zoning out. It is as if someone is holding my head underwater and, every now and again, I come up for air and catch a disconnected snippet: isn't it hot for this time of night... Did you see the football... Nightmare client...

A joke Phoebe told me pops into my head. What's a rubbish zoo with one animal? A Shih Tzu. It made me laugh even though I don't normally like rehearsed jokes.

Helen is telling us she has her twenty-week scan next Tuesday. I will write a reminder in my notebook to ask her how it went.

Other people seem so good at remembering stuff like this but, without conscious effort on my part, I know I'd forget.

Maybe if I'd done that as a child, I would have been happier at school, although, in my defence, I did move schools an insane amount of times because of Dad's job as a cameraman. And I did even have brief periods of popularity. One time, the teacher assigned Lucy Harper to be my first-week buddy. Lucy was the blonde-haired, smiley, clever-but-not-too-clever girl we all wanted to be, and for those heady few days just being in her axis made her golden light reflect on me. But then both my novelty and Lucy's attentions wore off.

'Hey,' Robbie, one of the account planners, says, appearing beside me. 'I haven't seen you since… y'know… that day. It must have been awful.'

'Nothing happened to me.'

'Well, yes, but still. It must have been upsetting.' He licks his lips which have a faint purple red-wine crust. 'It's all so tragic.'

I dig my nails into my palms and fight back the urge to tell him that this wasn't some stupid computer game or action movie. A real person lost her life. A young child has been left without a mother. 'Excuse me, I'm going for a glass of water.'

I gulp down the lukewarm liquid, hoping it will quell the heat inside my brain. I am being ridiculous. It would be odd if people didn't mention what happened.

You may find it difficult to process the trauma. Shut up, I almost scream out loud.

When I go back to the group, Zoe is talking about the miscarriage she had last year and, although I am grateful the focus is no longer on me, I am also uncomfortable with the raw emotion on display. Do other people not worry about showing so much vulnerability, particularly in a professional environment? Does Zoe not feel awkward as she wipes tears from her cheeks in front of these people she barely knows?

I want to get out of here. I picture myself at home on my sofa. Robert is holding me tightly and I am crying like Zoe is now. I confess all the things that are swirling around my brain, from the fact I can't seem to get Phoebe and Kate out of my head to my shame about what Greg really said at my appraisal. I tell him I am terrified by all these feelings I can't seem to control, and I keep thinking back to when I was a small child and our dog died. The look on my mum's face as she told me not to upset myself *so* much. This is nothing more than a fantasy, though. Thursday is Robert's night to play squash and then have a drink with the boys. He'd probably skip it if I told him I needed him, but I can't imagine being so, well, needy. And, even if he was there, I would no more tell him those things than I would poo in front of him.

'Are you sure you're okay, Loretta?' Maddie says. 'You're awfully quiet.'

'It must take a while to recover after an ordeal like that,' Zoe adds.

'Really, I'm fine.'

'I wonder how that poor little girl is?' Maddie says.

Terrible, I should imagine.

'The mother was the same age as me,' I blurt out. 'Thirty-one.'

They know this already, of course. They've asked me a million questions about Kate and what happened. Questions that keep me awake at night but which I have no answers for.

'It's no age at all,' Zoe says.

'Such a tragedy,' Maddie adds.

The voices around me merge with the clink of glasses and the laughter of a nearby group.

I need to get out of here.

Chapter Nineteen

'Loretta?'

My mind snaps back into the present. Everyone in the meeting room is staring at me.

Greg's eyes are fixed on mine. 'We were talking about how this new TV commercial could help us to gain traction with younger consumers...'

'Yes,' I say gratefully. 'The truth is Kitkins has become a bit invisible to millennials. Other brands are seen as more exciting and disruptive...' With each word I force myself back into the meeting room. I am not at Heathrow Airport. I am not dragging a terrified six-year-old away from her mother's lifeless body.

You may find it difficult to process the trauma.

I finish talking. My mouth feels as if it has been swabbed with cotton wool. I swallow hard in an attempt to magic up some saliva. Why did I tell Zoe I didn't need her in this meeting? Why did I lose focus and have to be rescued by Greg, who wouldn't normally be in a meeting like this, but is here because I told him the clients are cutting up rough and could do with seeing a face from senior management?

Why am I like *this*?

I take a few deep breaths to calm my heart rate and look around the room, trying to use detail to pull myself back into it. I am at the Holborn offices of one of my biggest clients, Kitkins. We are about to present a TV commercial script for a range of gourmet cat food they are launching. The noise that made me jump just now was nothing more sinister than someone in the next meeting room popping open a bottle of Prosecco. Happy Friday!

An action-replay of that day at the airport can unfold inside my head at any minute and there is no 'stop' button. As if everyone fussing over me on Monday wasn't odd enough, at lunchtime on Wednesday, in a staggeringly embarrassing bit of role-reversal, Maddie found me crying in the loos at work. Last night, at agency drinks, I acted weird even by my standards, and this morning I wanted to beg Robert not to leave me when he kissed me goodbye (instead, I smiled and told him to have a good day).

You may find it difficult to process the trauma.

That cannot happen. My day-to-day life is perfect. I am within sniffing distance of this promotion, I am getting married. The death of a stranger can't derail me – I won't let it.

'... And now I'll hand back to Loretta to take you through the work,' Greg says.

I stand up to speak, my legs gelatinous. What the hell is wrong with me? I am the queen of client presentations.

I take a deep breath. Think about the young creative team whose work I am about to show. Often creative teams present their own work but Rod and Roland, although conceptually brilliant, are not what you'd call client-facing. Rod is pathologically shy and Roland, well, Greg always says you wouldn't want to be his character witness in court.

I pull up the storyboard. 'We open on a young, smartly dressed woman setting the table for a very special dinner. Think the finest china, flowers, candles...'

As I speak, I watch the face of Hayley, who is the client who told Zoe they had been disappointed in the last round of creative work. As ever, I can't tell whether she likes what she is hearing. She is either an excellent poker player or a cold, hard bitch.

I keep talking through the script but it's as if my spirit has floated up to the ceiling and is watching my body go through the motions. '... And there you have it,' I say. 'A table for two.'

I glance at Alistair, the senior client, who is watching me like a lion watches an antelope. 'Thank you for sharing. Megan, what do you think?'

Megan, as the most junior client, doesn't have the power to say yes to anything but has plenty of authority to 'voice concerns'. She rarely wastes an opportunity to use this so I am not surprised to hear her launch into a string of negatives.

This morning, one of the designers came into the office with a yoga mat under her arm and I had to bite back tears. I pictured Phoebe contorting through the poses, talking me through each one with her earnest no-pause sentences.

Megan has stopped speaking and everyone is looking at me. Christ!

I glance at Greg who is pulling at his tie as if it is a noose.

I have no idea what Megan said. My palms sweat. 'Err... shall we wait for the collated feedback before we start discussing it?'

'Good idea,' Alistair says.

I am safe. For now.

I let myself breathe again.

You may find it difficult to process the trauma.

But Denise doesn't know me.

Chapter Twenty

After that dreadful meeting, I told myself all this had to stop. What happened to Kate is incomprehensible and I don't like things I can't understand. More importantly, it's a tragedy and the thought of Phoebe growing up without a mother is heartbreaking. But it isn't my tragedy or my heartbreak. Obsessing doesn't bring Kate back to life.

The heatwave has broken, replaced by violent storms, so the same people who complained about the insufferable heat now moan endlessly about the grey skies and torrential downpours.

I am running and I blink water from my eyelashes, struggling to see properly as I pound the oily black pavements.

I am pleased with how I've managed to keep myself in check in the last few days. I have called on the help of my old friend 'busy'. On Sunday, I batch-cooked seven separate dishes for the freezer, Monday evening, I ticked off every single wedding planning item in my app until 'two months before' (despite my wedding being six months away) and last night, I stayed up until 3 o'clock repainting the skirting boards.

A stitch starts to burn at my side, but I force myself to run through it. Faster, faster.

Running is good. Provided you go quick enough, you stop thinking about anything. You become nothing more than screaming legs and a pounding heartbeat. You can literally outrun your feelings.

My colleagues are a problem. I hoped they would have grown bored of talking about what happened by now. After all, it's nearly two weeks ago. But it remains a topic of conversation. They wonder how that poor little girl is doing, speculate as to how Kate could possibly have died and frequently say 'it makes you think'.

I don't want to think.

Normally, I could avoid this being an issue by avoiding my colleagues, limiting all interactions to work-related ones. But, of course, at the moment, I'm supposed to be proving I can Mesh With The Team. Tonight, God help me, I am going to agency softball. Zoe messaged me first thing, reminding me not to forget my kit. It will be such fun, she said.

Hmm.

As if softball isn't bad enough in itself, emotional bloodhound Chris is the team captain, and I am fearful he may make another attempt to force me to open up (horrible expression – makes me think of surgery). Not only was there that interrogation in the kitchen that day but, the next time I was trying to brief him on some copy, he made some weird remark about how you can't 'deal with bad shit by pretending it never happened'. He said he knew because he'd tried. Let's hope tonight he is too busy with the game to concern himself with my emotional wellbeing.

I slow to a stop, fold in half and rest my palms on my knees as I let my ragged breathing calm. I glance at my running app and am disappointed to see I was fractionally slower than my last run. Still, you can't go as fast in this kind of rain.

I put my hands against a wall and lean into a hamstring stretch, relishing the delicious agony. I think about what Denise the social worker said to me about processing the trauma, and tell her in my head that I'm managing just fine, that I had about a week of being wobbly, but refuse to allow myself a second's more self-indulgence.

And that's when I look up and see the small figure wearing fairy wings.

My tears mix with the rainwater.

What the hell is wrong with me?

It wasn't even Phoebe. Well, of course it wasn't. Millions of kids have fairy wings.

Didn't stop me running after her, though. The mother gave me a horrible look when I got close. Probably thought I was some weirdo.

Now the kid and the mother are long gone but I am standing in the street, wet, cold and shaking.

Finally, I find the strength to move.

I squelch up the stairs to my flat, determined to put on a happy face before I see Robert.

'Woah,' he says, as I walk in the door. 'You're soaked through.'

'Yes, no one can call me a fair-weather runner!' My tone sounds unnaturally bright.

I unlace my trainers and leave them on the front doormat to dry out.

Robert puts his plate into the dishwasher and fetches a cloth to wipe crumbs off the worktop. Yesterday at work, Zoe was saying that, much as she loves her husband, he's way too much of a neat-freak. Apparently, he has 'pass-agg frenzies' where he rounds up all the things she has left lying around. Robert and I don't have that problem because we're both super tidy (something he tells me is very unusual in a barrister). No piles of junk mail littered around our kitchen, no wet towels on the bathroom floor and no half-drunk mugs of cold tea by the bed.

Fairy wings crash back into my consciousness and I shake my head as if to dislodge my thoughts. 'What sort of day have you in store?'

'Oh, y'know, the usual – in court defending the indefensible.' Robert folds the dishcloth and puts it back in the cloth basket in the under-sink cupboard. 'You?'

'Busy.' I think about Phoebe in her broken fairy wings. The way she resolutely refused to take them off. 'It's all about this pitch now. No point in me doing well at that initial meeting with them in the States if I then fail to persuade them to move their account.'

'You won't fail.'

I force a smile.

The *Today* programme is burbling away on Robert's phone. There is an item on saving butterflies, and a memory drifts into my consciousness of walking through the forest when I was little and my father telling me and my sister that caterpillars turn into butterflies. It was as shocking to me as if I had been told that I would turn into a racehorse when I grew up.

'Are you okay?' Robert says. 'You look a bit pale.'

'I'm fine. Absolutely fine.'

Chapter Twenty-One

I am sitting at the kitchen table, still in my wet running clothes, tears streaming down my face.

As soon as the door closed behind Robert, I let the sobs rip through my body.

I have learned to regulate my emotions. As a child, I often felt like the odd one out in a family that seemed permanently set to neutral. If there was ever a raised voice in the house or tears, it was me. Even my laughter seemed embarrassingly big.

There were many times when I was reproached for 'ruining dinner'. Bad moods were no more acceptable at the family dinner table than a fart. (A bad mood being a catch-all term for sadness, anxiety, fear or pretty much any emotion my parents deemed unattractive.)

Anger was held in particularly low regard. My parents talked about people 'with a horrible temper' and observed how they 'always lost the argument'. I will never forget my mother's disgust when Mrs Atkins from number 23 put all her husband's clothes into black bin bags and hurled them from the bedroom window onto the front lawn. 'Imagine making such a show of herself.' It wasn't until years later that I found out that Mr Atkins had drained the family's bank account and then run off with the au pair.

Misery was better but only up to a certain point. After that terrible night we never speak of, I was allowed to cry. But, after a couple of weeks, my mother patted me roughly on the shoulder and said 'chin up'. The sell-by date for my tears had passed.

I learned strategies to be more like my mum, dad and sister. Mum didn't find herself driven to remark on me being 'so overemotional', people at school rarely called me 'cry-baby' and I saw much less of my father's 'concerned' face. I was finally a round peg in a round hole (no sharp edges).

I wipe the tears from my cheeks with the heels of my hands. I need to get out of these wet clothes and go to work.

I need to stop being like this.

Sad, terrible things happen every day. People live in war zones or go to bed hungry. Children die of cruel diseases after short, painful lives.

I can't unravel because I see a kid in fairy wings.

Chapter Twenty-Two

I have managed to get myself into work but, as I go through the double doors, I see that Kathleen, one of the new account execs, has seated herself at 'my' desk.

Like I don't feel bad enough already. I have an irrational urge to pick up Kathleen's keep cup and laptop and hurl them across the room because that desk is mine.

Maddie, who is talking on her mobile, spots me scanning the room and gestures to show me there's a free desk next to her. Terrific. Perhaps she senses that I have become a fellow crier?

I take a seat and a deep breath before pulling out my anti-bac wipes. Normally, I might be a little self-conscious about being seen doing this but there is no way I am using an uncleaned desk that anyone could have sat at the day before.

Several wipes later, I start to take my things out of my bag. I pull out my notebook and realise I forgot to write today's to-do list. What the hell is wrong with me? I always write a to-do list.

I need to make myself busy with work; survive the day. With any luck, agency softball will be rained off tonight.

I am reading through a presentation when Maddie says she

wonders how that little girl is doing. She can't get her out of her mind.

My shoulders stiffen. Not today, Maddie. Please, not today.

'It's awful,' Pete says. 'And I still can't understand how the mother died.'

My stomach clenches. When are they going to stop talking about this? When are they going to get it into their heads that them dissecting everything changes nothing.

'That poor little thing without a mother,' Maddie says. Her eyes are full of unspilt tears now.

Don't, please don't.

It's Zoe who delivers the fatal blow, though. 'Have you thought about going to see the little girl, Loretta?'

'No,' I say, even though that's a lie. 'I can't see it would help in any way.'

'The grandmother could give you some answers about what happened,' Pete says. 'And it might be comforting for the little girl to have a visit from you.'

'Yeah,' Kathleen pipes up. 'I'm sure it would.'

Even the desk-stealer has a view on this.

'I don't even have her address,' I say.

'There's probably a way we could find it,' Zoe says. 'Perhaps the police could get a message to the grandmoth—'

'I don't think it's a good idea.' I know sometimes my tone can be sharper than I intend it to be and, by the look on Zoe's face, I think this must be one of those occasions.

But I need to shut this conversation down.

Chapter Twenty-Three

If there are such things as rain gods, they can't like me. All day, it poured and all day, I prayed softball would be rained off. But then, minutes before the decision had to be made, the sun came out. 'Can you believe our luck?' Zoe said to me. I told her truthfully I could not.

The less said about the actual softball the better, but suffice to say it brought back memories of school sports and I was absolutely horrible at it. What was different today was that the people around me had to pretend not to care. As an adult, you can't get away with open hostility when your teammate repeatedly fails to hit the ball.

We are now in a pub that's packed with people who are talking too loudly. I would have dearly loved to give this post-match drink a miss but then I remembered adding 'Go to softball and the pub afterwards' to today's to-do list (when I eventually wrote it). No pain, no gain, right?

Zoe and Chris are sorting out the drinks order and she asks me what I'd like.

Hot chocolate in my bed.

It's been a very long day. I feel a lump rise in my throat and force it back down.

'So,' Maddie says to me. 'How did you enjoy your first agency softball game?'

My brain struggles to form an acceptable answer. 'Yeah—'

'Don't worry,' Maddie says, putting her hand on my arm. 'You'll get better.'

Patronising cow. Let's see how smug you feel when I get the promotion.

Zoe and Chris arrive with drinks-laden trays and the conversation turns to a dissection of the game. I mean dissection too. Every inning is pulled apart and relived strike by strike. It's deadly boring but I am only too happy to zone out and give in to the bone-numbing exhaustion that engulfs me.

Perhaps I will have a long hot bath when I go home? I can break into the expensive bath oil that Robert's parents bought me for Christmas. It's been sitting there by the side of the bath for ages, too nice to actually use.

'Loretta is thinking of going to see that little girl,' Maddie says to Chris.

What?

'Yes,' Zoe says. 'It might give the poor little thing a bit of comfort.'

My chest tightens. I know where Zoe and her posse are coming from, and the truth is, I've been wondering ever since that day at the airport if I should visit Phoebe, if only because it would make me feel as if at least I was doing something. Realistically though, how on earth would me visiting Phoebe make the slightest bit of difference to her? It's the universe's shittest deal – you've lost your mum but, hey, don't worry because you've an awkward visit with a near-stranger to look forward to.

'Like I said (I resist the urge to add *multiple times*), I really can't see how it would help.'

'Oh, I think it could,' Chris says.

Of course, he does.

'Well, I have no way of getting in touch with her,' I say, hoping to strike an air of finality.

'I'm sure we could find a way,' Zoe says.

'Yes,' Chris chimes in. 'The pol—'

'I don't want to talk about it anymore,' I snap.

A silence falls across the table and I think what an irony it is that I wasted two hours of my free time playing some stupid game in the drizzly rain (the sun lasted about twelve minutes) but now I can't even manage to be nice in the pub. 'Sorry.'

Chris puts his hand on my shoulder. 'No worries. You're obviously very upset.'

Chapter Twenty-Four

'Hey,' Robert says. 'Are you okay? You don't seem yourself.'

I bite hard on my lower lip and swallow down the tears that are rising. We are in a wine bar on the Southbank and, as I walked here alongside the snaking river, meandering tourists and people blowing gigantic bubbles, I resolved to put Kate and Phoebe out of my mind. What has happened is awful but, whatever people at work say, there is nothing I can do that will make the slightest bit of difference. It's not as if Phoebe and I can be friends. What would we do together? Grab brunch, neck the bottomless Prosecco and discuss the relative hotness of the two Ryans?

'I'm fine. Just in need of a large glass of Viognier!' I try to force a laugh but it comes out as a strangled sob.

Robert looks horrified. 'Whatever is the matter?'

Treacherous tears roll down my cheeks. I cannot believe I am crying, especially in such a public place. People from work come to this wine bar. I once saw a client of mine in here.

Robert is staring at me and I wonder for a second how I can explain all this to him and if I should even try. It sounds bonkers when I voice it in my own head: I'm in bits because a woman I barely knew died. I don't want Robert to think he is marrying a basket case.

A waiter appears at the table and I dip my head. As he walks away, I wipe away the tears and take a deep breath. 'I'm being a bit ridiculous, to be honest. It's just, you know that thing that happened at the airport, well, I'm struggling to get it out of my mind.'

'It must have been awful.'

I feel fresh tears prick the back of my eyes. 'All I can think about is the little girl – Phoebe. Her mum was a single mum and so Phoebe doesn't really have anyone left. Well, she has her grandma but that's not the same, is it?'

The waiter comes back with two glasses of white wine. If he notices my tears, he is too professional to show it.

I take a sip of my wine. 'The people at work said I should go and see Phoebe.'

A small crease appears between Robert's eyebrows. 'Do you even know where the grandmother lives?'

'No, but I expect the police would pass on a message.'

Robert takes my hand in his and massages my palm with his thumb. I know the case he is working on at the moment is really taking it out of him and, up close, I can see that he has dark circles under his eyes. This is the *last* thing he needs.

'You hardly know these people,' Robert says. 'What's happened to them is very sad but they're strangers to you.'

I look at the couple at the next table who are clearly on a first date. She is laughing a little too loudly at everything he says and he is acting all confident but his hands are shaking every time he picks up his beer glass. I am so glad to be past that stage. Not that I am a huge fan of behaving as I am now. I am a great believer in your partner seeing the best bits of you. Dragging them down with your problems or venting your frustrations on them seems like the equivalent of turning up to date night in your grubby sweatpants. I take a sip of my wine and resolve to change the subject and lighten the mood. Instead, though, I find myself blurting out, 'If I'm finding it hard to process what happened, how must it be for Phoebe?'

'Extremely, I imagine. But what can you do about that?'

'I don't know. Something?'

Robert puffs out his cheeks and pushes his hair back off his forehead. 'Do you remember that woman I was defending on the shoplifting charge? The one with the shitty partner who I was convinced was hitting her? Well, one day I plucked up the courage to say that she didn't have to stay with him and that there were refuges she could go to and people who would support her. And she went totally apeshit – told me to mind my own f-ing business and that she wanted a new brief.'

'That was different.'

Robert sips his wine. 'It was different, but the point I'm making is that you can't help everyone, and these people are total strangers to you.'

I glance at the woman on the first date and wonder idly how many outfits she considered before settling on that dress. I look at Robert. 'Yeah, I know you're right, really.'

Chapter Twenty-Five

I'm not the sort of person to believe in signs, but if I was, I might be more than a little freaked out by Phoebe's address just dropping into my lap.

I stand holding my cardigan and the headed notecard from Phoebe's grandmother.

Dear Miss Martinelli,

Please find enclosed the cardigan you kindly lent to Phoebe. I am sorry it has taken me so long to wash it and return it to you but, as you can imagine, things haven't been easy.

May I take the opportunity to thank you again for looking after Phoebe on that dreadful day and for staying with her until I arrived. I am forever in your debt.

All my best,

Sylvia Harris

I stare at the small, neat handwriting. Things haven't been easy. Tears spring to my eyes. God, what is wrong with me? I think I've cried more in the last four weeks than in the previous four years. I'm turning into Maddie.

But this is impossibly sad. It is so unfair that Phoebe has been robbed of a mother. What can she possibly have done to deserve such a fate?

I picture her that day at the airport swamped by the cardigan I am now holding, her fairy wings broken and askew and her face ashen and tear-stained.

Her life will never be the same again.

My hands shake as I look back down at the notecard. The grandmother lives less than fifteen minutes away. Phoebe is less than fifteen minutes away.

I know Zoe and the others would see that as a good thing but the reality is that physical proximity doesn't change anything. It doesn't mean I can help.

I pick up the jiffy bag and stuff the cardigan and the notecard back inside it.

'I thought you'd already left for work?' Robert says, appearing in the hallway.

'I'm going now.' I force a smile.

'I think it might be a late one tonight,' Robert says. 'This case is a nightmare.'

I give myself a mental shake. Yes, I have Phoebe's address now and, yes, I happen to live close by. It doesn't change a thing, though.

Chapter Twenty-Six

I am nervous as I make my way to visit Phoebe and her grandma. Why did I let my colleagues talk me into something I know isn't a good idea? I am terrified of saying the wrong thing. This is one of my superpowers at the best of times and I know from bitter experience that I am terrible around grief.

As it turns out though, I don't even have to open my mouth to upset Phoebe. The minute I walk through the front door she says I am wearing a top 'just like Mummy's' and starts to cry.

I curse the ubiquity of the Breton.

'She cries all the time,' Sylvia explains. 'It's overwhelming.' She puts her hand on Phoebe's arm. 'C'mon now, don't upset yourself. This nice lady has come all this way to see you.'

'Oh, it's not that far.' Why did I say that? What on earth is my point here?

Sylvia gives me a wan smile and ushers me into a living room that is so stuffed with furniture it resembles some kind of storage facility. 'Tea or coffee?'

It may only be 10 o'clock but I have rarely felt more in need of gin. 'Tea, please.'

Sylvia disappears, leaving me alone with the still-snivelling Phoebe. She is a husk of the person who was singing in the queue to go through security. It's hard to imagine the breathless no-pause sentences.

Well, what did I expect? The child is hardly likely to be bouncing around like Tigger.

'How's school?' I cringe as I trot out this standard adult-to-child question.

Phoebe shrugs through the tears.

We sit in silence, every second stretching out like an hour.

'Here we go,' Sylvia says, reappearing with a tea tray. 'Oh, Phoebe, I forgot the biscuits you made. Would you like to go and get them?'

Phoebe doesn't look as if she'd like to do anything very much but she heads towards the kitchen.

'What happened to your daughter?' I say, as soon as Sylvia and I are alone. I wince at the baldness of the question but I have to know.

'It was a sudden cardiac death,' Sylvia says. 'They happen more often than you might think, even to apparently healthy young people. Kate had a heart condition that we didn't know about called hypertrophic cardiomyopathy. Her first symptom was dying.'

What she's saying doesn't stack up. I mean, you hear about the odd marathon runner or professional footballer who drops dead because of an undiagnosed heart condition but Kate wasn't exactly at peak exertion. I refuse to believe it happens 'more often than you might think' too.

I am just about to ask Sylvia if Kate was a drug user when Phoebe returns, carrying a plate of slightly burnt biscuits. She is followed by what might be the largest cat I have ever seen outside a cage. 'Phoebe made those because she knew you were coming,' Sylvia says. 'It was kind of you to make the effort.'

'Oh, well, as I said, I don't live very far away.'

105

Phoebe strokes the giant cat.

'I can't believe she's gone,' Sylvia says, her voice breaking.

Dear God, is this my fault for asking her about how her daughter died? Also, is there destined to be one person in tears the whole time I am here, like some awful kind of crying relay?

'I'm sorry,' I say, watching Sylvia's shoulders start to shake.

The cat jumps up onto the coffee table and I just about manage to grab my mug of tea before it can stick its nose into it.

'She was just so full of life,' Sylvia sobs.

I glance over at Phoebe whose small head is bowed. Surely, it can't be good for her to see this?

'I'm sorry,' I repeat limply. What else can I say, though? I don't even know these people.

I say nothing and there is silence apart from the sound of Sylvia's sobs.

The cat is sniffing the biscuits now. Sylvia doesn't even seem to notice.

'Shall we get you down from there?' I say, trying to keep my voice oh-so casual.

The cat fixes its eyes on mine and arches its back.

'He's called Atticus,' Phoebe says, wiping her snotty nose with her fingers.

I don't care what its name is, I just want it a million miles away from the tea and biscuits.

Phoebe lifts the cat off the table. It looks comically huge in her small arms and I'm a bit worried it might scratch her but it's surprisingly compliant.

'Atticus misses Mummy,' Phoebe says.

This is hell. Actual hell.

I take a sip of my tea and try not to focus on the sound of Sylvia's sobbing.

After what seems like an eternity, she stops crying and wipes her eyes. 'Sorry about that. You can be okay one minute and then suddenly it just all hits you.'

I nod in what I hope is a suitably sympathetic manner.

'Anyway,' Sylvia says, her tone falsely bright. 'How about one of Phoebe's biscuits?'

I think about the cat whose nose was all over the biscuits just minutes earlier. 'That's very kind but—'

'Phoebe made them specially.' Sylvia smooths her hair and turns to her granddaughter. 'Phoebe, why don't you give Loretta one of your biscuits?'

I watch in horror as Phoebe makes her way towards the plate of cat-infused foodstuffs. But it gets worse because then she picks up a biscuit with the fingers she used to wipe her snotty nose.

'Thank you,' I say weakly, as she hands me the biscuit. I picture the bacteria swarming all over it. 'Looks delicious.'

Chapter Twenty-Seven

On Monday morning, my colleagues ask me how the visit to Phoebe went. I tell them it was unbearably awkward, that Phoebe and her grandma both became very upset, I said all the wrong things and I don't know why I went.

Nothing I say can shake the version of events they have concocted in their own heads, though.

'I'm sure they were glad you cared enough to try,' Zoe says.

'Yes,' Maddie says. 'That must have been a comfort.'

'It was a lovely thing to do,' Zoe says.

Lovely for who?

'Did you find out why she died?' Helen asks.

'It was a sudden cardiac death. Apparently, Kate had an undiagnosed heart condition called hypertrophic cardiomyopathy.' When I returned from visiting Sylvia and Phoebe on Saturday, I immediately took to Google and was shocked to find out that the old woman hadn't actually got the wrong end of the stick. Every week in the UK, twelve apparently fit and healthy people, all aged thirty-five and under, die from a previously undiagnosed heart condition.

'God, how terrible,' Zoe says.

'Awful,' Maddie says, her voice cracking.

'Is that what happened to that footballer?' Helen asks.

'Yeah, but you don't have to be exerting yourself.' I'm quite the expert on all this, courtesy of the internet. 'It actually happens more when people aren't doing anything much.'

Zoe blows out her cheeks. 'Terrible.'

Samira walks in and I feel a surge of relief as the focus shifts and people welcome her back and quiz her about her wedding and honeymoon. Was the wedding day as perfect as it looked on Insta? How was it to have a whole four weeks off work? What does it feel like to be Mrs Halliday?

'And how are you doing?' Samira says to me, suddenly. 'So awful what happened.'

'I'm fine—'

'She's a trooper,' Zoe says, interrupting me. 'She has even been to visit the little girl.'

I feel a heat start to rise through my chest. 'It was nothing. I probably did more harm than good.' I stare at the floor. 'The three of us should catch up on Kitkins.'

'I've already put some time in our diaries for this afternoon,' Zoe says. 'And, of course, you didn't do more harm than good.'

'Yeah,' Samira says. 'Don't be silly.'

Pete walks in and, for once in my life, I am delighted to see him. I know he'll briefly ask Samira about the wedding before launching into a 'story' about his journey. We are treated to the latter on an almost daily basis – as if Pete has scaled a polar ice cap rather than got himself from Peckham to Southwark.

I bury myself gratefully in my work and don't look away from my screen until Danielle, our office manager, starts clapping her hands and bleating about how it's time to put out our cakes for the charity coffee morning. These happen regularly and I have always had issues with them on so many levels. First of all, they aren't cost-efficient. It would be much better for the charity if people just donated what they would have spent on ingredients. Secondly, these coffee mornings are very disruptive to the working day and, thirdly, I dislike eating anything that has been made in the kitchens of people whose hygiene standards are completely unknown to me. For example, Pete does not look like a man who washes up thoroughly, Kathleen didn't even bother putting her sausage rolls in the fridge this morning and Zoe has been known to stick her fingers into other people's buttercream.

For all these reasons, I normally don't get involved, neither buying nor making cakes. But, of course, we're in a post-appraisal world now. Which meant that yesterday I opened my notebook and, right at the top of my to-do list, was 'Bake cakes for coffee morning'.

I reach for the Tupperware now. Is it bad form to buy your own cakes? I made brownies which I am particularly keen on. Plus, of course, I know they have been prepared in hygienic conditions.

It's probably not the right spirit, though.

'Ooh,' Danielle says. 'Not like you to bake. What have we there? Brownies? Ooh, my favourite. Shall we say 50p each?'

As an Account Director, I spend a lot of time talking to my clients about return on investment, or ROI, so I can't help calculating that, as I spent over a fiver on the chocolate alone, 50p a brownie represents very poor ROI indeed. But I force myself to return Danielle's smile and tell her that sounds great.

People flock eagerly to the tables, their work forgotten as they dive into cakes and chatter.

My dad and I used to bake cakes together when I was little. My mum took my sister to ballet on Saturday mornings (I had pleaded to be allowed to stop as I found everything about it excruciating) which left my dad in charge of me. I can picture myself, standing on a chair at the kitchen counter, creaming the butter and sugar while my dad told me stories about growing up in Genoa. Chasing his friends around the tiny cobbled streets, the delicious smells coming from the pasticceria, the sound of clattering coffee cups. I loved the time just the two of us and, even when my sister eventually gave up ballet, my dad and I continued our Saturday morning baking sessions.

'Great brownies, Loretta,' Zoe says. 'What with baking these and going to see that little girl, you really had a very productive weekend.'

'Yes,' Samira adds. 'Good work!'

Sweat prickles under my armpits. 'Like I said earlier, it wasn't "good work" going to see Phoebe. I think it just upset her even more and I kept saying the wrong things.'

'Nonsense,' Zoe says firmly. 'There's no "right" thing to say in situations like these.'

'Exactly,' Maddie agrees. 'These brownies really are incredible. I reckon we're going to have to ask you to bring a batch to the agency summer fun day.'

I point to my mouth to indicate I've just taken a mouthful of flapjack. It's actually quite tasty but it's turned to sand in my throat at the mention of the summer fun day. I think back to Robert asking me if I minded that he wouldn't be able to come with me. How my cheeks stung as I forced myself to keep smiling and say it couldn't matter less.

'It's so lovely we can bring our families this year,' Samira says. 'Tom is super excited, and it's great for people with kids. There's even going to be a bouncy castle.'

'Hey,' Maddie says to me. 'You know what you should do?'

I have a strong feeling I don't want the answer to this question.

'You should bring that poor little mite to the agency family fun day.'

What? Is Maddie insane? Has she forgotten that Phoebe is not my family at all and is instead a virtual stranger?

'There's no way her grandma would agree to that,' I say. 'You have to remember she doesn't really know me.'

'It sounds as if the two of you have developed a bond, though,' Zoe says, popping the last bit of brownie into her mouth.

'Exactly,' Maddie says. 'I think it's a lovely idea to bring her along.'

'Me too,' Samira agrees.

Chapter Twenty-Eight

I sit on the number three bus, gritty-eyed with tiredness and bubbling with resentment. Why on earth did I let myself be talked into taking Phoebe to the agency summer fun day?

It's bad enough that I have to go. That I have to give up a whole Sunday which is normally my day to do everything, from laundry to meal prep, so I am ready for the week. Robert says I am like a soldier preparing for battle. Today, there will be none of that, though. Instead, I will fritter away the day with people I already see far too much of.

The woman in front of me is pulling chips from a paper bag, blowing on them and then handing them to a red-faced baby in a pushchair who carefully smushes each one in his chubby fist before putting them in the vague direction of his mouth. Meanwhile, his older brother is clambering all over the seat and ignoring requests to 'sit properly'.

I was convinced Sylvia would say no. If I was in her shoes, I certainly wouldn't entrust my granddaughter to some random woman, and Sylvia will have seen enough of me last Saturday to know I am no child whisperer. So, when Maddie, Zoe and Samira kept banging on about how 'there was no harm in asking', I decided I would do just that and make the call in front of them.

113

But Sylvia threw me by agreeing immediately. 'I'm sure it will do Phoebe the world of good.'

The bus lurches to a stop and the little boy in front is propelled off the seat and into the lap of his baby brother, causing them both to start wailing. 'I told you to sit properly,' the mum says.

It must be exhausting having kids. I can't even begin to imagine the relentlessness of it all. Here I am feeling irritable because I have to give up one Sunday. I could be sitting in bed with Robert now, sipping a cup of coffee and flicking through the newspapers. Not that we ever really do that. Notionally, we could, though.

The two of us have hardly seen each other this week, which is the usual way of things. Once, I jokingly asked him if he reckoned we'd drive each other nuts if we saw each other more. 'We might be like those couples you read about who have been married thirty years but then they both retire and immediately divorce.'

'Why are you talking about divorce before we've even married?' Robert said.

I stare out of the window. The heatwave is back and it's an obscenely beautiful day, the kind where you feel the weather is almost showing off. You wanna see a blue sky? I'll show you a blue sky. There is a queue of people waiting to enter Brockwell Lido. I have always meant to go but never got round to it. I wonder if there were lots of things that Kate wanted to do but never managed to? At the age of thirty-one, she would have had no reason to think she was running out of time.

It's been a particularly tiring week at work. I am used to being consumed by the actual work but not accustomed to the extra emotional labour that comes with being involved with the dramas that seem to surround my colleagues.

I am nearly at my stop now. I give myself a mental shake and tell myself I am going to adopt a more positive attitude to today.

Perhaps people will see me in a new and flattering light? Kind Loretta who is great with kids. And perhaps it will cheer Phoebe a little? That's what you call a win-win, right?

Sylvia seems to open the front door before my finger has even left the doorbell. She is heavily made-up and dressed in a wafty hot pink and red dress that looks as if it has been made from stitched-together scarves.

'She's still getting ready,' she says. 'It has been *such* a difficult morning. I don't have any help, you know. Her father isn't in the picture.' Her voice drops to a stagey whisper. 'One-night stand.'

Why is she telling me all this?

'And as for my own ex-husband?' Sylvia continues. 'Useless.' She turns to call up the stairs. 'Phoebe, Loretta is here. Hurry up now and don't keep her waiting.'

The world's largest cat appears from the kitchen and gives me a hostile stare.

'I'll have Phoebe back by 4 o'clock.'

'Four?' Sylvia says, her voice going up an octave.

'Yes, is that too late? I could probably—'

'Not too late *at all*. I was imagining you'd be later. You said it was a summer fun *day* so I imagined you'd be back around six.'

Oh. *Oh!*

'PHOEBE!' Sylvia yells up the stairs. 'Come on now. You are keeping Loretta waiting.'

'I can't find my butterfly hair clip.'

Sylvia closes her eyes and tips her head back. 'She loses everything.' She heads upstairs.

I stand in the hallway, alone apart from the malevolent cat, who is still staring at me. I would like to leave now. I am a pathologically punctual person and it hadn't occurred to me that Phoebe wouldn't be ready.

Eventually, after what seems like forever, Sylvia and Phoebe come downstairs. Phoebe is in a most unsuitable outfit that comprises a swimming costume, her silver boots and a tutu. I don't want to make us any later by suggesting she change, though.

We are just about out of the door when Sylvia remembers sun cream.

'Great,' I say, snatching the bottle from her hands.

'We need to put it on now,' Sylvia says.

'Really?' I say. I know this is supposed to be a 'fun' day but I still don't like the idea of being late. Sylvia has already dolloped cream into her hand, though.

'No!' Phoebe squeaks, ducking away from her. 'Mummy always lets me put on my sun cream myself.'

'Well, Mummy isn't here.'

Wow, even I wouldn't have come out with something that brutal.

Sylvia goes to put the cream on Phoebe's shoulder but she dodges out of the way and the cream ends up on the carpet.

'NOW LOOK WHAT YOU'VE DONE!'

Phoebe bursts into tears and then, suddenly, so does Sylvia and I stand in horrified silence as Sylvia sinks to her knees and pulls the child to her as they both sob.

How on God's earth did I get myself into this?

After what seems an eternity, they stop crying, Phoebe applies some sun cream and we leave the house. It's now eleven o'clock which is the time we were supposed to be there. What's more, I feel as if my soul has been put through one of those old-fashioned mangles.

Phoebe is as incapable of sitting still on the bus as the little boy I saw on my journey here. She also seems to be on a mission to trail her hands over every available surface and then stuff them into her mouth. I keep thinking of a newspaper article I read which said that 90 per cent of surfaces on public transport have traces of faecal matter on them. Faecal matter! Our conversation is a rinse-and-repeat version of:

How's school?

Okay.

Take your hands out of your mouth. What have you been doing at school?

Nothing.

Take your hands out of your mouth.

Is your teacher in— Take your hands out of your mouth.

Things are even worse at the station. Phoebe can't seem to stay behind the yellow line and I start to experience the very real fear that I may not be able to return her to Sylvia alive.

I am very grateful when we are safely in our seats on the train and my breathing starts to return to normal. I tell Phoebe a little about who will be there later. I know some of this information will mean nothing to her but I like to be prepared before I am thrust into any kind of social gathering so think I should extend her the same courtesy. Plus, it's better than the two of us passing the whole journey in total silence. 'I think there'll be quite a few children there as well.'

Phoebe nods. 'Grandma's friend Patty told me my mummy is in a better place.'

The woman sitting opposite looks up from the book she is reading.

'But Mummy always says she's most happy when she's with me so, if she's not with me, then how can it be a better place?'

My head spins. What the hell am I supposed to say? 'Erm… umm…'

Phoebe scratches her head. 'I don't really like Patty.'

When we get off the train, Phoebe asks me if she can put the ticket in the machine. Her mummy always lets her.

I find her use of the present tense in relation to her mother discombobulating. 'Sure.'

When we reach the barriers, a member of staff ushers us through the disabled gate.

'I didn't put the ticket in the machine,' Phoebe says.

'Oh, sorry. It's because that nice man let us through the special gate.'

Phoebe has stopped in her tracks. 'You promised.'

'Well, I wouldn't say I promised.'

'YOU PROMISED!' A fat tear rolls down her face.

'Come on now, Phoebe. Don't be silly. Let's go and have some fun.'

But Phoebe stays right where she is in the middle of the busy station, getting in everyone's way. She has started to properly cry now too. Shoulder-shaking, snotty wailing that makes passers-by stare and me want to scream, I DIDN'T DO ANYTHING.

I can feel the sweat start to bead above my top lip. 'Come on now, Phoebe. It's not worth being upset about.'

Phoebe achieves the seemingly impossible by wailing even louder. An old lady with tight white curls stops and shakes her head.

'Phoebe,' I say, gingerly placing my hand on her arm. 'Don't get so upset.'

At a point where I am genuinely afraid a passer-by might be about to call social services, Chris appears with a mop-haired little boy who must be his son.

'Loretta,' he says, stopping.

'Hi,' I say, trying to sound calm despite the screaming banshee at my feet. 'Phoebe is just having a bit of a moment because she didn't get to put the ticket in the machine.'

'And she pr... pr... promised I could,' Phoebe says, through choking sobs.

'I didn't exactly promise.'

'Zack likes to do that too,' Chris says, kneeling down to Phoebe's level.

'Well, I used to,' Zack says.

Within a couple of minutes, Chris has managed to persuade Phoebe to calm down. He tells her she can definitely put the ticket in the machine on the way back.

The four of us step outside the station, where the sun is beating down, and it's the kind of heat that feels like it will melt the pavements.

'You go to my school,' Phoebe says to Zack.

Zack looks appalled by this information. 'What year are you in?'

'One.'

'Hmm,' Zack says, sniffing. 'I'm in year two.'

'Isn't that a funny coincidence?' Chris says.

I make noises to suggest that it is, but really I'm still trying to process the humiliation of a few minutes ago. All those people who witnessed that hideous scene.

'The fun day is being held in our boss's garden,' I say to Phoebe, hoping to convey the message that I would like her to be on her best behaviour from now on. No more stunts. It's bad enough that Chris had to witness Loretta the frazzled mess. I need the rest of my colleagues to see kind, fun, got-it-under-control Loretta.

Greg's garden is absolutely massive and still has plenty of lawn leftover despite there being a pop-up bar, BBQ station, boules court, bouncy castle, softball pitch and what must be about sixty people.

'Chris,' Greg says. 'And Loretta. I didn't think you'd come.

119

You've both met my wife, Elspeth, haven't you? And my son George?'

George eyes Phoebe and Zack warily.

'Can we play boules?' Zack says to Chris.

'Sure thing. Anyone else want to join us?'

We all shake our heads.

'And who is this?' Greg says, looking at Phoebe.

I wait for Phoebe to introduce herself but she has jammed her thumb in her mouth and is staring at the ground.

'This is Phoebe.'

Elspeth sinks down to her haunches. 'Lovely to meet you, Phoebe. We're going to have a fun day today. Would you like to have a go on the bouncy castle?'

Phoebe shakes her head.

I wish she wouldn't act so sullen. Doesn't she realise this is my boss's wife?

'No? Well, maybe later.' Elspeth stands up and looks to me. 'Do go and find yourselves a drink.'

We are on our way to the bar when we are intercepted by Zoe, Maddie and Samira who cluck effusively over Phoebe.

'I love your outfit,' Zoe says.

'Thanks,' I say, before realising she was speaking to Phoebe.

There's slightly awkward laughter which is interrupted by the arrival of Pete and his wife. I didn't even know he was married, actually. Truly, there is someone for everyone.

'Is this the man you said was boring?' a previously mute Phoebe pipes up.

I feel the heat rise through my chest and know I will have turned the colour of the geraniums. 'I don't think I said th—'

'Yes, you did. On the train.'

'Just joking around,' I say weakly.

Pete and his wife both laugh, frostily.

'I think I want to go on the bouncy castle now,' Phoebe says.

'Oh, okay. Well, off you go, then.'

'Bless her,' Zoe says, as Phoebe runs off.

'What she's been through,' Samira adds.

Maddie's eyes are wet with unspilt tears. 'Poor little thing.'

'It was lovely of you to bring her today,' Zoe says to me.

'Oh, well, it's nothing, really.' I look at Greg's magnificent garden and huge house. I could have a home like this one day if I keep working hard. I'd love my parents to see that. They may not approve of advertising very much but surely they'd be proud if I achieved this sort of success?

My thoughts are interrupted by the sounds of an altercation and I look towards the bouncy castle to see that Greg's son and Phoebe are hurling abuse at each other.

I run across the lawn at the same time as Greg and his wife.

'SHE PUSHED IN!' George shouts.

'NO, I DID NOT!' Phoebe shouts back.

'YOU'RE LYING!' George turns to his parents. 'SHE'S LYING.'

'Sweetheart, you know what we've talked about,' Elspeth says. 'No shouting and no name-call—'

Phoebe, who has turned almost purple in the face, hurls herself at George, knocking him off his feet and pummelling him with her balled fists. 'I AM NOT A LIAR! I AM NOT A LIAR!'

I watch, frozen with horror, before it dawns on me that I am responsible for this child.

And that this is not going to help my chances of promotion.

Chapter Twenty-Nine

Luckily, Phoebe's punches injure no more than George's pride but I can't help noticing that, when the two of them are ushered on to the bouncy castle, he keeps a safe distance away from my pugnacious charge, as do the rest of the bouncing kids.

'I am so sorry,' I say to Greg and Elspeth. 'I don't know what came over her. I don't really know her at all, if I'm honest.'

Elspeth waves away my apology, saying she has been told what Phoebe has been through recently so it's understandable that she's 'a little emotional'.

'Absolutely,' Greg adds, looking decidedly less forgiving.

After a few minutes, Phoebe hurls herself off the bouncy castle and declares she's had enough.

My God, all that fuss for nothing!

She pulls on the silver boots and we go back to the others, who are sitting on a big picnic blanket. Samira is talking about the floating market that she and Tom visited on their honeymoon and he is looking at her as if he thinks she could walk across that water. Does Robert ever look at me like that? Or, for that matter, me at him? It doesn't matter. We are different sorts of people.

'Was the bouncy castle fun?' Zoe says to Phoebe.

'Super fun,' Phoebe replies.

Really?

Samira moves briefly away from Tom to pour me a glass of wine. 'Reckon you could do with one.'

I could do with considerably more than one. I take a big glug and try to force my shoulders down from under my ears. Everything is going to be okay. This awful day is going to come to an end. I will soon be back to my simple child-free life.

The conversation swirls around me and, after a few minutes, I realise that the sunshine and the wine are doing their work and I am starting to feel slightly more relaxed. What's more, Phoebe suddenly seems to be having a great time. She is talking in the breathless no-pause sentences I remember from when I first met her and looks to be charming all the adults around her.

'I got a joke,' she says. 'What do you call a rubbish zoo that only has one animal?'

'I don't know,' Zoe's husband says, grinning. 'What do you call a rubbish zoo that only has one animal?'

'A Shih Tzu.'

Everyone roars with laughter.

'Can I go for another drink?' Phoebe says to me.

'Bless her,' Samira says, as soon as she's out of earshot.

'She's an absolute darling,' Zoe adds.

'And so brave,' Maddie says, her voice breaking.

Phoebe returns with a glass of lemonade that's almost as big as her head. I wonder briefly if she's allowed fizzy drinks but nobody has told me otherwise, have they?

She downs it greedily and then goes back into social mode. It's extraordinary to watch, actually – she could certainly teach me a few things about making small talk.

'You know the only thing that's missing from today?' Zoe's husband says. 'A swimming pool.'

Everyone makes murmurs of agreement. Wouldn't that be amazing? They could so do with cooling off right now. There's plenty of room for a pool in this garden too.

'I wouldn't like a pool because I can't swim,' Phoebe says, suddenly looking serious. 'Mummy was going to take me to Little Fishes swimming lessons in Dulwich—'

'At Dulwich Leisure Centre?' Chris says.

When did he pop up? A minute ago, he was playing softball with a bunch of the kids.

'We used to go to Little Fishes, didn't we, Zack?'

'Yeah, when I was like four.'

Phoebe is pulling at a patch of grass. 'I asked Grandma to take me to Little Fishes but she says she can't.'

Maddie's face looks as if it's folding in on itself.

'Grandma might change her mind,' I say.

Phoebe shakes her head so hard it's a wonder it doesn't fall off. 'She says she's too old and too tired and she has spent enough of her life taking people to swimming lessons.'

'Food is ready,' shouts the man behind the BBQ.

We queue up for burnt sausages and flaccid-looking white buns.

If Phoebe is upset by talking about the swimming lessons, it does not affect her appetite in any way. She puts away an unfeasible amount of sausages and buns and then wolfs down two bowls of ice cream and chocolate sauce in seconds. 'Can I have another one, please?'

'Umm—'

'Oh, go on,' Samira says to me. 'It's a special day after all.'

I'm not sure special would be my word for it. 'Okay, but just a small bowl.'

Phoebe comes back with a bowl of ice cream that's bigger

than the other two put together. She gobbles it down and then launches into some complicated story that appears to have started in the middle and doesn't actually have a point.

The other adults still appear utterly charmed by her, though.

Phoebe's story reaches a crescendo and, before I know it, she has fallen asleep with her head in my lap. This suddenly going from on to off is exactly what she did at the airport that day.

'Bless her,' Zoe says.

I look down at Phoebe. I have to admit she does look rather angelic when she's fast asleep. And it is quite nice feeling the weight of her in my lap. I stroke her hair. It's soothing – a bit like stroking a puppy.

'You and David are both so good with kids,' I say to Zoe. 'I hope the IVF works for you.' As I say this, I am struck by the realisation I really mean it. I have always liked Zoe, but now I've been making a bit more effort with her, I'm what the Americans would call 'invested' in her life.

'You know what you should do?' Pete says to me. 'You should take Phoebe to swimming lessons.'

What? Is he serious? Surely he can't expect me to take Phoebe to swimming lessons week in, week out? I mean, today is one thing, but I can't make a regular commitment.

There is a chorus of approval.

'There's absolutely no way I can do that,' I say, trying to keep my voice even. 'I go to work for a start.'

'The lessons are at the weekend,' Chris says.

'I'm sure her grandma wouldn't let me take her,' I say firmly.

'I bet she would,' Maddie says.

'Yeah, she'd probably be glad of the break,' Samira says.

'No harm in asking,' Chris says.

'No harm at all,' Zoe agrees. 'And she clearly adores you.'

Clearly adores me? What are these people on? I look at the sea of expectant faces.

Phoebe squirms in my lap and then opens her eyes, blinking in the sunlight. 'I don't feel so good.'

'What—' I say, as she vomits copiously all over my thin white skirt.

Chapter Thirty

It's been so long since I spoke to my sister, I can barely remember her voice. Her laugh is still crystal clear in my mind, though. Too big for her body, occasionally turning snorty so that our dad would call her his 'piccolo porcellino'.

I miss that laugh.

Chapter Thirty-One

'She's not on the list,' the weaselly-looking receptionist at the leisure centre says.

I don't dare look at Phoebe. We've already had a scene this morning because she didn't want to walk 'all the way' to the leisure centre.

'Could you look again, please?' I say. 'Phoebe Harris.'

'She's not on the list.'

'She must be.'

The receptionist shakes his head. 'Did you book the lessons online?'

'It wasn't me who booked them.' I give the receptionist a look to suggest he shouldn't push me on this subject.

'Well, then perhaps you should call whoever did.'

Great, so much for the look. I glance at the turnstiles that lead towards the pool and briefly consider vaulting them. 'Do you have any spaces left?'

'On the Little Fishes course?'

No, Zumba. I dig my nails into my palms. 'Yes.'

The receptionist consults his computer screen. 'Yes, we do.'

'Then could you book her in now, please?'

'Are you members?'

'No.'

'You need to be members.'

'Mummy booked the lessons but then she died,' Phoebe pipes up.

The weasel's eyes bulge and he scratches at his thin white neck. 'We could do the membership now.'

In the changing room, the scents of lots of different bodies fight with disinfectant and chlorine. Phoebe starts undressing and I use the moment to look at my notebook and see what tasks I have to complete today. It's quite a long list but mercifully, as it's a Saturday, there is nothing on there against Operation Mesh With The Team. This is a huge relief as it's become easily the most exhausting part of my working life, especially as I so often seem to get it wrong. Pete has been decidedly offish with me since Phoebe dropped me in it about calling him boring, I've made Maddie cry twice recently (not hard, to be fair) and even Zoe, who I genuinely like, often seems a bit disappointed in me, saying things like 'you don't give much away, do you?'. The only time people seem to properly warm to me is if they're talking about Phoebe and the burgeoning relationship they imagine the two of us share.

I look up from my notebook to see Phoebe is still half-dressed. What on earth has she been doing all this time? 'Do you need help?'

'I'm not a baby.'

'Remind me again why you're taking a child you barely know to swimming lessons?' Robert said to me earlier.

I mean, where to start really? 'It's not as if I'll have to do very much. I'm not teaching Phoebe breaststroke myself, I'm just sitting there by the side of the pool. I can use the time to do some work or read a book or something. You know I'm always saying I wish I had more time to read.'

Finally, Phoebe is in her swimming costume.

'Right,' I say. 'Enjoy the lesson.'

'I don't want to do it.'

'What?'

Phoebe's head dips. 'I'm scared.'

A woman who is lifting one of her pendulous breasts to dry underneath it glances over.

I can feel myself starting to sweat. 'You're going to be absolutely fine.'

'But I don't know how to swim.'

I resist the urge to say that is rather the point of us being here. 'Nobody in the class will know how to – and the swimming teacher will be very good at helping you to learn.'

Nine long minutes later, I take my seat on one of the blue plastic flip-up seats by the side of the pool.

'Excuse me,' says a very young-looking girl wearing a Little Fishes swimsuit. 'Are you Phoebe's mum?'

There really ought to be some kind of badge that kids with dead parents wear. 'I'm looking after her.'

'She needs a swimming cap.'

'Ahh, okay. I'll bring one next week.'

'She needs one now. It's the rules.'

I briefly consider arguing or even playing the sympathy card but then I remember seeing swimming caps on sale in reception. I glance at Phoebe who is shivering by the side of the pool while her classmates bob around in the water with floats and noodles.

After a mercifully brief interaction with weasel-face and taking off my own socks and shoes (trying not to think about the verruca risk), I am by the side of the pool with the swimming cap.

'Ouch!' Phoebe wails. 'Ouch!'

I pull harder to try to get the yellow latex cap over Phoebe's head. Did I buy the wrong size? Is Phoebe's head preternaturally big?

'YOU'RE HURTING ME!'

I suddenly feel as if every pair of eyes in or around the pool is on me. 'You need to stand still.'

'BUT YOU'RE HURTING ME!'

I give the cap a final sharp tug. 'There. All done.'

A hard plastic seat has never felt so good. Why on earth am I doing this, I think, as I yank my socks and shoes back on, lean back and close my eyes. It is unbearably hot in here and my efforts with the swimming cap have left me covered in sweat. The over-powering smell of chlorine, combined with the tension, is making me a bit nauseous too. Never mind, Phoebe is in the pool now. As soon as I start to feel semi-normal, I can get on with some work.

'Loretta.'

I open my eyes to see Phoebe standing in front of me, dripping and shivering.

'I need a wee.'

'What, now?'

Phoebe nods.

'Why didn't you have one before we left the changing room?'

'I didn't need one then.'

I resist the urge to point out this was all of six minutes ago. No sense in setting her off, though. I am quickly discovering she is only ever seconds away from meltdown. 'Do you need me to come with you?'

'Of course not. I'm just telling you.'

'Oh, okay.'

'Hello.'

I turn around to see Chris. What the hell is he doing here? Didn't he say he *used* to bring Zack to Little Fishes?

131

As if he can read my thoughts, Chris points in the direction of the deep end and explains Zack is in Little Sharks. He sits down next to me.

Great, now he's going to want to chat and I'm not going to be able to do any work.

'Those swimming caps are a bugger to put on,' he says.

Despite myself, I feel a blush rise. First, he witnesses me failing to cope with Phoebe's epic train station tantrum and then he sees me being equally inept poolside.

'The swimming lessons here are great,' Chris says. 'All the kids from their school come here.'

'Good. You'll have to excuse me. I've a bit of work I need to do.'

'Right, yeah. I remember when I used to work at weekends.'

Is he patronising me? Or, worse still, pitying me? I jab angrily at my keyboard.

Chris, meanwhile, seems to be focused entirely on what is going on in the swimming pool. It's overkill if you ask me. There is already a swimming instructor and a lifeguard watching his son.

I try to concentrate on the briefing documents I am reading but Chris's words keep eating away at me. 'So you never work weekends now then?'

'Hardly ever.'

'Is that why you refuse to work on pitches?' I want him to know we can all judge each other's choices. That if the rest of us didn't work on pitches, the agency would soon go out of business and he wouldn't be able to pay his mortgage.

'Yeah.'

I go back to reading through the briefing documents but Chris's words are still niggling me. 'I remember when I first started at the agency and you were there all hours. What brought about the change of ways?'

'Err—' He swats his hand through the air. 'Long story.'

Yeah, I bet it's actually a very short story: guy becomes lazy and decides to coast. I go back to my work.

'Loretta,' Chris says, a few minutes later, pointing towards the pool. Phoebe is out of the water and is hunched over in tears. She is flanked by the swimming teacher who is patting her arm ineffectually.

'What's the matter now?' I mutter, snapping my laptop shut and pulling off my socks and shoes again.

'You okay?' I ask, which is a pretty stupid thing to say because Phoebe is now a shuddering mass of snot and tears.

Phoebe can barely get the words out to answer and, without thinking, I find myself glancing across at Chris with a 'what do I do now' expression. He is barefoot and on the other side of Phoebe within seconds.

'I… I… mis… I miss my mummy.'

Where did that come from? Just minutes earlier, Phoebe was holding onto the edge of the pool and happily kicking her legs to see who could splash hardest.

'Of course you do,' Chris says. 'And sometimes you're just doing normal things and it's really bad, right?'

Phoebe looks at him through the tears and nods.

'It's okay to feel sad,' Chris says.

Eventually, Phoebe stops crying and announces she is ready to go back to her swimming lesson.

'Are you sure?' I say. 'There's only five minutes of it left now.'

'I'm sure,' Phoebe says. She waddles back towards the pool, her armbands keeping her arms far from her body. She inches her way down the steps and I can't help noticing that some of the other kids in the class are staring at her, presumably intrigued by the tears. I feel a wave of protectiveness that makes me want to tell them that she's been through a lot and to wind their necks in.

'Thanks,' I say to Chris, as we sit back down. I may not want him to be here but I definitely needed him in the last few minutes. 'I wasn't really sure what to say to her. I'm rubbish with kids.'

'You're not rubbish. It just takes a bit of practice.'

'Hmm, well, I was certainly out of my depth back there.' I smack my hand to my head. 'Whoops, unintentional pool pun.'

Chris laughs. 'You should be a copywriter. It is difficult to say—'

He is interrupted by the arrival of Zack who wants to know if Chris saw how fast he swam 50 metres and how he was 'so much quicker' than Arthur and could they have a hot chocolate, please – with whipped cream because he has worked really hard.

'Yes, I did see it, yes, you were faster than Arthur but don't be horrible and yes, we can have a hot chocolate.' Chris picks up the bag at his feet. 'Nice to chat, Loretta. I guess I'll see you at work. And here next week.'

Oh my God, he's going to be here *every* week.

I don't have time to dwell on this unpalatable piece of news because Phoebe has appeared before me. 'Did you see I put my head under the water, right under the water? I was the only one who would and the teacher said I was a very brave girl. Did you see, did you see?'

'Yes,' I lie. It is almost impossible to reconcile this child against the sobbing little person of just five minutes beforehand.

In the changing room, Phoebe pulls off her swimming cap, saying loudly and cheerfully it squeezed her head way too tight and pulled her hair the whole lesson so she doesn't think I can have put it on right.

'I don't think you can put them on wrong,' I mumble, wondering if it is my imagination or if there are now several pairs of inquisitive eyes on me. Yes, yes, I feel like shouting, I'm an amateur at all this – busted. 'Change as quickly as you can.' I am desperate to be back at home now – and child-free.

'I can't put my leggings on,' Phoebe says.

I bend down to help her but it is as if she has been swimming in glue and not water. 'I don't think you have dried yourself properly.'

'Well, you told me I had to hurry up.'

I feel a small stab of guilt. Being around a small child seems like one long demonstration of my inadequacies.

'There are a lot of people in here with no clothes on,' Phoebe says loudly, taking the towel I have handed back to her.

I breathe a sigh of relief as we finally emerge from the fetid changing room, my own brow only marginally less damp than Phoebe's.

'Did you bring snacks?' Phoebe asks.

'Err, no.'

'It's just I'm very, very hungry now. Too hungry to get all the way to Grandma's house.'

I sense another imminent meltdown. 'I'll buy you a small snack at the café. Something healthy, though.'

The pair of us stand in the café looking at the clingfilm-shrouded plates of sweaty cakes and the sorry-looking brown bananas.

'I could have crisps.'

I hesitate. It seems mad to fill her up with palm oil and E numbers when she has just been for a swim. 'How about an apple?'

'They're not very nice.'

I look at the wizened, yellow-green offerings and am forced to concede she has a point.

'Lucy the swimming teacher said I got 9 out of 10 for my swimming lesson today,' Phoebe says, as we queue to pay for the crisps. 'She said I was good to go in the water when I didn't want to and brave to put my head under.'

'That's great,' I say, thinking I'd give myself about 3 out of 10 for my childcare skills.

Chapter Thirty-Two

Weekdays are spent trying, and mostly failing, to conquer my ever-growing to-do list. The way things are going, the trusty Moleskine notebooks may have to be jettisoned for something fatter. The tasks have a Groundhog Day quality about them. I am always in discussions about our strategy for this pitch, I am frequently finding new ways to tell creative teams their work sucks and, if I have to write one more report about 'agile' working, I think I might throw myself off the roof terrace. My Mesh With The Team tasks are equally repetitive. Go to a social occasion I'd rather not, take time I don't have to eat lunch with people, and remember to ask how their date/evening/doctor's appointment went. At least my work tasks are within my comfort zone. But when I'm interacting with my colleagues, I often get the sense there's a code I have yet to crack. How was I to know Zoe wouldn't want me asking about her egg harvesting in front of other people?

Robert and I pass like the proverbial ships in the night, stopping to converse briefly as we wolf down a piece of grilled salmon or yet another takeaway. Often the conversation turns to Phoebe and the swimming lessons. He simply can't understand why I would give up most of my Saturday when I am already so busy.

I can't answer that, of course, so instead just protest it isn't most of my Saturday and the course only runs for eight weeks.

I would never admit that I wake on Saturday mornings with a ball of panic in my stomach. It's not that Phoebe can't be very endearing. And I have to admit it is gratifying how much she seems to like me. I can't say I deserve this. All I have done is show up, produce the right snacks and laugh when she said Sylvia's stew looked like dog food. If only relationships with proper human beings were this easy.

What makes spending time with Phoebe hard is that I am in constant fear of one of her meltdowns, which arrive without warning.

I do my best to mitigate any upsets. We take the bus to the leisure centre rather than walk (God, Phoebe loves the bus – telling her we are going to hop on the number 37 sparks the sort of reaction I'd expect if I said I was taking her to Disneyland), I always have snacks about my person and, after the debacle with the swimming cap the first week, I spent ages watching how-to videos on YouTube. I was actually watching one at work when Greg crept up behind me, and I was mortified, especially as, earlier that day, I had been telling him how insanely busy all my projects seem to be at the moment.

One thing I have come to accept is that I am never going to do any work while I sit poolside. Instead, I have fallen into the habit of chatting with Chris. He's actually pretty good company, even if I do find his total lack of drive and ambition mystifying.

Today, he surprises me by turning up with a latte for me. 'Double shot, just how you like it.'

How does he even know that? 'Thanks.'

'You're welcome,' he says, flipping down the blue plastic seat. 'How are you doing?'

'Good. Just hoping that Phoebe makes it through the lesson without something upsetting her. It's a bit like taking care of Beyoncé. I'm half expecting her to demand I fill the changing room with white roses, scented candles and massage tables.'

'To be fair, that does sound pretty nice,' he says, laughing. 'How is the pitch going?'

'Hmm, it's going. The initial round of creative work isn't quite there yet.'

He nods. 'Have you told Dillon your concerns?'

'I tried to.'

Chris says nothing and I wonder what he's thinking. The truth is, Chris would be a way better Creative Director than Dillon. If he'd shown even a hint of commitment, he'd have outranked him ten times over by now. Eventually, he says, 'You know how you can be quite... erm... well... direct—'

'Do you mean rude?'

'I didn't say that. The thing about Dillon is he has quite a fragile ego. If you make him feel as if he's under attack, you won't get anything out of him.'

'That's ridiculous,' I say, sighing. 'This is work we're talking about. It's not personal.'

'Riiiiight. How would you feel if Dillon said you screwed up a client presentation?'

'That's different.'

'How?'

I am struggling to formulate an answer when I hear a howling coming from the direction of the pool. I look over to see that Phoebe is out of the water and ripping off her swimming goggles.

'Oh God,' I say, taking off my shoes and socks.

'What happened?' I say when I reach Phoebe. 'Did you hurt yourself?'

'No one wa… wa… wa… wants to be my partner to do the noo… noo… noodle work.'

'Oh, okay. Listen, don't get so upset. Maybe you can do the noodle work on your own?'

Phoebe shakes her head. 'I wa… wa… want to go home.'

'But it's only halfway through the lesson.'

'I WANT TO GO H… H… HOME.'

I try to persuade her, I really do, but two minutes later I find myself back in the hot, smelly changing room. How do parents do all this on a daily basis?

Another thought crashes into my consciousness: Phoebe is like this right now *because* she has no parents. I bend down and put my arms around her, even though she is still wet. 'It's okay, it's okay.'

Eventually, she stops crying and manages to dress.

I am used to leaving the leisure centre feeling tired and inept but this is different. Today I'm just very, very sad.

We sit on the bus in silence, Phoebe turning down my offer of a snack. 'Are you sure? I've got hummus. And carrot and cucumber cut in very thin sticks, just how you like them.'

'Nobody ever wants to be my partner.'

'Oh, I'm sure that's not true.'

'It is true. Nobody wants to be my friend. I'm not even invited to Olivia's birthday party. Everyone else is but not me.'

My mind cartwheels. I am desperately sad for Phoebe and I know all too well what it's like to not feel in with the in-crowd at school (or even now, for that matter). My sister always made friends so easily and, even though we constantly moved schools as kids, she always seemed to have people to hang out with. I was – am – someone who you need to get to know, and even then I'd question whether I'm worth the effort.

'There will be other parties.' It's a stupid thing to say. The kind of thing my parents always used to say to me, which never made me feel in the slightest bit better.

Phoebe jams her thumb into her mouth. Seconds earlier, her hands were all over the bus window. I know I should tell her buses are dirty places but I just don't have the heart right now.

Chapter Thirty-Three

Since leaving Phoebe on Saturday, I've felt like I have a sadness hangover I can't shake. Robert and I went to see a movie on Saturday evening but my mind kept drifting to Phoebe and I suddenly looked up at the screen and realised I had no idea what was going on.

I spent Sunday working on the pitch but, although there is plenty there to demand my full attention, I couldn't stop seeing Phoebe's little face or hearing her telling me that everyone but her was going to Olivia's party. Like the kid hasn't been through enough.

It's now Wednesday and Phoebe is still very much on my mind. It doesn't take a psychiatrist to work out why, of course. Phoebe and I may be polar opposites in many ways, but her friendship difficulties are all too close to home.

I force myself to concentrate on what's on my computer screen. I have my weekly one-to-one with Greg in a minute and I know he'll want an update on where we are with the pitch (short answer: nowhere).

Maybe I should try to speak to Sylvia about Phoebe's friendship troubles? It's hard to imagine her being much help, though. She already seems overwhelmed by looking after her granddaughter, and never misses an opportunity to tell me this is not what she signed up for and it's 'a lot' for someone of her age. It might be different if she wasn't on her own, she says, but given that her feckless husband ran off with their accountant, and her son and his wife live in Edinburgh, she has no backup whatsoever. She loves Phoebe, she really does, but she is just so *tired*. Other people her age play bridge and go to the theatre, not stand around playgrounds, help with fractions and navigate a six-year-old's patchy understanding of death. Some fool had seen fit to tell Phoebe her mother was sleeping, too, and, while she is far too bright to buy that, it has resulted in her having an irrational fear of sleep. So, Sylvia is up with her at all hours of the night. *At her age!*

I can't keep obsessing about Phoebe. I anchor myself back into the present. Maddie is telling Zoe and Samira about how Alex has told her he just needs a bit of space right now. 'I think if I give him that, he'll come back to me,' she says, a tear plopping onto her keyboard.

I'm quite pleased with myself for not jumping in to tell her she is utterly deluded.

'He says he knows what we have is very special but there is just so much going on in his head at the moment,' Maddie says.

Yeah, right. I'm glad it's time for my meeting with Greg as I really don't know how long I can keep my mouth shut.

'Hey,' Greg says. 'How's the person who's going to end up taking my job?'

I laugh and launch into an update, tackling my regular accounts as quickly as I can. I know Greg will want to have plenty of time left over to discuss the pitch and I also know, for all his outward affability, he won't allow me to go one second over my fifteen-minute time slot.

'Great,' he says. 'Sounds like you're on top of everything, as usual. Also, I've noticed since your appraisal that you've been working hard to… erm…' He steeples his fingers. 'To swim with the dolphins. Very important in a small agency.'

I feel myself blush and not just because Greg is once again spouting his cringeworthy swimming-with-dolphins stuff. It's good that he has noticed I've been more social – indeed, I need this to happen – but I can't help feeling a bit ashamed that, at the age of thirty-one, I am being praised for trying to make friends.

'Tell me about the pitch,' Greg says.

I tell him the good bits first. The Account Planners and I have been working hard, our strategic proposition is looking strong, and I'm confident we're going to be able to demonstrate that we will be a better fit for their business than the other agencies on the roster. 'It's the creative work I'm a bit worried about. It seems Dillon isn't happy with the strategy and he keeps giving the creative teams a different steer.'

'That's not good,' Greg says. 'I assume you've talked to him?'

'I've tried but he's pretty set on his way being the right way.'

Greg leans back in his chair and puts his hands behind his head. 'Let's go back to basics. You met with this client in New York. What would you say are the main pain points for their business? How can we as an agency help them to meet their business objectives…'

My mind drifts back to Maddie talking her deluded nonsense about Alex a few minutes ago and how, for once in my life, I managed not to step in and tell her what I think. And that's when it hits me. Phoebe's problem is that she is way too unfiltered. When she's sad or angry, the world knows about it. She must be *a lot* for her fellow six-year-olds to handle. I need to teach Phoebe to hide her emotions. Excitement courses through my veins. I am the world expert on suppressing and hiding feelings.

Greg's voice snaps me back into the present and I realise I haven't been listening to a word he has been saying and that he has asked me some sort of question.

My mouth is dry and my body flooded with panic. What the hell is wrong with me? 'I... err... well—'

'Do you think that's the way forward?' Greg says, irritation seeping from every pore.

'Yes.' I still don't know what the question was but I do know that Greg has suggested something. Which means that yes is the safe answer.

'Good. I'll leave you to organise it, then. Bring the whole team in here on Saturday morning. We can soften the blow with expensive croissants, coffee and orange juice. But it makes sense to have everyone in together, and weekend working always has more of a relaxed, informal vibe. Y'know, gets everyone out of their silos and feeling the whole "one team, one dream" thing.'

'Absolutely.'

Greg stands up and I follow suit.

'Wait,' I say, as I reach for the door handle.

Greg looks at me expectantly.

'Umm, Saturday mornings are a bit tricky for me at the moment.' I can't quite believe the words that are coming out of my own mouth. Am I seriously prioritising Phoebe's Little Fishes lesson above this pitch when I'm within sniffing distance of a promotion? Surely, she could miss one week's lesson? But then I think of how unhappy she is at the moment. Greg will understand – he's a father. 'It's just, you know the little girl I brought to the summer fun day?' Great idea, Loretta, remind him this is about the feral child who tore lumps out of his son. I clear my

145

throat. 'Phoebe. Well, I take her to swimming lessons on a Saturday morning.'

The smile falls from Greg's face. He is not used to me saying no to him. Or, for that matter, me having any sort of a personal life. 'I see. Well, maybe someone else could take her this one week? As you are leading on this very important pitch.'

The right answer to this is yes, of course they could. But that is not what I say. 'It's just there is no one else, really, and I'd rather not let her down at the moment because she's been through such a lot and, I know it sounds weird, but she has got kind of attached to me.'

Greg's eyes bulge. 'I see.'

'The lesson is from ten to eleven so I could be in here by 1 o'clock at the latest. I'll sort out the croissants and orange juice and coffee the night before and have it delivered.'

Greg says nothing for what seems like the longest time and I have to fight the urge to say of course I will let Phoebe down on Saturday and I will be here at 7 o'clock and bake the sodding croissants myself.

'Whatever you think is best, Loretta.'

'Thanks,' I say, wondering if I have just made the biggest mistake ever.

Chapter Thirty-Four

In the end, I manage to achieve the worst of both worlds. I take Phoebe to her swimming lesson but am snappish and irritable with her.

I moan when she makes us miss the bus, hassle her to put her swimming costume on faster and forget the wisdom imparted to me by YouTube when it's time to put the swimming cap on her. 'Ouch,' she yells, 'OUCH!'

'Don't fuss,' I say, tugging at the latex.

Phoebe stares at me. In her swimming cap, armbands and goggles, she looks like a small and rather angry alien.

I sit on one of the flip-down chairs, ruing the fact they are so uncomfortable. Surely, it wouldn't kill the leisure centre to install chairs that don't leave their users in agony for the rest of the day? Maybe whoever picked the seats has some kind of deal going on with the leisure centre's physiotherapists?

'Morning,' Chris says, sitting down beside me. Despite myself, I can't help liking him. He's funny and easy to talk to.

Too easy to talk to, if anything. I find myself telling him things I'd never normally share. One week, my mother phoned in the middle of the swimming lesson and, instead of dismissing it when he said I seemed upset afterwards, I found myself telling him that, sometimes, I feel there is just no pleasing her and that I hate myself for trying so hard when I'm thirty-one years of age.

I'm still guarded when it comes to talking to Chris about work, though. It's obvious we have such different attitudes to it and I know he wouldn't understand how, right now, I'm tying myself up in knots about the fact that everyone on the pitch team apart from me is at the agency, Greg included. They will probably all have decided on a new strategy before I even arrive. And, of course, they'll be bonding madly. Perhaps they'll even agree it's been me who has been holding the project back.

Chris starts telling me about some fantastic new adventure playground he's taking Zack to this afternoon. Yesterday, Zoe was asking me about the swimming lessons and I mentioned that Chris was there at the same time. 'Nice you have someone there to chat to,' she said. 'He's such a sweetie too. And it doesn't hurt that he's not unkind to look at!'

'Zoe!' I laughed. 'I'm getting married in five months.'

'And I am married. But it's nice to have a bit of eye candy.'

I suppose Chris is a good-looking guy. He has blue eyes that are almost violet, a smile so big it seems to split his face in two and, when he's animated, he kind of sparkles.

He says I should bring Phoebe to the adventure playground, that she'd love it.

'Oh, I'll be at work.' Reclaiming my territory; showing them they can't manage without me.

'Shame.'

There's no shame about it. I can't wait to be there.

'And then tonight I'll be whipping up the house special, chicken fajitas.'

'Very nice,' I say. 'You're the cook in the family, then – not your wife?'

Chris goes a bit quiet. 'Well, actually, she's not around anymore.'

Well, that was awkward. One of the disadvantages of taking no interest in the agency gossip mill for all these years is that I had no idea Chris was divorced. I quickly change the subject back to lighter topics.

The swimming lesson passes with only one minor strop from Phoebe. So minor the teacher manages to coax her out of it. 'First lesson she's had where I haven't had to take my shoes and socks off,' I say to Chris, at the end.

He smiles. 'Enjoy the rest of your weekend.'

In the changing room, Phoebe seems slower than ever. 'Can we go a little bit quicker, please?'

Phoebe scowls at me. She pulls on her sweatshirt but then realises it's back to front and takes it off again.

'Here, let me help you.'

'I'm not a baby.'

Sheesh, she's so touchy. I stare at the clock on the wall as if doing so might cause time to slow down. If we don't have a long wait for the bus, I reckon I could make it to work for about 12.45. That will be okay. I bet a lot of people were late in this morning, anyway. Except Greg. Like me, he's never late.

'*Phoebe,*' I say, realising that she is still only half-dressed.

Her face falls and I realise my tone must have been more nakedly impatient than I meant it to be. I force myself into children's TV presenter jolly. 'Come on, pickle.'

Not sure where the 'pickle' came from but, in my defence, I have never claimed to be good with kids, or, for that matter, people. I didn't plan to get involved in any of this.

We are just about to leave the leisure centre when Phoebe's small hand clamps to her head and she says she doesn't have her butterfly hair clip. I resist the urge to say my app has told me there is a bus in three minutes and never mind the hair clip. It's okay, I tell myself, there's another bus in seven minutes.

The hair clip is nowhere to be found and I try not to hyperventilate as we miss both buses. 'Are you sure you had it?' I say, as I scrabble around on my hands and knees looking under the benches (yes, I am so desperate I am on the floor with the microbes, soggy plasters and verrucae).

Phoebe nods. Her lower lip looks dangerously wobbly now.

'I'll buy you a new hair clip.'

'Mummy bought it for me. That day at the airport.'

It's in that moment that I know I am doomed. How the hell am I going to explain this to Greg? I take a deep breath. 'Perhaps someone has handed it in to lost property?'

Someone has not. Phoebe starts to cry and it's all I can do not to join her.

'I'm sorry,' I say, as we wait for the bus.

Phoebe cries harder.

'How about a snack?'

'I don't wa… wa… want a snack, I want my hair clip that Mummy bought me.'

I try to ignore the stares of the other people in the queue. You try stopping her crying, I feel like screaming at them. I glance at my phone and see it's nearly midday. I am so late now. I'll be lucky to get to the agency by 2 o'clock.

We sit down on the bus. This was the time I had earmarked to chat to Phoebe about her friendship difficulties and how she needs to rein in her emotions a little. Unfortunately, with an irony that totally fails to amuse me, she's way too emotional right now for me to even try.

'Your nose could do with a little wipe,' I say. 'Here, let me find you a tissue.'

'I ha... ha... have some,' Phoebe says, reaching into the pocket of her denim jacket. She pulls out a crumpled tissue and, with it, a pink butterfly hair clip. 'My hair clip!'

I don't trust myself to speak because, although I am happy Phoebe has found the missing treasure, I am also more than a little irritated it was in her pocket all the time – and that the sodding thing may well cost me my promotion. Who doesn't look in their pocket? I manage a tight smile.

The traffic is achingly slow and I am sorely tempted to suggest we jump off the bus and run back to the house. Phoebe wouldn't, though. Or rather, she would for about thirty seconds but then she'd say she couldn't go any further, and she'd be all loud and dramatic and people in the street would stare at me as if I shouldn't be in charge of a child (to which the only appropriate response would be that I completely agree).

It's fine. Within fifteen minutes, I will have returned Phoebe to Sylvia and I can run as fast as my legs will take me to Herne Hill station. I'll get to work by 2 o'clock and make up for lost time.

I decide that, now Phoebe has calmed down, I may as well use the time productively. 'So, I have been thinking about school and what you told me. You know, about feeling like you don't have any friends – although, I'm sure that's not true.'

'It is true.'

'Right, well, I think we can change things.'

Phoebe turns to look at me, her eyes huge and round.

'Maybe we can even have you invited to Olivia's party?' I hate myself as soon as those words are out of my mouth. I have no right to raise her hopes. 'Maybe. Anyway, we can certainly make things better in general.'

'How?'

'Well, I've been giving it a bit of thought and you know sometimes you become quite… quite upset or cross?' She nods. 'The thing is that it can make other people feel upset or cross.'

Phoebe says nothing but sits staring at me. Eventually, she speaks. 'But I can't help feeling sad or angry.'

'I know, but we don't always have to show people what we're feeling on the inside.'

'You mean pretend to be happy?'

'Well… I like to think of it more as having strategies to cope with your feelings.' I've been thinking about this for a few days now and looking at the things I use – running, wine, being insanely busy. Obviously, these aren't all suitable for a six-year-old, but I've done a bit of research and there are things Phoebe could do, from punching a pillow when she's angry to having a distraction box that's filled with things like colouring pens and stickers. I tell her some of my ideas now.

'And that will make people like me?'

I shift uncomfortably in my seat. 'I think sometimes people find it hard when they see others getting very upset or very angry. They don't know what they should do and then they become upset or angry.'

'I would like to have friends.'

Minutes later, it's our stop. I'll leave the conversation at that for the moment, and then pick it up again with Phoebe next week. Apart from anything else, time is against me now.

Phoebe decides she will avoid all the cracks on the walk from the bus stop back to Sylvia's. I ball my fists against my sides and remind myself that, even at this languorous pace, we will be there within a few minutes and then I can hightail it to work.

When Sylvia's front gate looms into view, it's all I can do not to break into a run and, as I finally put my finger on the doorbell, relief courses through me.

But Sylvia does not come to the door.

'Granny isn't answering the doorbell,' Phoebe says, unnecessarily.

I ring again, pressing for longer.

No answer.

'Granny must be out.'

'She can't be out. We're already late back.' I ring the doorbell again and then hammer on the glass in case the ringer is broken.

Nothing.

I call Sylvia's mobile but it goes straight to voicemail.

The sweat starts to bead on my upper lip. I cannot afford to be any later to work.

'Maybe something has happened to Granny?' Phoebe says. 'Maybe she's dead?'

'No,' I say firmly, registering that I seem to have fallen into a nightmare. 'No.' I type out a message to Sylvia, trying to avoid both the caps lock and expletives.

'Grandma always hides a spare key under that big plant pot over there.'

I feel like kissing Phoebe! I practically skip towards the pot, where I instantly find the key. I really must talk to Sylvia about her lax attitude to security, but right now I am way too happy to think about that. 'We're in!' I say to Phoebe.

And that's when it hits me. I might have the key to the house but it doesn't make the slightest bit of difference. Phoebe is six years old – I can't leave her on her own.

I try Sylvia's mobile and squash down a stream of very un-child-friendly words when I reach her voicemail again.

I sink to my haunches and put my head in my hands.

'Don't get upset,' Phoebe says, placing a small, hot hand on my shoulder. 'You know you said that sometimes when people are very upset, they make other people upset? Well, that's what's happening to me now.'

Her earnestness almost breaks my heart and snaps me out of my inaction. 'How would you like to see where I work?'

Chapter Thirty-Five

I remember my cousin Maria telling me that, once, when her little girl was sick and she couldn't go into work, she told her supervisor her boiler had blown up rather than admit the truth.

'That's ridiculous,' I scoffed at the time. 'Why is a plumbing emergency more valid than a kid-related one?'

Seeing the look on people's faces when I turned up at the agency with Phoebe today has made me a lot more sympathetic to what Maria was saying, though.

No one directly remarks on Phoebe being with me, and most of them are pretty friendly towards her, but there's a distinct undertone that the grown-ups are up against it and it isn't helpful to have a child around.

I'd kind of expect this attitude from the people who aren't parents, but it's Greg who makes a pointed comment about how he imagines Phoebe is going to be bored out of her mind.

She has actually been very good. She had a bit of an impromptu yoga session which everyone appeared to find endearing, and then Zoe fetched her a layout pad and some coloured pencils from the creative department; since then she has sat quietly drawing while I have gone into 'making up for lost time' overdrive.

'That man over there is wearing very funny trousers,' Phoebe suddenly pipes up, pointing at Dillon the irascible Creative Director.

I tell her to shush but I can't help giggling and nor can any of the people within earshot (which, luckily, doesn't include the man whose fashion choices are being debated). Dillon is wearing what look to be some sort of baggy harem pants, the crotch of which hangs somewhere near his knees. The trouble with weekend working in an ad agency is, because the dress code is usually pretty casual, especially for the creative department, people don't have far to go in terms of taking it down a notch. I wouldn't be entirely surprised to see someone come in wearing their slippers and pyjamas.

After about an hour, Greg announces we should 'huddle' and look at the different campaign ideas.

'Look at my drawing,' Phoebe says, as I rise from my chair. She thrusts a piece of paper under my nose. 'It's a picture of me and Mummy and I am in my party dress because I am going to Olivia's party because you're going to show me how to make friends and get invited.'

There is so much to unpack in that one sentence, I can't even begin. 'I'll be back in a minute.'

I feel a spiralling panic as I walk towards where my colleagues have gathered. I should never have given Phoebe the impression I can get her invited to Olivia's party. Or even help her to make friends. I hate parties and am rubbish at making friends. Phoebe deserves better grown-ups than me in her life.

Right now, I must put all that out of my mind and focus on work, though. Everyone is gathered around a wall that has been plastered with concepts.

Dillon jabs at one of the pieces of paper. 'This first route is probably the safest of the lot…'

I zone out from what he is saying because I am fine with the work he is currently talking about but much less happy with route two.

My mobile rings and I see Sylvia's name flash up. I am torn because I would never normally answer my phone in these circumstances but I have been trying to track down Sylvia for the last two hours. 'Excuse me,' I say, jabbing the green button and taking myself off to one side.

I can immediately tell from Sylvia's voice that she is drunk. She says she is sorry she is a bit late back. The trains were all completely buggered.

My jaw clenches. A bit late back? She has been AWOL for hours. I don't have time to row with her now, though. I will have it out with her when I drop Phoebe back later.

I go back to the concepts wall where route two is now under discussion.

'I don't think this approach is right,' I say.

Dillon pulls at the waistband of his ridiculous trousers and gives me a look. 'But it's by far the strongest creatively.'

'It doesn't align with the strategy we agreed on.'

'Yeah, but we talked about that strategy and decided we could deviate from it a little. This morning, when you weren't here.'

One–nil to Dillon.

Everyone is looking at me expectantly. I want to tell Dillon not to be such a bloody baby, that cheap point-scoring about me not being here is irrelevant. I want to say it doesn't matter if the concepts on the wall would scoop every creative award this self-congratulatory business can throw at them, and if he cares so much about being creative, he should be an artist or a poet and not in advertising, but I suddenly remember Chris telling me it's important not to make Dillon feel as if he's under attack. 'It is brilliant creatively,' I say. Surprise registers on Dillon's face. 'I just wonder if we could make it work a bit harder strategically? Maybe we could look at combining what we like about this route with some of the things that worked from the first route?'

I wait for Dillon to say that's impossible and he doesn't want to ruin both routes by smashing them together to make Frankenstein's monster but, to my surprise, he says it could work, and it's all I can do not to dance a little jig.

'Loretta,' Phoebe says, suddenly appearing at my side and tugging at my sleeve. 'I need the toilet.'

'Oh, okay. Well, I showed you where it was, didn't I? Don't forget to wash your hands.'

'I can't open that door.'

Of course, she needs a security pass. 'Just tap that against the little pad by the door,' I say, handing her mine.

'Please can you come with me?'

She never normally needs me to take her to the toilet. What happened to 'I'm not a baby'? 'You'll be fine on your own. The toilets are just the other side of that door and tapping your card against the thing is exactly like what you did at the tube station earlier.'

Phoebe stares at the floor. 'I need you to take me.'

'Umm—'

'Take her,' Greg says, cutting in.

I'm probably imagining the irritation in his voice.

Chapter Thirty-Six

On the train journey back to Dulwich, I picture myself tearing a strip off Sylvia for what she did today. How dare she take advantage of me like this? Going out and getting drunk with her mates. She could have jeopardised my job. Also, how appalling to treat Phoebe that way. She has already lost her mother, she does not need Sylvia to let her down.

But I take one look at Sylvia's swollen eyes and splotchy red face and I don't say any of that. I tell Phoebe to go upstairs and put her pyjamas on and that I'll be up in a minute to read her a story. Miraculously, she does as she is told.

'I am so sorry,' Sylvia says, dissolving into fresh tears. 'I didn't mean for this to happen, I promise. It's just—'

'We'll talk later,' I say. 'Let me make you a cup of tea and get Phoebe to bed.'

This makes Sylvia cry even harder. 'You're so kind.'

I feel a bit disingenuous given all the deeply unkind thoughts I have been harbouring.

Phoebe is already on the bed, in her pyjamas. She is surrounded by books and talking away softly, presumably to her raggedy-looking stuffed penguin. For a nanosecond, just a nanosecond, I wonder if it would be nice to have a child of my own one day.

But I am being silly. It's easy to romanticise the idea in moments like this but there have been many times today where I would have happily agreed to having my fallopian tubes tied on the spot.

'Is Grandma okay?'

'I think she's a bit sad.'

'She misses Mummy.'

I feel I need to say something here, but what? 'Would you like me to read you a story?'

Phoebe snuggles against me as I start to read and, a few pages in, I notice her eyes have closed. I guess it's been a long day for both of us.

Sylvia is still sitting at the kitchen table where I left her, the cup of tea in front of her untouched.

'She's asleep.'

'That's amazing. I normally have a huge struggle trying to get her to bed. You must have the magic touch.'

'Beginner's luck.'

'Listen, I really am sorry about today. I didn't mean it to happen. I'd arranged to meet a few of my girlfriends for a coffee in town. I haven't seen anyone in the last few weeks and I thought it would do me good to go out and have a change of scene. But, of course, as soon as I arrived, I started to talk about Kate and how, even though our relationship was difficult, I miss her so much.'

I wonder if my parents would describe my relationship with them as difficult. It's hard to imagine them describing it as anything at all, of course. They are not people who talk about emotions. Feelings are something to be managed discreetly and decorously.

I remember the first time I met a child who was adopted. Her name was Niamh, and she had an impossibly exotic Irish accent. Even more captivating than the sound of her voice, though, was what she actually said. The family she lived with were not her birth family.

I had only recently joined the school and was feeling particularly isolated and miserable, but Niamh's words sent a jolt of excitement through me. Maybe my family were not my actual family? That would account for why I always felt as if I didn't quite belong.

'What was Kate like?' I'm surprised to hear this question come out of my mouth. My intention coming here this evening was to read Sylvia the riot act and then escape as soon as possible. Yet suddenly, I am filled with curiosity about this woman who was the same age as me but will never again blow out candles on a birthday cake.

'She was a brilliant mum,' Sylvia says, through her tears. 'I wasn't sure she would be, given the pregnancy was unplanned, but she adored Phoebe right from the start. She didn't seem to worry about being on her own either. Said it meant she could do things her way with Phoebe. That was so typical of Kate. She was fearless about the way she lived her life. She always said it made her sad when she saw people staying in relationships that didn't make them happy – settling. Or putting up with jobs that sucked the life out of them.'

Sylvia pauses, unable to speak for a moment. 'She was funny too. Even when she was a little girl, she could make us all laugh.' She shakes her head. 'Not that I'm saying she was perfect, of course. She was the most stubborn person I've ever known. If she thought she was right about something, she wouldn't let it go.' She starts to sob. 'I even miss arguing with her.'

I am not quite sure what to do. Truthfully, this display of raw emotion is making me want to run out of the door and not look back.

Sylvia wipes the tears from her face and blows her nose loudly. 'It was my friend Min who suggested a quick glass of wine this morning. And, somehow, one became two and, the more I drank, the more everything I've been feeling over the last few weeks just flooded out of me. I didn't even look at the time until Min said we should probably have some food to soak up some of the alcohol.'

'I know it must be very difficult for you right now but what happened was totally unacceptable. I had to go into the office today because I'm working on a very important project and I ended up not only being horrendously late but having to take Phoebe with me.'

'I'm so sorry.' Sylvia presses her fingers under her eyes as if she can manually stop the tears that are coming. 'The thing is, I don't think I can do this. I love Phoebe very much but I'm her grandma, not her mum, and looking after her is just exhausting. I don't think I'd have the physical energy to cope at the best of times but that's not even the half of it. It's just so emotionally draining. She is so unhappy, and I have no idea how to help her, particularly as I'm so miserable. How the hell can I explain what happened to Phoebe when I can't begin to make sense of it myself? Kate was a thirty-one-year-old woman who rarely had so much as a cold. And, suddenly, she's dead.'

She trails off and I realise that this is meant to be my Oprah moment. I am no Oprah, however, so we sit listening to the cat which is loudly licking its genitals.

Sylvia blows her nose again. 'You must think I'm an awful person.'

'I don't think that.' But I do think I can't deal with this. That this was just supposed to be about taking Phoebe to a few swimming lessons. I never intended to get *involved*. Not like this. 'I should be going.'

'Of course,' Sylvia says, although she looks disappointed.

For a moment, I waver. It feels a bit mean to leave Sylvia like this. But it also seems like a very long time since I left the flat this morning – and I barely know Sylvia, let alone how to help her. I picture myself and Robert snuggled up on the sofa with an Indian takeaway on our laps, watching telly and talking about nothing very much. My perfect Saturday night.

I pull on my jacket. 'I know it must feel impossible right now but I'm sure you'll get through this.' The words sound hollow and meaningless. I'm sure of no such thing. I know all too well that grief can change people forever.

Sylvia nods and gives me a wobbly smile. 'Sorry again about putting you out so much today. You will come back next week to take Phoebe to swimming, won't you? She looks forward to it all week.'

My guts clench and I'm not sure if it's because that makes me feel pressurised or happy or both. 'Yeah, I'll be here.' I put my hand on the front door handle. 'And, listen, if you're ever really desperate, you can always ask me for help.'

I know I shouldn't say that but the woman looks so desolate, I feel I have to offer something. And it's not like she is ever going to take me up on it, is it?

Chapter Thirty-Seven

Three weeks whizz by and, although I am very busy, I'm pleased with how things are going on all fronts.

At work, the pitch seems to be coming together and, bar the odd blip such as me telling Samira her new trousers don't do anything for her (she asked), I am still managing to rub along better with people.

Out of work, things also seem under control. Robert and I are fine, of course, and I am relieved that Sylvia has kept to her word and always been at home when I've taken Phoebe back from swimming. What's less welcome is that, having opened her heart to me once, Sylvia now seems to see me as something of a confidante. She tells me she had just started to put her life back on track after her divorce. That she had taken up jewellery making, started going to parties, having sex. Do I know how much she misses sex?

As well as taking Phoebe to swimming every week, I continue trying to coach her in 'emotion management' and find her to be a delightfully eager student. I teach her deep breathing, counting to calm down, punching her pillow when she's angry and removing herself from situations when she needs a break. We put together a calm-down kit packed with coloured pencils, stickers and a new glittery notebook I bought her, and we talk about mood boosters such as reading her joke book or listening to an upbeat piece of music.

Today, within seconds of me picking her up from Sylvia's, Phoebe is proudly launching into a story to demonstrate her progress. 'Ben said Mummy would probably have been eaten by worms by now and I wanted to shout at him and tell him he's a horrible meanie, but I just shut myself in the toilet and did my deep breathing.'

'Good girl,' I say, while also making a mental note that Ben sounds like a right little shit.

'When I opened my packed lunch and dropped my hummus on the floor, I felt like crying but I counted the tiles on the ceiling until I was okay.'

'Brilliant.' I feel a warm glow of pride. As this is the weekend before the pitch, I really shouldn't be taking Phoebe to swimming today, but seeing her like this makes any extra pressure I'll be under later worthwhile. Plus, things are in pretty good shape on the pitch and I'll be in the office for the rest of the weekend.

When we reach the leisure centre, I tell Phoebe I need to nip to the loo and she should start changing. In the cubicle, I allow myself to daydream about winning the pitch. 'Imagine if we win the first pitch you've ever led on?' Greg said to me yesterday. 'I don't think that could hurt your chances of promotion, could it?' We both laughed at the way he was making it sound as if this was nothing to do with him.

I wash my hands and go back towards Phoebe, who is engaged in conversation with someone no one can see. I've noticed this on several occasions now and, with the benefit of hindsight, I think it was this imaginary friend and not her stuffed penguin that she was talking to on the night of Sylvia's meltdown. This doesn't worry me in any way. I had an imaginary friend as a child too. He was called Ralph and I found his affections to be considerably less fickle than other people's.

'Look at you,' I say. 'All changed already.'

Phoebe has her head in her bag looking for her swimming cap so I can't hear her answer properly, but it sounds like she says her mummy helped her.

Chris is already sitting on the blue plastic seats. 'How are you doing? Still moonlighting as a sex therapist?'

I laugh. Last week, I told him I was flummoxed about why people keep talking to me about their sex lives. Not just Sylvia but people at work. Zoe tells me how IVF really puts the kibosh on spontaneity, Maddie tells me about the 'epic' break-up and make-up sex she and Alex have, and Danielle regales the whole office with a story about the guy she met on a dating app who wanted her to dress as a soft toy.

It seems you only have to be slightly friendly towards people and they will tell you everything.

'Thankfully, this week has been sex-free.' I realise what I've said and laugh. 'Sex-talk free. Oh God, I give up.' I take a swig of my water. 'Sylvia dropped a hint the size of a blimp this morning when she told me she has been invited to a party she really wants to go to next month.'

He grins. 'Subtle. Are you going to step up to the babysitting duties?'

'I'm not sure.' The truth is, Sylvia's comment raised questions in my head about more than that one night. There are only two more Little Fishes lessons after this one and I have been trying to ignore the dilemma about what contact, if any, I should have with Phoebe after that. It seems a bit brutal to sever ties completely and I do genuinely like her. However, realistically, what's the long-term future for our relationship? Am I really still going to be part of Phoebe's life in six months' time, a year's time, five years' time? Robert is obsessed with this question and keeps telling me it's unfair to 'let the kid become too attached'.

'Never mind whether I offer to babysit or not, what really perplexes me is why anyone would want to go to a party.'

Chris laughs. 'You're kidding, right?'

'I am most certainly not. I *hate* parties.'

'How can anyone hate parties?'

A memory pierces my consciousness, sharp and jagged – fragments of a party on the worst night of my life. I push it away. 'Easily. The worst thing about them is you're expected to mingle. How does anyone do that? I have never learned the knack, which means as soon as I start talking to anyone, I can neither concentrate on what they're saying nor think of anything to contribute, because I am too distracted by this giant flashing neon red light in my mind's eye saying: MINGLE! The worst thing is, I'm sure there is some secret signal that draws people who are crap minglers together, because I am always stuck with people for ages and have to listen to their boring stories about how their child's piano lessons are going or how they have literally shrunk since they cut out wheat. At times, I've even considered taking up smoking because, yes, it will kill me, but at least at parties I'll have a watertight excuse for getting away from people – just nipping out for a fag.'

Chris laughs. 'You really are one of a kind, Loretta.'

I look over at Phoebe who has just swum a width of the pool, her legs kicking wildly. She has made so much progress since she started these lessons.

'The only party I care about right now is Olivia's,' I say.

'How is that all going?'

'Well, not to tempt fate, but apparently Olivia sat next to Phoebe at lunch yesterday.'

Chris high-fives me. 'Excellent news.'

A harassed-looking man appears, says hello to Chris and then says he has to go and feed the meter and would we mind keeping an eye on his bags.

'That's my mate, Finn,' Chris says. 'He's a bit fragile at the moment because he's going through a divorce.'

The way Chris says this, and everything I know about him as a person, tells me he'll become involved, not in the prurient way some might, but because he genuinely wants to help. 'Well, it's nice he has you for support. It must be good to talk to someone who has been through the same thing.'

Chris's face crumples. 'I've never been divorced.'

'But you said Zack's mum wasn't around anymore.'

Chris looks at his shoes. 'Lara is dead.'

The words are so shocking I can't say anything, even though I feel like I should.

'She died of acute myeloid leukaemia. Within three weeks of being diagnosed.'

'I'm sorry.' The words are woefully inadequate but what else can I say, really?

'LORETTA!' Phoebe says, hurtling towards me.

'Don't run!'

'DID YOU SEE ME? I SWAM TWO WHOLE WIDTHS!'

'Amazing, well done you!'

'Thanks,' Phoebe says, peeling off her swimming cap. 'Come on, the lesson is finished now and you said you were in a big, big hurry today.'

I look over at Chris who, although he is smiling at Phoebe, still looks as if his head is somewhere else entirely.

'See you,' I say.

'Yeah. And good luck with the pitch on Monday.'

'Thanks. Also…'

He looks at me. 'What?'

'Nothing.' Because, really, there's no neat way to resolve the conversation we've just had. I doubt even someone considerably more socially adept than me would manage that.

Chapter Thirty-Eight

I wake up bathed in sweat. I was dreaming about my sister. She turned up at my wedding and I was so happy to see her. I hugged her too hard, and she was laughing and telling me to stop crying because it was my wedding day, and I was ruining my make-up.

I told her I didn't care about my make-up.

Chapter Thirty-Nine

It's the night before the pitch. Apart from when I took Phoebe to swimming yesterday, I've been in the office all weekend and am pretty shattered. That said, I am very pleased with how our presentation is looking.

It's now nearly 8.30 p.m. and I have just returned home. Robert is making me dinner – something light and plain because I get a nervous stomach before big meetings like this. Robert is brilliant in these kinds of situations. He may be in an entirely different field to me but because he is equally work-focused, the two of us have a well-calibrated routine for any 'night befores'.

We will have our dinner in front of the TV, choosing one of our lighter programmes that doesn't demand too much of my attention. I will have one small glass of wine to help settle my nerves and be in bed for 10 o'clock.

I open my wardrobe, which is divided into colour-coordinated sections, with three quarters of the space being work clothes and the other quarter 'weekend me'. I pull out the navy silk dress I'm planning to wear tomorrow and hang it on the wardrobe door. I take out the clear plastic box containing my red suede kitten heels.

'I'm going to have a quick shower,' I shout through to Robert.

I have just taken off my clothes when my mobile rings. My stomach clenches in case there is some last-minute pitch panic. What though? The documents are already printed, the presentation rehearsed several times over and I even made the IT department come in to do a dry run of the tech.

It's Sylvia's name that flashes up. Whatever can she want?

Sylvia is sobbing so hard she is almost incoherent and my stomach lurches. Something must have happened to Phoebe. 'Slow down,' I say, trying to sound more calm than I feel.

'I cut my ha... ha... hand cooking the supper,' Sylvia wails. 'And I ne... ne... need to have stitches.'

I sink down onto the bed, a wave of relief flooding through me. Phoebe is fine. But, also, what the hell? Sylvia has cut her hand. I mean, I know it's not the nicest thing to happen but it doesn't warrant her being in this sort of state or, for that matter, calling me.

'I ne... ne... need to go to the hospital for stitches but Phoebe has thrown a big tantrum and says she won't come with me because that's the hospital her mum died in. And I tried so hard to persuade her and tell her that it's a different bit of the hospital and she wouldn't even know it's the same place. Then I said we could go to a different hospital.' Her words become indecipherable again for a minute. 'I even tried to bribe her. But you know what she's like.'

'Can't you ask someone to look after her while you go to the hospital?'

'What do you think I've been trying to do while I've been sitting here bleeding profusely?'

Jeez, don't snap at me.

'I asked the au pair who works at number 25 to come but she said her boyfriend is over from Croatia and they have tickets for a gig tonight. I asked my friend Min's daughter but she babysat for Phoebe once before and Phoebe had one of her epic melt-downs. I asked Min but she said her arthritis has really flared up this weekend and she just isn't up to it.'

I suddenly know where this is leading. But it's the night before the pitch.

Sylvia blows her nose so that I am treated to a loud honking sound down the phone. 'The thing is, Loretta, like I told you before, I have no one.'

Silence buzzes down the line and I stare at a crack in the ceiling that Robert and I have been saying for months we ought to ask a builder to look at. 'Okay, I'll look after Phoebe while you go to hospital. Do you think you could bring her over to my house, though?'

'Absolutely. We'll take a taxi and be with you in fifteen minutes.'

I pull a towel around me and go into the kitchen where Robert is meticulously halving baby corns. 'Umm, slight change of plan.'

Chapter Forty

Robert, it has to be said, is chopping the peppers rather furiously.

'Look,' I say. 'I can't pretend I'd have planned this the night before my pitch, but it will be nice for you to meet Phoebe. I know the two of you are going to love each other.' I know no such thing, actually, but surely it pays to think positive?

'I still don't understand why you said yes.'

I scratch at a patch of eczema on my arm, noting vaguely that I haven't yet managed to have a shower. 'Because there is no one else.'

Robert picks up the strips of pepper and lays them on a plate next to the baby corn and mangetout. His serried ranks are something to behold. 'I realise that, but I don't see why the grandmother couldn't have insisted the child goes with her to the hospital. She's six years old, for Christ's sake. If I had a child, there is no way I'd let them dictate to me.'

Yes, I think, it's easy to be the perfect parent in the abstract. Before I started taking Phoebe to her swimming lessons, I used to judge anyone who I thought wasn't doing it properly, be that a father with an absurdly dressed child in the park or a mother giving in to a tantrum in the chocolate aisle. After a few weeks of looking after an actual child, albeit only occasionally, I'm a lot more humble.

'I don't think it's so odd that Phoebe feels uncomfortable about going to the hospital where her mother recently died.'

Robert makes a 'pfft' noise.

I am about to say more when the doorbell goes.

Sylvia looks greyer and older than I've ever seen her. Phoebe, by contrast, is bouncing with energy and is up the stairs before her grandmother has had a chance to say she'll be back as soon as she possibly can.

I catch up with her just before she reaches the front door of our flat.

'I was invited to Olivia's party!' she says.

'That's amazing! See, all those tips and tricks we've been learning have worked.'

Phoebe is beaming and I allow myself to feel a small swell of pride. I have actually done some good.

We go into the flat and I introduce Phoebe and Robert. There's a slightly awkward moment when Robert says he's heard a lot about her and she replies saying she hasn't heard a lot about him. Robert laughs but it sounds a bit forced.

Phoebe starts prowling around the flat, picking up random things to examine them. She takes the hideous cut-glass vase Robert's mother gave us for Christmas and holds it up to the light. 'Look, it makes patterns on the ceiling.'

'Be careful with it,' Robert says.

I don't know if I am imagining the edge in his voice but, if there is one, Phoebe doesn't seem to notice and has already moved on to her next object of interest, which is Robert's wig. 'What's this?'

'It's my wig I wear in court,' he says. 'You can try it on if you like.'

She puts it on and we all laugh. See, this is going fine. Robert may not be mad about kids but he's a kind person.

'Have you had your dinner?' I say to Phoebe.

'Not really. Grandma was cooking fish pie but then she cut her finger so she didn't finish it properly and I wouldn't eat the fish in the sauce on its own because it looked a bit yucky and also she probably got blood in it.'

'Robert is making a stir-fry.'

'I like stir-fry.'

'Good.' I don't dwell on the conversation Robert and I had before Phoebe arrived where I said we'd have to offer her some dinner and he said by this time of night she would definitely have been fed ('fed'? Like she's a dog).

'Can I play on your iPad, please?' Phoebe says, picking it up before I can answer.

'Yes, you can play until dinnertime.' I turn to Robert. 'Okay if I have a very quick shower?'

He nods but I can't help noticing he doesn't look very happy. He probably doesn't like the sounds of the iPad game because he's very noise-sensitive. 'Phoebe, can you turn the volume down a little bit, please?'

She gives me a look that's pure 'tiny teenager' but does as she is asked.

I stand in the shower, letting the hot water course over my rock-solid shoulders. I hope Sylvia doesn't have a long wait in A&E because I really need to go to bed early.

I have just started shampooing my hair when the door bursts open. 'What's wrong?' I say, attempting to cover my nakedness.

'Nothing,' Phoebe says, sitting down on the loo and starting to wee.

I think about my cousin Maria who once told me that when you have a child, you surrender all your privacy and me time. I thought she was being hyperbolic.

'See you in a min,' Phoebe says, blissfully unaware of how happy I am to see her walk out of the door.

I condition my hair and shave my legs.

As soon as I turn off the hot water, I hear the sounds of a commotion coming from the living room. Robert is saying something, and although I can't hear what, he definitely doesn't sound happy and Phoebe, oh God, is Phoebe crying?

I throw a towel around me and run into the living room. Phoebe *is* crying. She has somehow managed to knock over one of the glasses of red wine that Robert had put on the table and it has gone all over the cream carpet, Robert's wig and my pitch notebook.

'It was an accident,' Phoebe wails. 'I was just trying to have some water because I was thir… thir… thirsty.'

'Shush,' I say, kneeling down beside her. 'Of course it was an accident. Don't get upset. It won't take long to clear up.'

Of course, that's a total lie and fifteen minutes later, I am still on my hands and knees wrapped in my bath towel, scrubbing at the carpet. I tackled Robert's wig first and that's now hanging up in the bathroom, looking mercifully okay if a little soggy.

'Is it coming out?' Robert says, looming over me. I refused his offers to help, insisting he should carry on making dinner and that I am fine. Phoebe, meanwhile, is in the bedroom with the iPad. I think her imaginary friend is with her too because I heard her chatting away.

It takes me nearly half a bottle of carpet cleaner and a considerable amount of elbow grease to remove the wine stain from the carpet. When Robert's brother first saw this flat, he teased us about how absolutely everything was cream or white. He said he bet it wouldn't all look so pristine in a couple of years' time. It does though (or it did).

I turn my attentions to my pitch notepad. It's so soaked it's almost tempting to throw it out, but that feels like it might be bad luck. I settle for just wiping it down the best I can and leaving it on the draining board.

Dinner is a rather stilted affair and I suddenly feel way too exhausted to facilitate the conversation between Phoebe and Robert. It doesn't improve matters that Phoebe picks at the stir-fry with a look of disgust.

'I thought you liked stir-fry?' Robert says.

'Not this stir-fry.'

I take a large glug of wine and another mouthful of my very small dinner.

After we have eaten, Phoebe goes back to the iPad in the bedroom and Robert and I clear up.

'I expect she'll be picked up any minute now,' I say, drying the wok and putting it in the cupboard.

As if on cue, my phone goes and I see it's Sylvia.

'I'm so sorry but I still haven't been seen. It seems as if there has been some kind of major incident.'

I turn my back to Robert. 'No problem. See you soon.' I end the call. 'Shouldn't be too much longer.' Great, now I am blatantly lying.

'Can we play Cheat?' Phoebe says, appearing in the doorway.

'What's Cheat?'

She explains it's a card game and she will teach us how to play. We will all be dealt a hand of cards which we will take turns to place face down, saying what the cards are. We can lie about what we're placing but we risk another player calling 'cheat'. If they're right, the cheat has to pick up the discarded pile but, if they're wrong, the caller does.

The game is completely bonkers and just what we needed and,

within minutes, we are all laughing as we try to call cheat on each other.

'Three tens,' I say.

'Cheat,' Robert says.

'No,' I say, showing him the three tens.

Phoebe squeals with delight and Robert smiles and picks up the discarded pile.

'Two fives,' Phoebe says, a little later.

'Cheat,' I say.

Phoebe's face lights up as she turns over two fives.

'Oh no!' I say, going for the discarded pile.

'Wait,' Robert says. 'You played three cards, Phoebe.'

'Yes, but Loretta didn't notice and there were two fives.'

'But that's cheating.'

'Robert,' I say, grinning and putting my hand on his arm. 'The game is called Cheat.'

Phoebe giggles but Robert looks distinctly unamused. I reach for the discarded pile.

'No,' Robert says. 'The game may very well be called Cheat but there are still some rules. Phoebe lied about the number of cards she put down. What's more, she did not tell us when she explained the rules that you were allowed to lie about the number of cards placed.'

It's at times like this I wish I wasn't marrying a barrister. 'She's six, Robert.'

'I don't want to play cards anymore,' Phoebe says, standing up.

I follow her into the bedroom where she is sitting on the edge of the bed, looking forlorn. 'Robert didn't mean to be grumpy. He just likes to do things properly.'

Phoebe nods.

'Want to go on the iPad again?'

'Okay.'

Phoebe starts playing *Fledgling Heroes* and I sit beside her, stewing with annoyance and not wanting to go back into the sitting room. Why did Robert need to make such a thing? Does he really care that much about some silly card game? How is my life going to look in twenty years' time?

Stop it. Robert is lovely. I am just stressed because of the pitch tomorrow and because I had a very different kind of evening in mind.

I turn to look at Phoebe and see she has fallen asleep. I prise the iPad gently from her hands and switch off the light.

'She's asleep,' I say to Robert, sitting down next to him on the sofa.

'Oh, I don't suppose she'll appreciate being woken up when her grandma arrives.'

I shrug.

'Want to watch a bit of telly?'

I want to ask you why you made such a fuss about some silly card game. Why it was worth upsetting a child over? 'Yeah, why not?'

'It will do you good to relax a bit before tomorrow.'

We are ten minutes into the programme when Sylvia calls. She is sorry but she is still waiting to be seen.

'Oh, I was kind of hoping to go to bed soon. Sorry, I know you can't help it.'

'Maybe Phoebe should sleep here tonight?' Robert says. 'We could make up a bed on the sofa for her. That way, at least, you can go to bed now and have a good night's sleep before your pitch tomorrow?'

'But what about in the morning?' I say, covering the handset. 'I don't have time to take her home before I go into the office.'

'I'll do it.'

I feel a rush of love and gratitude. Also, guilt for thinking those bad things about Robert before.

Chapter Forty-One

I lie in bed all cosy and warm. I made up a little bed for Phoebe on the sofa and, somehow, Robert managed to pick her up and carry her there without waking her. He tucked the covers over her with such care too.

My mind swirls with thoughts of the meeting tomorrow and I start to feel nervous again.

I tell myself that it will be okay, that these are the same clients who declared themselves 'bowled over' by my presentation in New York. What's more, I know what we have in store for them tomorrow is impressive. I just need a good night's sleep.

I must drift off shortly afterwards because, the next thing I know, I am woken by a tugging on my sleeve. I prise open my eyes to see Phoebe standing in front of me with tears streaming down her cheeks. 'I had a nightmare.'

I take her hand, guide her back into the sitting room and lie down with her on the sofa. Her whole body is trembling. 'Shush,' I say, stroking her hair. 'It's okay.'

'I had a nightmare and she didn't come.'

'Grandma?'

'Mummy.'

Oh.

Phoebe starts to cry again. 'I was frightened and I kept calling her and calling her but she didn't come.'

My head spins. I feel desperately sorry for Phoebe but also a little sorry for myself. It's 1 o'clock, which means I have had all of two hours' sleep. I don't need this the night before the pitch.

'Why am I still here?' Phoebe says. 'Did Grandma die at the hospital?'

'NO!' I lower my voice. 'No. Grandma is absolutely fine. There was just a bit of a wait for the doctors to look at her hand. You're going to sleep here tonight and then Robert will take you back to Grandma's in the morning, before school.'

'I'll need to change into my uniform.'

'Yes. Don't worry, we have it all worked out.'

'The nightmare was scary. I was at Olivia's party but then Olivia was lying on the floor and she was dead and everyone was telling me that it was my fault because people just die when they're with me.'

Wow, I'm not sure my sleep-addled brain is up to this. 'You're okay now. It was just a bad dream.'

'Please can I have a glass of water?'

'Okay,' I say, getting up. 'And then we should try to go back to sleep, okay?'

I fill a glass of water, wondering vaguely if anyone else on the pitch team is awake right now. I'd put money on the fact that, if Greg's son has a nightmare, it will be Elspeth, not Greg, who will deal with it.

Phoebe gulps down the water and tells me she's 'a bit hungry'.

'Really? Listen, I have a very busy day tomorrow.' I look at her small, sad face and feel a wave of remorse. 'I'll make you some toast, but then we have to go back to sleep.'

'Okay, after the toast you won't hear another peep out of me.'

The parroted expression makes me smile. Everything is going to be fine. I will be back in bed within no time.

Chapter Forty-Two

I sit on the tube with my eyes closing. Last night turned into a total disaster. Phoebe didn't go back to sleep for another hour after I'd made the toast.

When I finally climbed back into bed, I was exhausted but also utterly wired and I lay there for what felt like forever until I finally succumbed to sleep.

Then, after what seemed like seconds, I was woken by the sounds of screaming. Phoebe had had another nightmare and was shaking with fear.

Poor Sylvia, I thought, as I tried to calm Phoebe down. I wasn't particularly sympathetic when she moaned to me about how badly Phoebe sleeps but, witnessing it first-hand, I saw it's brutal – and I am half Sylvia's age.

I didn't even try to go back to my own bed after that, deciding I would get more rest if I stayed with Phoebe. What I hadn't counted on was quite how much space one small person can take up on a sofa.

I was quite relieved when my (wholly unnecessary) alarm went off at 5.30 a.m.

The tube shakes me from side to side. I wish I wasn't so tired. I will be okay, though. A strong coffee and adrenaline are all I need.

I come to with a jolt and wipe a streak of drool from my chin. The tube has just pulled into Canada Water.

Canada Water! I have missed my stop. This cannot be happening to me.

I hurl myself through the doors just before they close and run to the platform that will take me back in the direction that I have come from.

It's okay, I tell myself, I still have time to reach the office.

Perhaps I should call someone to say I am running a little late? But, of course, there is no signal down here. I guess I could run upstairs and do it but that seems like a waste of valuable time.

I stand on the platform, tapping my foot impatiently.

The ping ping of an announcement comes through. There are severe delays on the Jubilee line. Passengers are advised to seek alternative routes where possible.

Panic courses through me. How on earth could this happen? Today, of all days.

I need to stay calm, to think. I can still be there on time. I will catch the DLR to Whitechapel where I can jump on the District line…

There isn't time. My heart is racing now and I feel as if I might pass out.

I will get a cab. It will be expensive but it's the only answer.

I run up the escalator, sweating and saying 'excuse me' to the countless people who insist on standing still, despite the fact they are on the left. Don't they know the rules?

Outside, it is pouring with rain. I reach for my umbrella but it isn't in my bag. It is always in my bag. Never mind, there is no time to worry about niceties. I will look like a drowned rat but I will be a drowned rat who is on time.

There are no cabs anywhere. I run along the street, trying hard not to cry.

Eventually, I see a taxi, flag it down and hurl myself gratefully into the back seat. The meeting starts at 8 o'clock. I have twenty-six minutes before that. I might just do it.

I remember a taxi driver once telling me how much he hated it when people got into his cab and told him they needed to be somewhere as quickly as possible. 'Like I was thinking of going as slowly as possible,' he said, rolling his eyes.

I push this to the back of my mind and tell the driver I'm in a desperate hurry.

The traffic is awful and I sit there feeling sick as the minutes tick away. I try to call Zoe, Greg and, in total desperation, even Dillon, but their phones go straight to voicemail. I picture them all sitting in the meeting room without me. As long as I arrive there before the clients, I will be okay.

We pull up outside the agency at 8.06 and I shove my card against the card reader and throw myself into the building.

'Good morning,' says the man on reception. 'Have a nice day.'

Chapter Forty-Three

At first, when Greg tells me we didn't win the pitch, I think he's winding me up. It's only four days since the meeting, which is much sooner than we thought we'd hear. Plus the meeting went perfectly, despite my slightly late and damp arrival (which I blamed on travel problems, leaving out any mention of my sleepless night with Phoebe). Remy, the senior client, even started to talk to us about his long-term business objectives. After the meeting, their team stayed for drinks, accepting our offers of Prosecco with jokey questions about whether we were trying to get them drunk before they went to see the next agency on the roster.

I look at Greg, slumped in his chair, and realise he is deadly serious.

'I really thought we would win,' I say.

'Me too.'

We sit in silence. On the one hand, I am grateful that Greg has called me in on my own to tell me this before the others, but it does mean the mood is intense, and it's clear we are both locked in our own private despair.

It crosses my mind Greg might think that me being late was a factor in the decision but I know that's ridiculous. He was obviously annoyed with me about it, as I would have been in his position, but no rational person can think it was a factor in the client's decision. And I know my presentation was good.

'Did they say why?' I say, trying to stop my voice cracking.

Greg shakes his head. 'The usual BS about it being a close race and a tough call.' He puffs out his cheeks. 'Please could you bring the pitch team together so we can tell them?'

I nod and am halfway out of the door when I turn back and ask the question I hardly dare voice. 'Will this affect my promotion?'

'Your promotion was never tied to us winning the pitch,' Greg says.

Chapter Forty-Four

Phoebe's last-ever Little Fishes lesson comes two days after I find out we haven't won the pitch. I have decided that this is the perfect time to let my contact with her fizzle out. I will still visit her occasionally – to take her a Christmas present, for example – but being a regular part of her world isn't sustainable. I need to focus properly on my own life again. I'm 99.9 per cent sure that my involvement in Phoebe's life isn't what cost the agency the pitch, but there's no denying I haven't been quite as 'on it' as I normally am, and that cannot continue, especially since I'm on the cusp of promotion. My involvement with Phoebe is clearly affecting my relationship with Robert too.

I am a little nervous about how I will tell Phoebe what I've decided, especially since she has been talking for weeks about starting Little Seahorses. It's better to make a clean break now rather than stringing her along, though, and at least I can come away with the knowledge that, not only have I facilitated her learning to swim, but I have also helped her to regulate her emotions.

Whatever progress she has made on this front, though, I don't want to risk upsetting her before the lesson. Right now, she has to concentrate on swimming 10 metres and gaining her badge and certificate.

Chris is already sitting on the flip-down seats. As I make my way towards him, I have the uncomfortable realisation that, apart from passing him in the corridor at work, I haven't seen him since the awful revelations about his wife dying. I hope things won't be weird. I would definitely feel odd and self-conscious if I'd told a near-stranger something that personal.

Chris seems cheerful enough when he says good morning, though. 'How has your week been?'

'Eurgh, not great, to be honest. We didn't win the pitch.'

'Yeah, I heard. I'm sorry.'

'Thanks.'

'I know it was very important to you.'

I understand that he is trying to be nice but this irritates me. The pitch wasn't some little pet project of mine. 'It was important to the whole agency, actually. It's a huge account and one that would have paid a lot of people's mortgages.'

Chris just nods. A message flashes up on his screen and his face changes. 'Excuse me,' he says, standing up. 'I'll be back in a bit.'

I have to admit I am a little intrigued. Chris's whole demeanour changed when he saw that message, and it is very unlike him not to watch Zack's lesson. I wonder idly if it's some dating drama.

Phoebe is inching across the pool, a plume of white water behind her as she kicks extravagantly. It seems like a lifetime ago that I met her and Kate at the airport. I remember how desperate I was to get away from them, and I certainly never would have imagined that Phoebe would start to become part of my life. Not that that is set to continue, of course.

'Sheesh,' Chris says, when he comes back. 'That was that mate of mine who asked me to watch his bags the other day, the one who is getting a divorce. He doesn't even have his son this weekend but he came here just so the two of us could grab a coffee. He is in a bad way.'

'It must be tough, but it's nice he has you for support.'

'I guess. I wish I could do more, though. It's obvious the guy is really hurting. He's such a good bloke too. The irony is I thought he was an advertising tosser when I first met him, but that couldn't be further from the truth. I've known him for twelve years now and the two of us are more like brothers than mates. We tell each other everything.'

I've always wondered if the 'tell each other everything' thing is a myth. Don't we want to show our friends the best of us? I certainly can't think of anyone I tell everything, not even Robert.

'He was incredible when Lara died. Lots of people keep away, you know. He kept turning up whether I wanted him to or not. He would tidy up the flat, force me and Zack out to the park with him and his little boy, and then make us all something to eat. He's the worst cook in the world, mind you. I think I'd rather eat a real toad than his toad in the hole!'

Phoebe is running towards me.

'Don't run!'

Phoebe pulls at her swimming goggles. 'My teacher says I am doing *very* well and that I should keep going *exactly* like this.'

'Don't run!' I shout, as she heads back towards the pool.

'Big day for her today,' Chris says.

'I can't believe she has come so far so fast. I'm really proud of her.'

'It's brilliant,' he says. 'And you wait to see the progress she makes when she becomes a Little Seahorse.'

'Actually, I won't be bringing her to Little Seahorses.'

Chris looks surprised. 'Really? I thought she was super keen?'

Okay, this is a guilt trip I could do without. I am already

nervous about telling Phoebe and Sylvia what I have decided, and I don't want to have to justify myself to Chris. I take a sip of my coffee, which is cold and bitter.

'It's actually my decision. I never planned to become quite so involved with Phoebe. She's a lovely kid but I have my own life to lead.'

This is a conversation I had with Robert on Thursday evening and, indeed, something he has been pushing me towards for a while, but Chris, although he says nothing, looks unconvinced.

'I've done a good thing bringing her to swimming lessons week in, week out,' I say, hating the defensiveness in my tone.

'You have.' Chris rakes his hands through his hair. 'Does Phoebe know yet about Little Seahorses? It's just the way she talks about it, it's as if she assumes she's going to be doing it.'

A muscle starts to pulse under my eye and I put my fingers over it. 'I'm planning on telling her today, after the lesson.'

'But Sylvia knows already, right?'

Jesus, who does this guy think he is? Sure, we have chatted a bit over the weeks but he is not my mate and this is none of his business. How bloody dare he stick his beak in like this? Besides, although I haven't told Sylvia yet, I have been thinking about a plan to take the pressure off her a bit. 'I'm going to suggest to Sylvia that she gets an au pair to help out for a couple of hours each day. She has the money and plenty of space. I chatted to a few of the mums at work and I have a whole list of au pair agencies.'

'Sounds like a good idea.' Am I imagining this or is there a coolness in Chris's tone that doesn't match the words?

'The au pair might even be able to bring Phoebe to Little Seahorses,' I say, as the idea pops into my mind.

'Maybe. But I think what Phoebe really likes about the swimming lessons is the time she spends with you.'

Oh, he is just too much! Anger fizzes through my veins. 'Listen, I really don't have to justify myself to you—'

'I wasn't suggesting you do—'

'I'll have you know that, as well as bringing Phoebe to swimming over the last eight weeks, I have been helping her in other ways.'

'You're brilliant with her.'

I am not sure that I have ever been described as brilliant with anyone. Chris is probably only trying to backtrack after overstepping the mark, though. Also, I know he's talking rubbish. Most of the time I'm with Phoebe, I flounder around feeling utterly inept.

Phoebe comes towards me, flapping her arms.

'Don't run,' I say.

'It's my turn to swim the 10 metres. WATCH ME!'

'Of course.'

Phoebe heads back towards the pool where she and her classmates line up and listen to the teacher's instructions.

'I told you about Phoebe's friendship difficulties at school,' I find myself blurting out. 'And how I worked out that it was because she's so overemotional.'

Chris's brow furrows. 'Wait, what? You did tell me that Phoebe was having friendship difficulties and that you were helping her to deal with her feelings, but I didn't realise you had linked the two things in your head.'

'What? *Of course* they're linked. If Phoebe is in floods of tears the whole time or losing her temper, that's bound to be off-putting to other kids.'

'Umm, but surely you wouldn't want Phoebe to suppress all her emotions? It's a strength to be able to show vulnerability.'

Oh, trust him to come out with this sort of new-age guff. How can being vulnerable be a strength? Talk about an oxymoron.

'She has just lost her mother.'

'I am well aware she has just lost her mother, thank you.' Luckily for Chris, I don't have a chance to say any more because Phoebe's teacher is instructing the kids to jump into the pool. I lean forward in my seat, the irritating man to my left shoved to the back of my mind as I focus entirely on Phoebe. I watch as she lowers her small body into the water, waits for the teacher to give the command and then starts to make her way messily across the water, her legs and arms going wildly.

As she reaches the edge of the pool, I am surprised to realise that, as Chris and I both stand up to cheer wildly, I have tears running down my cheeks.

I am going to miss this strange, sad, funny little girl.

The revelation hits me like a punch to the stomach.

It doesn't mean it's not right to break off contact, though. It's kinder all round in the long term.

Chris flashes me a sympathetic look. I was desperately hoping he was too busy clapping to notice me falling apart but, of course, he's not a man to miss that kind of thing. Heat rises through my cheeks as I stare at the floor and try to compose myself.

I don't know why I'm so embarrassed, though. Chris can think what he likes. We'll probably never have a conversation after today unless it's about a copy brief.

'You okay?' His eyes are filled with concern.

'Fine.' I blink back fresh tears and stare straight ahead. Phoebe and her classmates are lining up by the side of the pool and being presented with their badges and certificates, and watching her makes me feel as if my heart is suddenly too big for my chest. I pull out my phone and take photo after photo. They will be lovely for Sylvia to keep.

Chapter Forty-Five

Telling Phoebe I won't be able to continue taking her to swimming lessons is awful.

We are on the bus, Phoebe clutching her badge and certificate and chuntering away happily about how she can't believe she can swim now, properly swim, and she could probably save someone's life now if they were drowning, she is sure she could. She is just going to get better and better too. Do I know in Little Seahorses they teach you *proper* breaststroke?

I know this is my cue and swallow down a lump that has risen in my throat. 'I'm afraid I'm not going to be able to take you to Little Seahorses. The thing is, you know I have a very busy job—'

'You don't go to work on Saturdays.'

'Well, sometimes I do. But, anyway, that's not really the point.'

'So you're not going to come next Saturday?'

'Err, no.'

'Or any Saturday?'

'Well… umm… I will come and visit you sometimes. I'm definitely going to come to see you at Christmas and I might even take you to that new ice cream place you're so excited about.'

Phoebe's eyes have filled with tears. 'Is it because I have been whiney and naughty sometimes?'

'No, of course not.'

'Because I will be very good from now on, I promise.' She lets out a small hiccupy sob.

'Phoebe,' I say, putting my hand over hers. 'Please don't cry.'

This makes her cry even harder. I feel my resolve wavering but then I remember something Robert said about it not being fair to let Phoebe become too attached to me. Her being so upset now is even more reason to stand firm.

Phoebe doesn't make that easy, though. She carries on crying all the way home, refusing to listen to anything I try to say to make her feel better.

She is almost hysterical by the time we reach the house (so much for my masterclasses in regulating emotions) so my plan to tell Sylvia what I have decided in a calm way is completely derailed. 'Loretta doesn't want to see me anymore,' Phoebe says, before her grandma has even opened the door fully.

'That's not what I said at all.'

But Phoebe is already up the stairs, her bedroom door slamming so loudly I fear for its hinges, and somehow I doubt she's looking for the calm-down kit we put together.

I don't stay long after that. Sylvia handles the news better than Phoebe (not hard) but tries to talk me out of the decision, explaining that her granddaughter has become 'so fond' of me. Meanwhile, the cat sits in the kitchen doorway, eyeing me malevolently.

When Sylvia sees she can't change my mind, she sighs, accepts the list of the au pair agencies and thanks me for being a big help in a difficult time. 'Phoebe,' she shouts up the stairs. 'Come and say goodbye to Loretta.'

'NO!'

'Phoebe,' Sylvia calls. 'Come on now, I know you're upset but where are your manners—'

'Honestly,' I say, turning towards the front door. 'It's fine. Just tell her I said goodbye. And that I'm very proud of her and all her hard work in Little Fishes.' My voice breaks and I give Sylvia a wobbly smile. I need to get out of here.

Chapter Forty-Six

I am standing in the queue in the coffee shop thinking about Phoebe and hoping she's not still sad.

I was in a mess when I arrived home on Saturday afternoon and, if it wasn't for Robert, I think I might well have run back and told Phoebe and Sylvia I'd changed my mind. 'Shh,' he said, stroking my hair. 'Just because something is hard doesn't mean it's not the right thing to do. You can't keep taking her to swimming lessons until she's twenty-five, can you?'

I know he is right, but I didn't factor in just how sad all this would make me. It's almost like I'm having some sort of physical reaction too. My whole body aches and I have a cold sore the size of a planet, which is painful enough in itself but also serves as a near-constant reminder that Phoebe calls them coleslaws and I always thought that was way too cute to correct her.

'Loretta,' Greg says, appearing behind me. 'Good weekend? I was actually hoping to have some time with you today, so why don't we grab a coffee together now? Otherwise, it may just never happen – the rest of my day is back-to-backs.'

It's a bit early in the morning for my brain to cope with this, especially as I am yet to ingest any caffeine, but the only reason

I can think of why Greg would need an unscheduled chat with me would be to tell me he's giving me the promotion.

My heart rate speeds up and I feel as if my tongue has suddenly grown too big for my mouth as I mumble something about that being a great idea.

The queue moves agonisingly slowly and, as Greg and I make awkward small talk, I inwardly curse Nadia's innate friendliness and seeming need to interact meaningfully with each and every customer in her coffee shop. I honestly think I could make dinner in the time it takes her to make a single coffee.

She is presently engaged in asking the woman at the front of the queue how her 'hot date with cycle guy' went.

Annoyingly, the woman is only too happy to spill all the details and launches into a long-winded download about how he was great and she knows it was only a first date but she really felt like they had a connection. He was pretty hot too and not dressed head to toe in Lycra, thank goodness.

Just order your damn coffee, woman. I am on tenterhooks here.

I study Greg's face, trying to gauge signs of his mood, but he doesn't give anything away. I really can't think of anything but the promotion he would want to talk to me about now, though. He always makes a huge deal about how his first hour in the office is his sacred golden time where nobody must disturb him because that's the only time he can focus and why he arrives so early. So, this must be important.

I am just about to come straight out and ask him to put me out of my misery and tell me what he wants to talk about when his mobile rings.

'The wife,' he says to me. 'Can you order me a double-shot latte and a croissant? You can expense it – and yours too, of course.'

'Sure,' I say, as he takes the call and heads towards an empty table.

Nadia is serving an oldish man in a suit now and the two of them are hooting with laughter about something. Come on, come on, I think.

Greg must want to talk to me about the promotion. He wouldn't give up his golden hour for anything else. A bubble of excitement grows in my belly. This is the moment I have been working towards for so long. Hell, I have even put up with agency softball for the cause. If that doesn't mean I deserve this, I don't know what does.

I allow myself to picture Robert and me celebrating this evening. Did we drink that bottle of champagne my parents gave me on my birthday?

Finally, I reach the front of the queue. 'Morning,' I say. 'Two double-shot lattes and a croissant, please.'

'Loretttttttta,' Nadia trills. 'How are you, my darling? Did you have a good weekend? You look a little tired this morning. I hope you haven't been overdoing it…'

On and on she goes, my cold sore cracking painfully as I force myself to smile.

I snatch the coffees and croissant out of Nadia's hands the minute she stops talking and rush over to Greg, who is tapping away on his phone.

'Just replying to an email from a client. Won't be a mo.'

I sit there, forcing myself not to drum my fingers or tap my feet. I should drink in this moment and remember every little detail. This is the place where I will be made a Board Account Director. I imagine the news being announced at agency drinks. That will actually be a social occasion I genuinely look forward to.

Greg looks up from his phone. 'You not eating anything? You

should always have breakfast, you know. Most important meal of the day.'

'I had something at home,' I lie, not wanting to admit I am too excited to eat right now.

Greg reaches for his croissant and I squash the urge to squirt his hands with some of my anti-bac hand gel before he touches it. I wonder how he travelled here today and if he realises how dirty public transport is? Stop it, I tell my brain. Greg is a grown man and, anyway, that is not what is important right now.

I watch as he pops a chunk of croissant into his mouth and chews slowly.

Finally, he starts speaking. 'So, you know how I have always been your biggest champion? How I have always pushed you forward?'

'Umm hmm.' With Greg, even when it's about you, it's about him.

Greg takes a sip of his coffee. 'You know I think you are very good at what you do and totally committed to the agency…'

Just say it! Just tell me you're making me a Board Account Director.

'The thing is, though, recently I've noticed a change in you. You don't seem completely…' He pauses, thinks and then makes air quotes with his fingers, 'on your game.'

What? I give everything to this bloody job. Greg should see the endless to-do lists in my notepads. I have even been 'meshing', for Christ's sake.

Greg lowers his head towards his shoulder in an extravagant stretch. 'You haven't been yourself, Loretta.'

My brain struggles to process. Of course I haven't been myself, I've been a sodding dolphin just like he told me to be. I have been swimming with the other dolphins with a great big dolphin smile on my face. (Never be fooled by a dolphin's smile, by the way. It's just the shape of their mouth. A dolphin can be 'smiling' when they're utterly miserable.)

Greg sends his head towards his other shoulder. 'You seem to have taken your eye off the ball a little.'

What? Okay, Greg has called me out on being distracted a couple of times, and there was that embarrassing moment when he caught me looking at YouTube tutorials about swimming caps, but I haven't exactly been slacking. 'I am just as committed as I have always been. I've been working twelve-hour days.' I hear my own voice rising and it suddenly crosses my mind that maybe Greg has actively chosen to have this conversation in a public place so I can't make a scene. That's ridiculous, though. This was a chance meeting. I am not being dumped, my promotion is not being dumped.

A memory crashes into my mind. Greg's obvious irritation when he asked me to come in to work on that Saturday morning and I said I couldn't because of Phoebe and then I ended up bringing her into the office with me. And, of course, I was late to the pitch.

'So, I am thinking you are not ready for this promotion.'

My breath catches in my throat and the world seems to tunnel around me.

I watch Greg's lips move. I am aware he is still talking but I don't take in a single word.

Because I am not getting this promotion. And there is nothing anyone can say that is going to make that okay.

Chapter Forty-Seven

I may have been teaching Phoebe anger management but I could do with a few lessons myself. I am a small ball of fury and hardly dare speak because, every time I do, the hurt and the bitterness come spewing out like vomit.

I am unable to be gracious to Maddie, to pretend I think she deserves this promotion – *my* promotion. For three days, I say nothing to her about it at all and then, after the formal announcement, when I can no longer act as if I don't know, I mutter some 'joke' about how she has stolen it from me. She looks as if she's about to cry. No change there.

Days inch past and I sit at my desk seething, with my noise-cancelling headphones jammed in my ears. I started wearing them again straight after my conversation with Greg in the coffee shop. I had actually started to like feeling more connected with my colleagues, especially people like Zoe and Samira, but, with Operation Mesh With The Team cancelled, I can certainly give up on the things I don't like. I won't be setting myself those kinds of tasks in my notebook every day and I won't be going to agency softball or drinks. Nor will I be listening to Pete's boring stories. Seriously, that guy. If he sat next to Lady Gaga on the tube one morning, he'd tell you, but not before telling you first that there were delays on the Bakerloo line, and isn't it chilly for this time of year and had he told you about the new bar he has found in town?

I keep going over and over the conversation with Greg. You don't seem on your game. You've taken your eye off the ball recently.

I veer wildly between being angry with him and angry with myself. I never should have started taking Phoebe to the swimming lessons. I have seen enough working mothers (and it is usually mothers) who have been sidelined and, however I might feel about that as a feminist, I should never have let myself be blown up by the same landmines, especially as Phoebe isn't even my child.

What is harder for me to process is that Phoebe is on my mind a lot. In fact, I'd go as far as to say I am sad at the prospect of not seeing her. I would never admit this to Robert. He stopped short of going down the 'I told you so' road when I told him I wasn't getting the promotion, but we both know he thinks my involvement with Phoebe is what cost me the job.

I am at my desk, reading the same paragraph of a client brief for what feels like the hundredth time. My brain is ignoring the words on the screen and instead rehashing the same things it has been busying itself with for days now: how could this promotion slip away from me? How could I have messed up so catastrophically? What the hell am I going to do with *all these feelings*?

A tapping on my arm makes me jump and I look up to see Zoe. I pull out one of my headphones.

'Lunch?'

'I'm actua—'

Zoe shakes her head. 'No excuses. We're going for lunch. Just the two of us.'

I suppose I do need to eat. And I actually like Zoe. I just hope she doesn't want to talk about my failure to get promoted.

'Want to go to Efes?' Zoe says, pulling on her jacket.

I shake my head. I do not want to go to Efes, the scene of my world coming crashing down around my ears. 'Let's go to the sushi place.'

As we walk there, Zoe tells me that she and her husband have come to a decision. They are going to have one more round of IVF and, after that, they will call a halt to the whole thing. Of course, they are desperately hoping they get their last-chance miracle baby, but they can't afford to keep on indefinitely, not just from a financial point of view but from an emotional one.

I nod and bite back the urge to say that if Zoe wants to get anywhere in her career, she shouldn't have a child. That even borrowing someone else's can screw things up for you.

We buy our sushi and find a table.

'Want some hand gel?' I say.

'No thanks. I washed my hands just before we left the office.'

Since then you have touched lift buttons, door handles and a credit card reader. I don't say anything, though. I don't want to provide further evidence of my 'weirdness' – even though I am convinced that, when it comes to things like this, it's actually other people who are being odd.

Zoe dips her sushi roll (and microbes) into a puddle of soy sauce and wasabi. 'I'm a bit worried about you. You're clearly very down these last few days and I know how much you wanted that promotion. How much it meant to you.'

'I'm fine,' I say, arranging my face into what I hope passes for a smile.

'Loretta.'

I take a bite of my sashimi and point to my mouth while I

think of how much I do and don't want to say. On the one hand, it's very tempting to talk to someone. I am so full of thoughts and feelings I'm convinced I could spontaneously combust at any minute, and the only analysis of all this has taken place in my own head. Robert and I have talked about me not landing the promotion, of course, and he knows I'm disappointed, but I've felt as if I have to play it down a little and act as if I am just focusing on the next opportunity (a lie – my head is completely mired in the now). On the other hand, I'm not sure I want anyone, Zoe included, knowing quite the effect this has had on me. 'Obviously, I'm disappointed, but there will be other opportunities.'

Zoe just raises her eyebrows and I realise she's not going to be as easy as Robert is to fob off.

'Okay, I'm more than a bit disappointed. I felt I deserved it, that I've worked for it.'

'Nobody works harder than you,' Zoe says.

'I really thought Greg rated me. To realise he doesn't…' My voice cracks and I feel tears pricking the back of my eyes. What the hell am I doing?

I am just about holding myself in check when I look up and see the kindness and concern in Zoe's eyes and it completely undoes me. 'Sorry,' I say, as I start to cry messily into my half-eaten sushi. 'Sorry.'

'Shh, don't apologise. It's natural that you feel sad.'

Eventually, I manage to bring myself under some sort of control. 'Sorry.'

'Hey, what did I say about apologising?'

I drag my hands through my hair. 'What makes it worse, of course, is Maddie getting it. I know I can hardly talk today, but Maddie is pretty all over the place most of the time, isn't she? I mean it's such an irony for Greg to talk about me not being "on my game" and then give the promotion to someone who never is.'

Zoe's face has changed. 'Don't do that, Loretta. I know you're upset but don't do that. I like Maddie and I think she's great at her job. I wanted to have lunch with you today because I can see you're struggling, but I am not going to let you sit here and bitch about Maddie. Come on, you're better than that.'

I'm really not. I force a tight smile.

Chapter Forty-Eight

My lunch with Zoe achieves the seemingly impossible by making me feel even more rubbish than I did before, and I decide that, for once, I will leave on the dot of 5.30. I cannot wait to be back in my flat. I will be home a good two hours before Robert and plan to wallow for every single second until he returns.

Of course, given the time of day, Chris is waiting for the lift. I swear to God it has been years since that man has been in this building at 5.31.

The lift arrives and it's packed. Chris and I are squeezed up next to each other so I can feel the warmth coming off his body.

'I'm sorry about the promotion,' he says. 'You must be very disappointed.'

I don't trust myself to speak so just shrug. I was aiming for insouciant but fear the effect is more sulky teen.

'Perhaps it's a blessing in disguise?' Chris offers. 'That role comes with a hell of a lot of pressure.'

Typical! Just because he lacks any drive and ambition, he expects the rest of us to be the same.

The lift spits us out at the ground floor and I breathe an inward sigh of relief. I cannot wait to escape from this building and get away from Chris and his nonsense platitudes.

'By the way,' Chris says. 'I know this is none of my business, but I can't stop thinking about Phoebe and wondering if maybe you might think again about taking her to Little Seahorses? It's just I can see she has become really attached to you.'

Guilt stabs at my guts and I picture Phoebe's small face as clearly as if she was in front of me. 'I thought you were of the opinion I am rubbish with Phoebe?'

'What? I never said th—'

'You said I was teaching her to suppress her emotions.'

'Oh, that. Look, I think you might be a bit off the mark by linking her friendship difficulties to her showing emotion; it's important she doesn't bottle up feelings. But that doesn't mean I think you're rubbish with her. Far from it.'

Despite myself, I feel a small jolt of pride. Chris and I have stopped walking and are standing in the middle of the lobby and right in the way of the stream of people who are trying to escape for the day. 'I can't keep taking Phoebe to swimming lessons indefinitely. I have my own life to lead.'

'I know you have your own life. It's just I remember Zack after Lara died and how fragile he was, and if there was anything – anything at all – that had helped him to deal with that, well, I wouldn't have wanted that thing to be ripped away.'

'Don't play that card.'

Chris's face hardens. 'It's not a card, Loretta.'

'You're not the only person to have lost someone, you know.'

'Wha—'

'Don't you think I've thought about how Phoebe feels? But if you're right and she is becoming attached to me, then surely it's better to just knock things on the head right now? Cruel to be kind if you like.'

Our voices have risen a little and, out of the corner of my

eye, I see Mr Have a Nice Day staring at us from his position behind reception.

'I think Phoebe needs you right now,' Chris says. 'I think she's extremely vulnerable and you can help her.'

I sigh heavily. 'You know what? You were right when you said this is none of your business.'

'I'm only trying to help.'

'Help who?' I say, my voice coming out much louder than I intended it to.

'Phoebe, of course. But maybe even you too.'

I roll my eyes. 'And how are you helping me, exactly?'

Chris shakes his head. 'Oh, forget it.' He turns to go. 'Have a nice evening.'

I have wanted nothing more than to escape from this man but there is something in him suddenly deciding he is done with me that makes me incandescent with rage (admittedly not difficult at the moment). I run after him into the street. 'What did you mean when you said you were helping me?'

'I didn't mean anything.'

'Yes, you did.'

Chris sighs as if I am a particularly tiresome child. 'I think, however much you pretend to yourself that you don't, you really care about Phoebe.'

A thousand images rush into my mind. Phoebe falling asleep with her head in my lap at the agency summer fun day, the two of us laughing when she tried on Robert's wig and I told her she needed to adopt a very serious face, her running over to tell me to watch as she swam her 10 metres in the last Little Fishes lesson.

'I think Phoebe brings out a side of you I've never seen before,' Chris says.

'What the hell is that supposed to mean? You haven't seen any *side* to me because you don't know me.'

'Exactly. We've worked together for over three years and I don't know you. Just like everyone else in the office. You take no interest in the people around you and give absolutely nothing away. But you're different around Phoebe – kinder and more human.'

I feel as if he has slapped me around the face, and my head reels, not just with his words but the ones I have heard my whole life. *Why can't you make more of an effort? Weirdo Loretta. Her sister is so nice.* 'How dare you?'

'Listen, I'm sorry that came off as harsh and I didn't mean it to. I was just saying I've got to know you better recently and it's been nice.' Chris puts his hand on my arm.

I shake him off, my whole body filling up with anger. 'You don't know me at all. And you can take your patronising "it's been nice" and shove it, because I have no desire whatsoever to be your friend. I talked to you at swimming because you gave me no choice. I could never be friends with someone who has zero drive and ambition in life. Someone who has just given up.'

Chris looks so hurt, I almost take the words back.

Almost.

Chapter Forty-Nine

The tiny silver charm stops me in my tracks. A miniature version of *Pride and Prejudice*. My sister's favourite book.

It's her birthday coming up.

The sales assistant swoops. Would I like to take a closer look? Isn't it darling?

My heart hammers in my chest. Suddenly the shop is too hot and too bright.

'No,' I snap.

Chapter Fifty

I have commandeered one of the meeting rooms, saying I need some quiet space. This is very much frowned upon despite the fact it's what Greg and the rest of senior management do all the time.

I defy anyone to challenge me on it with the mood I'm in, though. It's nearly a week since my lunch with Zoe and row with Chris and I feel as if present me looks back on that me as Little Miss Sunshine by comparison. Even Zoe seems to have given up on me now. As for Chris, we have hardly spoken since that day. I did have to debrief him on some client amends to his copy but neither of us deviated from the topic at hand. As I was about to walk away, I considered stopping to tell him that I do care about Phoebe, but I believe that me extricating myself from her life now is better for her in the long run. It's ripping off the plaster instead of drawing out the pain. But then I decided that I absolutely don't have to justify myself to Chris.

An unknown number flashes up on my phone and I consider not picking up.

'Is that Loretta?'

'Yes,' I say wearily, preparing to say I have not been involved in an accident or missold PPI and can they please delete my phone number from their system?

'It's Lucy Ching from Talentz.'

I sit forward so fast I practically give myself whiplash. Talentz is a big advertising headhunter and Lucy Ching has the nickname within the industry of Lucy Ker-Ching because she is known for securing people great salaries.

'I have a role I think you might be interested in at Hola.'

The agency that won the pitch – oh, this would be too perfect! I picture Greg's face as I tell him I am not only defecting but defecting to the agency that stole the pitch win from right under his nose.

'It's a Board Account Director role. I know that's a slight jump, but I reckon you could do it, don't you?'

If Maddie can be a Board Account Director, then I certainly can. She was crying in the toilets again yesterday (it's so common-place I recognise her cry) and I just stayed in the cubicle. What does she need comforting about? 'Absolutely.'

'Great. If you could send me over an up-to-date CV, I'll start making some calls.'

I end the call and sit there with a huge smile on my face. Imagine being able to tell Greg that he may not think I'm 'on my game' but someone else very much does. Imagine having a new job and the job title that has just been stolen from me. Imagine having a clean slate with new colleagues.

I open up my CV.

Chapter Fifty-One

Lucky-heather woman looks shocked, as well she might do. I must have passed her a hundred times offering her no more than a scowl. But today, I buy not just one but two of her lacklustre sprigs, one for me and one for Zoe.

'Morning,' I say to Maddie who is coming out of the coffee shop as I walk in. She looks almost as taken aback as lucky-heather lady. No doubt the friendliness in my tone is somewhat disconcerting. I have barely been able to look at her since she got the promotion.

I knew the meeting at Hola yesterday was going to go well when, just after we sat down, my interviewer Ruth reached for her anti-bac hand gel. 'Everyone laughs at me for being addicted to this,' she said, grinning.

'I'm just the same!'

It was a good start, the ice breaker that so often eludes me in social situations. It continued well too. I was prepared for every question – hardly surprising given I'd spent every waking hour since Lucy's call researching the agency and their clients.

Barely ten minutes after I walked out of Hola's door, Lucy called me. 'Ruth Levine loved you! There are still a few more hurdles to jump but she is already talking about you meeting the new MD. I can't say who it is, but they are announcing it soon. He's a good guy, but honestly, from the way Ruth was talking, I think the job is already pretty much yours. So, just keep on doing whatever you're doing.'

I reach the front of the queue in Efes.

'Someone looks happy today!' Nadia says. 'Want to see the latest pics of my grandbaby? She's such a little chubster.'

I don't really want to see photos of a baby I don't know and never will, but I'm in an indulgent mood and manage to make suitably convincing cooing noises as Nadia swipes through image after image on her phone.

I walk through the revolving doors to the office and wish Mr Have a Nice Day a good day before he can get the words out, then ride up in the lift aware I have a goofy smile on my face. I don't even let it flicker when I see Kathleen is sitting at 'my' desk.

Zoe's eyes well up when I give her the sprig of lucky heather.

'You remembered my appointment was today,' she says, giving me a hug.

'Of course.' I don't mention the truly extraordinary thing, which is that I remembered before I even looked in my notebook.

As I am wiping down the desk I'll be using, and unpacking my things, Pete comes in and launches into the tale of that morning's 'travel chaos'. This goes on for a full four minutes but I listen to the whole thing and even manage to laugh when we reach the 'punchline'.

'Right,' I say. 'I'm making tea. Who would like one?'

In the kitchen, Danielle introduces me to her daughter Amber who is apparently off school today because she's under the weather. Two thoughts occur to me at once. One, Amber doesn't look very 'under the weather' and, two, if she is, why has she been brought to the office to spread her germs to all of us? I keep my tea-making activities as far away from her as possible.

Amber prattles to her mother. She must be about the same age as Phoebe. She's not a patch on Phoebe, though. She doesn't talk in breathless no-pause sentences or have Phoebe's strangely adult take on the world.

My stomach clenches as I think about Phoebe and how upset she was when I told her I wasn't going to be able to take her to Little Seahorses. Just because something is hard doesn't mean it's not the right thing to do, though.

'Those mugs have been through the dishwasher, you know,' Danielle says, snapping me back into the present.

'Doesn't hurt to give them a little wash. I think the cleaners often just put the dishwasher on a quick rinse.' I look towards Amber who is standing at the fridge gazing sullenly at its contents. 'She's very sweet.'

'Aww, thank you,' Danielle says, beaming.

The two of them trot out of the kitchen, leaving me alone, and I am just stirring milk into the last of my cups of tea when Chris walks in.

'Hello,' he says. His eyes are no longer warm and friendly.

I feel a sharp sting of hurt. There was a time when I thought Chris and I had become friends – real friends. I talked to him in a way I rarely talk to anyone. We're definitely not friends now, though.

'Hi,' I reply, picking up the mugs and walking away. My convivial mood appears to have evaporated.

Chapter Fifty-Two

'Let's go out tonight,' I say.

'On a *Tuesday*?' Robert says. He arrived home before me and has already changed into his tracksuit and installed himself on the sofa with a huge pile of court papers.

'Why not? I feel like celebrating.'

'Isn't that a little premature?'

'Well, no, because we wouldn't be celebrating me getting the job at Hola – not yet anyway – we'd be celebrating that my meeting with the Head of Client Services went well.'

'That's not tempting fate?'

'Neither of us believes in fate.'

'Fair point,' Robert says, laughing. 'What about the salmon that's in the fridge? I think the sell-by date is today.'

'I'll freeze it.'

'Okay,' Robert says, looking back down at his court papers. 'But I have to push through some of this first. I can't go for at least an hour.'

I stand under the shower, wondering if it's weird that Robert and I aren't a bit more spontaneous given we're youngish and don't have kids. A picture of the two of us in ten years' time flashes into my mind. We will mix only with other couples in the

219

same postcode with the same views, we'll eat roasts or BBQs on a Sunday as is seasonally appropriate and sex will be on Saturday nights with a possible exception made for birthdays.

I squirt some shower gel into my hand, the room filling with the smell of grapefruit. Spontaneity is overrated and it's nice knowing what to expect from life.

My mind goes back to the conversation I had with Ruth Levine yesterday. It was after my chat with her and the Head of Client Services. Ruth insisted on 'walking me out' herself and, as soon as we were alone, she told me she could tell he had been 'blown away' by me. 'The next step will be for you to meet our new MD. That might not happen for a few weeks but don't read anything negative into the delay. His diary is absolutely chock-a-block with onboarding stuff and, because your role is mainly going to be running new accounts, for once we're not in a tearing hurry.'

I step out of the shower, imagining the moment I tell Greg that I am resigning and going to work at the agency that stole the pitch win from Burnett White.

The thought is as comforting as the big fluffy towel I wrap myself in.

'Where would you like to go tonight?' I say, wandering into the living room.

'You choose,' Robert says, not looking up from what he is reading.

I book a table at the Italian place down the road. I know we both like it and it's easy. Normally, I would fill the time between now and then with work – after all, there are always things to be done – but tonight I decide I will allow myself to relax, especially as I have a copy of the latest issue of *AdTalk* in my bag.

I prop myself up on the pillows and start to read while simultaneously imagining the announcement on the pages of this very publication if – *when* – I land the job at Hola. *Hola poaches Loretta Martinelli as Board Account Director. Head of People Ruth Levine says, 'We are delighted that super-talent Loretta Martinelli will be joining our team. Her role will include heading up several key accounts and helping to steer the business forward'*

'What time did you book the table?' Robert calls from the other room.

'8.30.'

I read about an agency who have rebranded after a legal dispute and skim a thought piece on how clients and agencies can elevate the impacts they have on each other.

The 'Campaigns We Love' section has a still from a supermarket TV commercial which features a little girl wearing fairy wings and my stomach knots. I hope Phoebe is okay, that she has friends beyond her imaginary one and that Sylvia is coping.

I turn the page and see the headline: *Finn Burrows takes the lead at Hola.*

So, that's the new MD, the final hurdle between me and my new job. There's a photo of him standing outside the agency, arms crossed and stony-faced. He looks familiar somehow but I guess that's just because a lot of men over thirty in ad agencies look the same.

I glance at my phone and see it's nearly twenty past eight, which means unless I am planning on turning up at the Italian in my towel, I'd better hurry. The restaurant is casual but not that casual.

'Please can you zip up my dress?' I say.

'Hmm?' Robert says, his eyes still locked on the court papers.

'Please can you zip up my dress?'

'Oh, yeah, sure. Is it time to go already? We'll need to be in and out of the restaurant fairly quickly. I still have lots to read through before tomorrow.'

I squash down the feeling that I'm taking my fiancé hostage this evening and he would much rather stay on the sofa with his court papers.

I look for the battered hoop earrings that go nicely with this dress. Finn Burrows really did look familiar.

'Ready?' I say.

'Ready,' Robert says, much as someone might say they are ready for a colonoscopy.

We walk to the restaurant, Robert telling me about tomorrow's case. The outside temperature seems to have dropped by several degrees since I came home from work and I shiver in my thin jacket.

After a few minutes, I see the welcoming glow of Osteria Toscana and we are greeted warmly by Fabio who, although he sounds more Croydon than Tuscany, definitely knows how to do the proper Italian welcome. 'You look fantastico,' he says to me.

'Thanks. Must be because I'm in a good mood. I shouldn't talk about it yet, but I'm close to getting a new job.'

Robert looks amazed and I must admit I'm slightly surprised at myself. It's very unlike me to divulge information like this and, even if I don't believe in fate, it seems unwise to tempt it so flagrantly.

Fabio makes exaggerated finger-crossing gestures and shows us to our regular table.

We look at the menu, although it's very likely Robert will have the bistecca and I will have the sea bass. We will share a portion of spinach-buttered, not creamed.

I am reaching into my handbag for my anti-bac hand gel when a piece clunks into place in my brain. I know exactly where I know Finn Burrows from.

He is Chris's mate.

Chapter Fifty-Three

I keep thinking about Chris saying he and Finn tell each other everything.

It's 3 o'clock and I am sitting on the sofa, having got out of bed in case my tossing and turning wakes Robert. The room is in darkness save from the yellowy glow of the street lights that is leeching under the blinds.

I cannot allow anything to come between me and this job at Hola. It's so close now I can smell it.

I have picked up Robert's court wig from where it was left lying on the coffee table and have started absentmindedly stroking it.

Chris was bubbling with excitement the other day because Finn's ex has agreed to let Finn have their son more often at weekends. Clearly, Chris and Finn talk. But I still question whether everything means *everything*? Surely it doesn't include mentioning a row with some insignificant woman you work with?

Except if said woman told you she could never be friends with someone like you because you totally lacked any drive or ambition.

You might well mention that. *Can you believe that's what she said to me? When I've sat chatting to her, week in, week out at swimming, helped her out when she was struggling to deal with the kid. That's another thing. Did I tell you she inserted herself into that little girl's life when it suited her and now she is dropping her? You're a father, how do you feel about somebody doing that to a vulnerable kid?*

And even if Chris doesn't have that sort of conversation with Finn, well, isn't it inevitable that, when Finn finds out the new candidate he is about to meet for the Board Account Director role currently works at Burnett White, he'll want to pick his mate's brain? What's she like? Give me the lowdown. Is she a good egg?

Anxiety bubbles in my stomach. I don't think Chris is a vicious person but he's hardly likely to answer these questions positively.

Maybe it doesn't matter, though? Even if Chris says I'm Satan in disguise, surely Finn won't want to come in and overrule all the people beneath him who think I'm right for the job?

Except there will be other people who are right for the job too and, however much Ruth and the Head of Client Services and everyone else I have met at Hola so far rate me, they will have a list of other well-qualified candidates. People who don't come with a whole host of red flags. I think of the Account Manager I interviewed earlier this year. I thought he was great until, at his third interview, he made a joke that wasn't really a joke about his current boss. Needless to say, I offered the role to someone else.

I stare at my notebook that is lying on the coffee table. In it is a long list of tasks for tomorrow. But there's one thing that isn't yet on the list that I know I have to do.

Chapter Fifty-Four

'Are there problems with that Kitkins copy?' Chris says, when I appear next to his desk.

'No, they love it. Actually, I wanted to talk to you about something else.'

'Oh?'

I can feel the eyes of several people in the vicinity on us as they pretend to be immersed in their work. Danielle is virtually reaching for the popcorn.

'Perhaps I can buy you a coffee?'

Chris's face scrunches. 'Umm, okay.'

He follows me in the direction of the lift and I force myself to breathe. I can do this.

Jim and Bella, one of the junior creative teams, are stepping out of the lift we are about to walk into. They ask Chris if he has time to look at their ideas later and he says of course, and that he'll pop by as soon as he can.

'I didn't know you are Jim and Bella's line manager,' I say, as the lift doors close.

'I'm not. I am just giving them some advice. They're a bit scared of Dillon.'

Okay, he is literally doing Dillon's job for him but without the status or the money.

We walk to the coffee shop, making small talk that is so awkward the trip feels as if it takes two hours rather than two minutes.

I pass Chris his latte. My hand accidentally brushes his and I quickly pull it away. 'I wanted to say… umm… I feel I should… umm…' I swallow hard. 'I owe you an apology. For saying I could never be friends with a person like you because you lack any drive and ambition and have given up.' That's right, Loretta, remind him exactly what you said. Elegant.

'You don't have to apologise. I know we are very different people. I think I used to be quite similar to you, actually.'

'Oh?'

Chris takes a sip of his coffee and runs his hand across his face. 'Lara's death changed everything for me, made me re-evaluate my priorities.'

I don't know how to respond to this so we sit in awkward silence until Chris speaks again. 'Sorry if that's a bit heavy for 10 in the morning. Listen, it's nice of you to apologise. You didn't need to but I imagine you don't want there to be an atmosphere between us at work, so let's draw a line under everything that has happened and agree that, while we don't need to be mates, we don't need to be enemies either.'

'I want to be mates,' I blurt out.

Chris looks palpably shocked.

I feel a sharp sting of hurt. I didn't know how much I meant that until Chris's face told me so plainly the feeling is not mutual. Every fibre of my being now wants to salvage what's left of my pride by backtracking – well, not mates, exactly…

Unfortunately, I have no such luxury. If Finn asks Chris about me, I need him firmly on Team Loretta. But that's not all. Chris doesn't realise it yet, but he is going to furnish me with an informal introduction to Finn before the two of us meet at my interview. 'Also, I think you were right and I should take Phoebe to Little Seahorses.'

'Really? But you seemed so adamant it was a bad idea?'

An ambulance drives past, its flashing blue lights bouncing off the café windows and its sirens filling the air.

'I was wrong.'

'Oh. Well, I have to say, Loretta, it takes a big person to admit that.'

I feel a little squeamish about the compliment. On the one hand, I would swear in a court of law that I genuinely care about Phoebe, that I have missed her more than I would ever have imagined, and I have been wavering about whether I made a mistake in telling her I wouldn't take her swimming anymore. On the other hand, I can't deny the catalyst here has been the chance to meet Finn socially before he interviews me (it has to help, right?). This feels morally questionable. Maybe it's okay if I am helping Phoebe at the same time, though? Sort of like offsetting your carbon footprint when you fly? 'I probably should be going back to work.'

'Yeah,' Chris says, grinning. 'Not like you to sneak out for mid-morning coffee. Maybe I don't really know you at all!'

I force myself to laugh. It's okay what I'm doing. It's one of those situations where everybody wins.

Chapter Fifty-Five

Phoebe hurls herself into my arms with a force that belies her small frame. 'Lorettttttttta!'

Her body feels as hot as a radiator and her hands are kind of sticky but it's hard not to be happy about someone being *this* pleased to see you. Perhaps that's why people have children. Or dogs.

Sylvia, while thankfully not hurling herself into my arms, also seems pleased. 'We were so excited when you called,' she says, as Phoebe disappears upstairs to fetch her swimming bag.

The oversized cat glares malevolently from its oversized basket. I know your game, say its narrowed eyes. I feel a pang of guilt knowing that, although I genuinely like Phoebe, it was the job at Hola that drove me back here today. The headhunter called me to set up the date for my interview with Finn. It's in a month's time which means I have four swimming lessons to try to charm him. This isn't, let's face it, my strong point, but surely the fact Chris and I are already 'mates' will make things easier? I have also researched Finn on social media so I have a few 'shared interests' I can mention. My biggest worry is acting surprised when he tells me he works at Hola. It is generally accepted that I have the sort of poker face that could bankrupt me. However, I have practised my surprised act in the mirror. *Really? You work in advertising too?*

'Tea?' Sylvia offers.

I shake my head. 'How have you been, both of you?'

Sylvia shrugs. 'Oh, y'know, it's tough going at times. I think Phoebe seems to be doing a bit better at school, though. She said you gave her some advice on making friends.'

'Umm, sort of. Listen, I know things are hard for you too. Maybe Phoebe could come back to my house for a sleepover after next week's swimming lesson?' It's the guilt talking and I know Robert will be horrified. We have already had a couple of tense exchanges about why I am 'reinserting myself into the child's life'. 'I thought we'd agreed it was a bad idea?' he said to me, wearily.

Sylvia smoothes back a wisp of hair that has escaped from her messy bun. 'If you're sure? I think a night off would do me the world of good. I might even go back on the dating apps. God knows, I could do with some sex.'

I'm not sure how to respond to this so say nothing.

'Would you take her back to your place straight after swimming?'

'I guess.'

'Phoebe would love it.'

'Love what?' Phoebe says, bouncing into the kitchen.

'Coming to my flat for a sleepover after swimming next week. We can have takeaway pizzas and ice cream and watch a movie – anything you want as long as it's not a twelve.' Wow, I really am feeling guilty.

'What about a fifteen?' Phoebe says.

I ruffle her hair. 'Some people are just too smart for their own good.'

On the bus, Phoebe catches me up with everything I've missed since I saw her last. She went to Olivia's party. It was okay but no one wanted to sit next to her and she didn't like the cake.

She is doing a Roman project at school. She wants to make a Roman soldier's helmet but Grandma says it's too hard and why can't she just make a Coliseum out of loo roll tubes like everyone else?

An old woman with a face like a scrunched paper bag and ankles that puddle around her feet looks over at Phoebe and smiles indulgently.

Phoebe says she has been doing all the things I taught her and now she doesn't cry or get angry in front of people – well, she did cry the other day in PE but that doesn't count because no one noticed.

'It's okay to cry sometimes,' I say, thinking back to Chris telling me I was teaching Phoebe to suppress her emotions and it wasn't healthy. 'And don't put your hands in your mouth. You've had them all over the handrails. Buses are very dirty.'

'Mummy's helping me learn my spellings and I got nineteen out of twenty on the last test and Mrs King was very pleased with me.'

I'd forgotten about how Phoebe often talks about her mother in the present tense. Perhaps kids of this age are not very good with their tenses?

At the leisure centre, Phoebe tells me she is going to undress very quickly because she knows I like her to do that and she doesn't want me to change my mind about taking her to Little Seahorses.

Another knife-twist of guilt. 'I won't do that.' I have already thought about my exit strategy and how I plan to phase things out gently this time. 'Are you okay by yourself if I nip to the loo?'

'I'm not a baby.'

I emerge from the toilet cubicle at the same time as a little boy in the stall next door but, whereas I go immediately to the sink, he runs straight out without washing his hands.

In the changing room, I see him with his mother and decide to do my good deed for the day. 'Excuse me,' I say to the woman. 'Your little boy didn't wash his hands after going to the toilet.'

'Right,' the woman says, her voice dripping with hostility. Honestly, you'd think she'd be grateful. I walk away, wishing I hadn't bothered trying to do the right thing. Clearly, I should have just let her dirty little grub make himself ill.

'All ready,' Phoebe says to me.

'Great.'

Chris is already by the side of the pool. 'Hey, stranger. I bought you a coffee.'

'Oh, you didn't have to do that.'

'Maybe I wanted to.'

Phoebe is hurtling towards me, her arms flapping wildly.

'Don't run!'

'Loretta!' she says, sounding almost breathless. *'Georgia is here!'*

'Umm—'

'Georgia is new in my class at school and she doesn't have any friends yet so I'm going to ask her to be my friend.'

My heart clenches. How do people with children even begin to function? How do they go to work and make dinner and laugh as if everything is normal when they have to take on all the hopes and dreams and fears of another human?

Chris and I start chatting. I'd forgotten how easy he is to talk to and the only thing that spoils it for me is the memory of his face when I told him I'd like to be mates in the café. He's a friendly person rather than my friend.

I'm also concerned there's no sign whatsoever of Finn. Perhaps he has stopped bringing his son to swimming lessons here? That would kind of serve me right, really.

The only people who come through the door that I recognise are dirty grub child and his mother.

'Georgia,' the woman calls out. 'You forgot your towel.'

Oh, crap, why does she of all people have to be Georgia's mother? She clearly took me mentioning the hand washing badly, and I just hope that doesn't put her off Phoebe when she inevitably connects the two of us. Honestly, trying to hook friends for Phoebe is making me feel like Mrs Bennet trying to secure marriages for her daughters.

I am distracted from these thoughts by another panic because, although people keep coming through the door, none of them is Finn. Eventually, after nearly half an hour, I can stand it no longer and try to keep my voice oh-so casual as I ask Chris if his mate still comes here; the one who left his bags with us that day. I can't remember his name now. Tom? Ben?

'Finn. Yeah, he still comes but his little boy had a bit of an accident in the playground at school the other day and he had to have a couple of stitches in his chin. They're giving swimming a miss today because they want to keep the stitches dry.'

'Oh no.'

Chris cocks his head to one side and looks at me. 'Goodness, Loretta, you look really upset. It's nothing serious – just a row with a climbing frame. Who would have had you pegged as such a big old softy?' He gives me a mock punch on the shoulder.

Chapter Fifty-Six

I often think of marriage as choosing the person you want to have the same rows with for the rest of your life. Robert and I definitely have the same arguments on repeat. This one is the 'I told you/no, you didn't' dispute.

We are making supper. Until a few minutes ago, all was domestic bliss. I was chopping onions and mincing garlic, Robert was making his signature salad dressing, and music that I don't love but don't hate was coming from his Spotify playlist.

Then I mentioned that I had invited Phoebe for a sleepover next Saturday night.

'What? But I told you my parents are coming up to London next Saturday night.'

'You didn't tell me that.'

'I definitely did.'

'Well, I don't remember. Maybe you just thought you told me.'

'I did tell you,' Robert says, vigorously shaking the jar of dressing. 'I told you on the night of your second interview with Hola because I remember you said you weren't sure if you should mention all that to my parents or if you should wait until it was a firm offer.'

Want to win arguments? My advice would be never to marry

a lawyer. 'Right, well, it needn't be a problem. We can combine the two things. I'm sure your parents would love to see Phoebe.' I am actually sure of no such thing. Robert's parents don't seem to love anything much, and that includes Robert and his brother.

'That's a silly idea,' Robert says, reaching for the tomatoes. 'You'll have to tell Phoebe she can come another time. Preferably when I'm out.'

'*Robert,*' I say, tipping the onions and garlic into a pan.

'What? You know I'm not a kid person, and neither were you until all this business. It's not me that's changed, Loretta.'

'I haven't changed,' I say, giving the onions and garlic a stir and sprinkling them with salt. 'Look, I really think we could all have supper together. It will be jolly.'

'Hmm, well, where would we go? My parents are not going to be happy with some burger joint with crayons on the table.'

'We can go anywhere you like,' I say, trying not to remember how I promised Phoebe pizza and ice cream. 'Or we could make a nice dinner here. You know how you always say it's murder to park in town on a Saturday night.'

'Well, that is true. And I expect Mum and Dad will be tired from the drive down.'

The kitchen fills with the aroma of onions and garlic. Is there any better smell? It makes a home feel like a home should, and always reminds me of my childhood. My mum may not be the stereotypical Italian mamma in many ways but she can knock up a mean plate of pasta. I have a sudden vivid picture of my sister aged about two, her small, smiley face covered in red pasta sauce. 'Messy baby!' I exclaimed, making my parents burst out laughing.

'Okay, let's have dinner at home. I still think we should keep it to just the four of us, though. We don't see my parents very often and I don't want an evening of chaos.'

'It won't be an evening of chaos.'

'It could easily be. C'mon, Loretta, even you would admit Phoebe is something of a loose cannon.'

'I can't just uninvite her. She is looking forward to it.'

Robert shrugs and there is something so dismissive and uncaring about the gesture that it's all I can do not to hurl a can of plum tomatoes at him. 'You're being unreasonable. Phoebe will be no bother at all and your parents might even enjoy seeing her. What's more, she has been through a lot recently, as you very well know.'

Again, Robert just shrugs. Clearly, the man has little regard for his own welfare. I pour the tinned tomatoes into the pan with the onions and garlic and start furiously wiping over the kitchen sides with anti-bacterial spray.

'Why are you doing that while we're still cooking?' Robert says.

It's not an unreasonable question but I don't bother to answer it. 'I want Phoebe to come here for a sleepover next Saturday evening.'

The row takes a steep turn for the worst after that and, before I know it, the onions are more brown than translucent and Robert and I – neither of us normally a shouter – are yelling at each other across the kitchen.

'This whole thing with the kid is ridiculous, anyway,' Robert says.

'What do you mean, "this whole thing"?'

'You know exactly what I mean. You never should have got involved. What has happened to her is awful – truly awful – but it's not something you can fix.'

'I never said I could fix it. But that doesn't mean I can't try to help.' I ignore the flash of guilt that, although I genuinely would like to help Phoebe, not all my motives are as pure as I'm making them sound.

Robert keeps his eyes fixed on the carrot he is slicing. 'The whole thing is ridiculous.'

'Well, maybe if you think I'm so "ridiculous", you shouldn't be marrying me.'

I wait for Robert to say of course, he doesn't think I'm ridiculous and of course, he should be marrying me, but he just carries on slicing the carrot.

'Marvellous,' I say, throwing the oven gloves on the worktop and walking out of the kitchen.

I hurl myself onto the bed and burst into tears. A few minutes later, Robert comes in and I feel a surge of relief. This is a row over nothing; we're going to be fine.

Robert sits on the edge of the bed. 'We could still get the deposit back on the wedding venue.'

Chapter Fifty-Seven

Robert vigorously maintains that him mentioning the deposit on the wedding venue was simply him 'presenting the options' and did not mean that is what he wants. However, one week on from the row, and despite us ostensibly making up, I still feel bruised.

He got to that pretty quickly.

I am sitting on the bus on the way to pick up Phoebe for Little Seahorses. It's raining heavily and the windows are misted up. A baby is crying and a group of teenagers seems to be locked in a dispute about a girl who isn't with them.

I walk to Sylvia's house, holding on desperately to the side of my umbrella to try to stop the wind blowing it inside out. I have to shake the mood I'm in. Not only is it unfair to Phoebe but I need to make a good impression on Finn.

Phoebe is bouncing with excitement. She tells me she has packed three games including poo Trumps. It's like Top Trumps but with poo!

I'm not really sure how to respond to that.

'Have you packed your pyjamas and toothbrush?' Sylvia asks Phoebe.

'I think I forgot my toothbrush,' Phoebe says, disappearing up the stairs.

'I have a date tonight,' Sylvia says to me, her eyes shining. 'He's a chartered surveyor and he looks very handsome in his photos. Do you think it's all right to have sex on the first date? I wouldn't normally but it's what people do nowadays, isn't it? Plus, if I don't do it tonight, I don't know when I'll have another opportunity. That child is up at all times of night so I certainly can't risk entertaining a man friend when she's around. Which makes me think if I like the chartered surveyor, I should go for it. That's okay, right?'

I am as confounded by this conversation as I am by the one about the poo Trumps. I don't know why Sylvia sees me as any sort of confidante, or, for that matter, an expert on relationships. Luckily, I am saved by Phoebe returning with a battered brown leather holdall that's almost as big as her.

'That's huge.'

Phoebe nods earnestly. 'I know because I had to pack Mummy's stuff too.'

I flinch and look across at Sylvia, but she is busy examining her roots in the mirror and seems unconcerned. I guess Phoebe must have a few things of her mum's she likes to have with her.

'It's very heavy,' Phoebe says, 'and you can't drag it along like you could my Timmy the Tiger suitcase because it doesn't have wheels.'

My mind flashes back to the small orange and black stripey suitcase that tripped me up at the airport. What a long time ago that feels like.

On the bus to the leisure centre, I tell Phoebe it will just be her and me this evening because Robert is going out to dinner with his parents.

'Yay!' Phoebe says, not bothering to hide her delight. 'And can we have pizza and ice cream and watch any movie I want, like you promised?'

I nod. Tonight's arrangements were a sensible compromise and it was me who suggested them so I have no business at all feeling sad about them.

The leisure centre seems hotter than ever and the air is soupy and oppressive. I take my seat by the side of the pool and rub the muscles in the back of my neck. Robert and I will be fine. All couples have rows.

I'm finding it hard to shake this gloomy mood, though. This whole week has been a struggle. Work, which is normally my refuge, feels tough going now I have mentally checked out. In my mind, I am already a Board Account Director at Hola. To be fair to me, this isn't completely fanciful. Lucy the headhunter says the job is mine to lose.

I watch Phoebe who is standing alone by the side of the pool in her goggles and swim cap. When I came back from the toilet earlier, I walked into the changing room to find her engaged in a voluble conversation with thin air. She looked – and there is no other way of putting this – *weird*, and I was tempted to say something. That it is fine for her to have an imaginary friend, that I had one when I was a kid, but maybe keep it on the down-low? I have learned you have to tread carefully with Phoebe, though. Even when she seems happy like today, that happiness is fragile and transitory. So, I said nothing because, truthfully, I feel too delicate myself today to cope with her falling apart.

Now, I watch as Georgia comes running out of the changing room and the two of them greet each other and start chattering. Please let Georgia be kind to Phoebe, not just now but always. I even made myself smile at her awful mother and dirty grub child of a brother earlier.

'Morning,' Chris says, flipping down the seat next to me. 'How are you?'

Hanging on by a thread. 'Good. You?'

'I'm good. I brought us some of my homemade croissants. I don't want to be immodest, but I think we can agree that makes me a domestic god, no? And, by the way, my kitchen is extremely clean and I washed my hands repeatedly when making these.'

'Why are you telling—'

'You don't have to be über-perceptive to know you're a germophobe, Loretta.'

'I wouldn't say germophobe,' I say, laughing and rolling my eyes.

'I would but that's fine. We all have our stuff.' He grins and holds the Tupperware box towards me. 'Looks like it's going well with Phoebe and Georgia.'

I nod. 'Yeah, so far, so good. These are delicious. Did you really make them or did you buy them from a bakery and then smash them up a bit?'

'How very dare you.'

I take another bite of the rich, buttery pastry and flakes fly all over my shirt. I hope this is not the moment Finn will choose to walk through the door.

Ten minutes later, though, there is still no sign of Finn. 'How is your mate's little boy, the one who had the stitches?'

'Arthur is fine.' He points in the direction of the pool. 'In fact, that's him over there racing Zack. I saw him earlier and it looks like the doctors did a great job on him and he's not even going to have a scar.'

My mind struggles to catch up. If Finn's son is here, where is Finn? I'm pretty sure seven-year-olds don't attend swimming lessons on their own. Silence hangs heavily in the air and I try to make my voice casual. 'So, where is Finn?'

'He only has Arthur every other weekend. Justine brings Arthur on the other weeks. That's her sitting over there. I think she's trying to move as far from me as possible. Sad, really, when you think we've been on holidays together and know each other...'

Chris's voice washes over me as I am filled with panic. Finn is not coming here today and he won't be here the week after next, which means I only have one more opportunity for this casual, friendly meeting before my interview with him. That's okay, though. One is all I need.

'You okay?' Chris says, cutting into my thoughts. 'You look lost in your own world there.'

'I'm fine.'

'Good.' Chris gestures towards the pool where Phoebe and Georgia are giggling every time they come up for air after diving to retrieve plastic seahorses from the bottom of the pool. 'Look at those two – they're thick as thieves.'

'Long may it continue.' I pull at the skin around my cuticle and a little spot of blood appears. 'Robert and I had a row, and it was a stupid one over nothing, but then he told me we could still get the deposit back on the wedding venue.'

I want to suck the words back into my mouth as soon as they are out. What possessed me to say such a thing? This is not me at all. I nearly did the same with Zoe the other day at work. We were on our own in the office very early one morning and she confided in me that she didn't want to tell everyone yet but my lucky heather had worked and she is pregnant. Before I knew it, and somewhat to my surprise, I had tears in my eyes and was hugging her. We talked for ages, Zoe admitting she was terrified the pregnancy wouldn't stick, and then I suddenly felt the confessional mood overtake me too. But then I shook myself, realising that the last thing I needed was for my row with Robert to be the subject of office gossip.

'Please don't tell anyone,' I say to Chris. 'I mean, not that there is anything to tell. All couples have rows, don't they? In fact, forget I said anything. Look, Zack's front crawl has really come on, hasn't it?'

Chris, of course, isn't so easily diverted. He puts his hand on my arm and I feel the warmth of his skin through my sleeve. 'That's quite a big thing to talk about, calling off the wedding. It must have been upsetting for you?'

I shrug. 'Robert is just very practical.'

'Hmm, and how did you feel when he said it?'

I feel tears start to rise and swallow them back down. What the hell was I thinking, bringing this up with Chris, of all people? 'I was upset at the time but I'm fine now.'

Chris makes a face.

'What? I *am* fine. Really.'

Chris looks unconvinced.

I look towards the door. A few minutes ago I was obsessing about when Finn was going to walk through it. Now all I can think about is when I am going to run out of it.

Chapter Fifty-Eight

'Loretta,' Robert says, appearing beside me in the kitchen as I heat up the soup I've made for lunch. 'I just walked into the sitting room and Phoebe is in there talking to herself.'

'Shh,' I say, shutting the door behind him. 'She's not talking to herself, she's talking to an imaginary friend. Didn't you ever have one as a kid?'

'Ermm, no.' Robert pours himself a glass of water. 'She looks weird.'

'That's not a very kind thing to say,' I snap, even though exactly the same thought had crossed my mind when I saw Phoebe chuntering away to thin air.

I reach for the Mickey Mouse cutter I bought yesterday, willing Robert not to comment on the fact that I used to be someone who laughed at people for pandering to children, but now think nothing of cutting toast into 'fun' shapes.

Lunch is tense. Phoebe is momentarily delighted by the Mickey toast and then takes three mouthfuls of soup before asking if she can get down. I say she can and Robert scowls at me. I don't mention that I gave in to the whingeing after swimming and bought Phoebe a brownie the size of her head.

The afternoon passes slowly. Robert says he has work to do

and won't join in any activities. This leaves me as the only adult participant in two games so mind-numbingly dull I'm surprised they don't have to carry a health warning on the box. I feel like I've reached a new low when I actually ask if we can play poo Trumps.

Phoebe is also spectacularly messy. In the short period that Robert and I were clearing up the lunch things, she asked me for some pens for drawing and I directed her to my work bag and then, when she found the sole pen within that unsatisfactory (too black), the drawers of my desk. When I went back into the sitting room, it looked as if we had been burgled, with all my navy Moleskine notebooks, various files and every stationery item you can imagine scattered over the floor.

Now, Phoebe is standing on the sofa, red-faced and feral, asking what we are going to do next.

To be honest, this is partly my own fault. As well as the afore-mentioned brownie, I also said she could have a few of the sweets she found in my bag, which I had intended to give to her after supper. By the time I noticed, she had hoovered up half the packet.

Phoebe starts reciting a nonsensical poem at the top of her voice.

'Is this what you meant when you said I'd be charmed by her?' Robert whispers to me.

It's all I can do not to hit him. Or point out that there is something about *him* that makes Phoebe different in his company. Perhaps if he didn't go around acting as if there is a stick up his bloody bum?

Whoa, I tell myself. Robert is great. He may not be the Pied Piper, exactly, but that's fine.

'Phoebe,' I say. 'Do you want to bake some cookies?' God

knows, she does not need more sugar, but she does need something to occupy her – not to mention keep her out of Robert's hair.

In the kitchen, Phoebe whisks the butter and sugar, sending big blobs of the mixture flying everywhere.

'You need to keep the whisk low,' I say, fighting to keep the irritation from my voice.

Phoebe has launched into a stream of consciousness about how she and Georgia are going to be best friends now and how they are going to put their names down for the inter-school swimming gala and how they couldn't do that without each other but together they can.

I heard all this as soon as we left the leisure centre and several times since, and I am delighted for her, really I am, but I also have to fight the urge to scream: YOU'VE ALREADY TOLD ME. I AM NOT A GOLDFISH AND CAN RETAIN INFORMATION. Also, does she have to speak quite so loudly? I can hear Robert huffing from behind his laptop in the sitting room.

'NO!' I shout, as Phoebe stuffs the chocolate chips meant for the cookies into her mouth. 'No more sugar.'

'Just a few. Mummy always lets me.'

I sigh wearily, trying not to calculate that there are still twenty hours before I return Phoebe to Sylvia. Admittedly, eight of those should be spent sleeping, but I know from previous experience that is not something I can count on.

'And don't put your fingers into the bowl,' I snap. 'Think of the germs.'

Phoebe's eyes fill with tears and I immediately feel like the most horrible person in the whole world.

'Sorry,' I say. 'Look, you can lick the bowl afterwards, okay?'

Somehow, we manage to get the cookies into the oven without any further upset and I tell Phoebe she can play on my iPad while I clear up. The black granite worktops are coated in a dusting of flour and sugar, and blobs of melting sugary butter are scattered far and wide. We also seem to have used a disproportionate amount of crockery and implements. I run a sink of hot water and pull on my rubber gloves. I am so disappointed in myself. I have been envisaging the cookie-baking for days and I imagined it would be a sweet and cosy moment where Phoebe and I worked side by side as the house filled up with tempting aromas. Perhaps Robert would come in at some point and the three of us would share a joke? The reality was so different to the expectation. I am all too aware of my limitations, but I thought even I could manage to bake some cookies with a six-year-old without reducing them to tears.

I rinse the big mixing bowl under the tap, thinking back to this morning when I told Chris about my row with Robert last week. I have no idea what possessed me, and the only explanation I can come up with is that this weird limbo-like state of thinking I've landed the job at Hola, but not being able to count on it for sure, is messing with my head.

Phoebe and I are making the paper fortune tellers that Emilia and I were so obsessed with as kids. I suggested the idea to Phoebe out of desperation. In this world of the internet and computer games and a crazy number of TV channels, I couldn't imagine a bit of folded paper that told you your 'future' would have much appeal. But Phoebe is very taken with them. Pick a colour, she tells me for the umpteenth time. (Seriously, what is it with kids and repetition?)

'Blue.'

'B-L-U-E. Pick a number.'

How can she not be bored of this by now? 'Three.'

'One, two, three.' Phoebe pauses for dramatic effect, puffing out her small chest. 'You will give Phoebe some ice cream.'

'Phoebe!' I say, laughing. 'It's supposed to be my fortune. You can't just write what you want to happen.'

'It is your fortune,' she says. But it's no longer Phoebe's voice I'm hearing, it's Emilia's: you will let your little sister play with your doll's house.

Emilia used to do exactly what Phoebe is doing now.

'Loretta,' Phoebe says, waving her small hand in front of my face. 'Why aren't you answering me?'

I shake away the memories that have flooded my brain. 'Sorry.'

I have only just cleared up all the detritus from the making of the fortune tellers when the doorbell rings. It must be Robert's parents, who are having a quick drink here before the three of them head off to dinner.

'Hello,' Robert's mother says to me, her lips fleetingly grazing my cheek. She looks over at Phoebe who is jabbing away at the iPad. 'And who have we here? Kids today are obsessed with screens, aren't they?'

I blanch at the implied criticism of Phoebe – and I suppose my care of the child – within seconds of her coming through the door. It's a good thing I don't want children of my own because Robert's parents would definitely make exacting and hypercritical grandparents. 'This is Phoebe. Phoebe, come and say hello to Fiona and Miles.'

Somewhat to my surprise, Phoebe immediately does as she is asked, peeking shyly from behind her hair to shake hands.

The drinks themselves are rather stilted. As they so often do, Robert and his father immediately lapse into talking about work, and Robert's mother, after the briefest of interactions with Phoebe about where she attends school and if she works hard there, ignores her completely while she tells me about her bridge club, the row over the church coffee rota and how the traffic on the way here was 'murderous'.

I'm bored so know Phoebe must be too and can hardly believe that she sits still and quiet. The hyper, sugar-rush version of her seems to have worn itself out.

I glance over at Robert and Miles. They look very alike, with the same sharp jawlines and pale blue eyes. They even have the same whorl of hair at the crown, although Robert's dad's is flecked with grey. The two of them are arguing over some finer point of the law, seemingly oblivious to the rest of us in the room.

'Don't keep fiddling with your buttons, Phoebe,' Fiona says.

It's the first thing she has said to Phoebe in about half an hour. Hasn't she noticed how well-behaved Phoebe has been? And what's the harm in her playing with her buttons? I think about Sylvia, who must be about the same age as Fiona and looks after Phoebe all day every day. I hope she's having sex with the chartered surveyor right now. Lots of hot, swinging-from-the-chandelier sex.

I take a large sip of my wine and try to make noises in the right places as I half listen to more on the church coffee rota saga.

'Of course,' Fiona says, 'Mary might not be making such a fuss about the rota if she wasn't upset about not being invited to the wedding.'

Oh, not this again. Fiona, much like my mother, is disappointed in me and Robert for insisting on a small, intimate wedding for thirty guests. They don't seem to understand that

I'm more than a little uncomfortable about being the centre of attention. I wasn't the type of little girl to clip a tea towel to my hair and play brides. Meanwhile, Robert would happily go to the local registry office. 'I know the venue we've picked is small but it's so lovely. Especially when they light all the candles in the evening.'

'Hmm,' Fiona says.

Robert, to my eternal gratitude, tunes in to where this conversation might be heading and cuts in to say he and his parents should start thinking about leaving for the restaurant.

'Thanks,' I whisper, as he kisses me goodbye.

He winks and I feel a small stab of pain that the two of us seem to have drifted off course recently. We'll be fine, though. All couples have their ups and downs.

There's a chorus of goodbyes, and Fiona asks Phoebe if she's going to 'look up from that screen' to say goodbye.

'Sorry,' I say to Phoebe, as I shut the door. 'That wasn't much fun for you, was it?'

Phoebe shrugs. 'Mummy told me I had to be a good girl.'

I ignore the use of the present tense. 'Well, you were a very good girl.'

'Because I want to come back here. I really like coming to your house and being with you.'

I feel, somewhat bizarrely, as if I might cry. Children are so forgiving. I played Phoebe's games without enthusiasm, snapped at her when we were cooking and radiated boredom for most of the afternoon – and yet in her eyes I still seem to be okay.

'Georgia is going to invite me over to her house next week.'

'That's nice.'

Phoebe nods. 'Because we are best friends now. We are going to be in the inter-school swimming gala together. And we sit together at lunch, and we are partners for everything you need partners for. We are going to stay best friends too because I am going to be nice and I am not going to cry or talk to Georgia about Mummy.'

'Umm—'

'That's right, isn't it? If I want to stay friends with Georgia, I shouldn't make her feel upset.'

I take a sip of my wine, buying myself time. Phoebe needs better grown-ups in her life than me. I am thirty-one years old and still haven't really got the hang of friendships. 'It's okay to be upset about your mum. That's a big, big thing. But, yes, sometimes it's hard for other people to hear how sad you are, particularly other kids.'

Phoebe nods earnestly. 'Can we order the pizza now and pick a movie? And can we have extra pepperoni?'

'On the movie?'

Phoebe laughs like I have said the funniest thing in the whole world.

Twenty minutes later, the two of us are snuggled up watching a just-the-right-side-of-cheesy movie about a kickass princess who chooses to save her kingdom instead of pursuing a man. We have a big box of also just-the-right-side-of-cheesy pizza.

I look over at Phoebe's small face laughing, the light from the TV reflected on it. And that's when it hits me – I would rather be here with her than with Robert and his parents in some stuffy restaurant.

It's a very weird feeling.

Chapter Fifty-Nine

Kathleen is at 'my' desk again, the infuriating woman. Still, I won't be at this agency for much longer.

I find another desk and take out my anti-bac wipes. I'm beyond exhausted. Phoebe and her nightmares kept me awake for most of Saturday night and, by the time I'd returned home after dropping her at Sylvia's on Sunday, I was too tired to even tidy the flat properly, chucking everything from my notebooks to kitchen equipment in vaguely the right places in the sort of slapdash manner I normally wouldn't countenance.

Then last night, poor Robert was up several times being violently sick. I am the world's worst nurse and not good around vomit, but even I am not so heartless as to be able to just stay in my bed, so I found myself hovering outside the bathroom door for a lot of the night, making soothing noises and offering to bring water.

'Morning,' Zoe says, plonking her oversized tote bag on the desk next to mine. 'How was your weekend?'

'Good. Yours?' I look around and confirm no one is within earshot. 'How are you feeling?'

'A bit sick, actually, but I guess I can't grumble.'

'Okay, you sit quietly and I'll make you some ginger tea.'

'Thanks.' Zoe looks quite surprised and, to be honest, I'm also a little thrown off by this nurturing version of myself, especially as Operation Mesh With The Team is a thing of the past.

A little while later, I am back at my desk and wondering if I should have made ginger tea for myself as well. I feel distinctly odd and am struggling to focus on the words on my computer screen.

Maybe Robert wasn't sick because of the restaurant Dover sole? Maybe he had a bug and gave it to me? I push the thought out of my mind and reach into my bag for my notebook. I haven't even made a to-do list for today as I was just too tired on the tube this morning.

I don't even manage to open the notebook before I am hit by a wave of nausea so powerful I have no alternative but to run to the bathroom as fast as I possibly can.

I am in a taxi on my way home, shaking and sweating, when I realise I am supposed to be interviewing a new account executive in half an hour. I tap out a message to Zoe, asking if she can phone him to put him off. His name is Simon and his mobile number is on the inside cover of my notebook.

The taxi lurches to a stop at the traffic lights and I scrabble for the 'just in case' carrier bag Samira shoved in my hands before I left.

Chapter Sixty

It's Wednesday before I make it into the office again. I can't remember the last time I took two days off sick.

'Morning,' the man on reception says. 'Have a nice day.'

I stand waiting for the lift, wondering how many times a day he says that.

'Morning,' I say to Maddie, as I walk through the swing doors.

'Morning.'

Is it my imagination or is her tone a little clipped? And why is she walking on without even asking me if I am feeling better? It's most un-Maddie-like. I expect she has had yet another row with Alex.

Thankfully, Kathleen the desk stealer is yet to arrive so I set about cleaning 'my' desk.

'Loretta,' Greg says, appearing beside me. 'I need to talk to you about Kitkins. Can you put some time in my diary, please?'

'Yes, will do.' Unlike Maddie, Greg often skips the pleasantries, and things have been a little off between us since he didn't promote me, but I still would have thought he would ask me how I am feeling, even if he then didn't properly listen to the answer.

I open my laptop and nervously hover the cursor over my inbox. On Monday, I was too busy with my head down the toilet to even check my emails and yesterday, although I had stopped throwing up, I felt so weak I only managed to skim them for the most urgent. Now, I have 56 unread emails, which is unheard of for me.

Pete comes in, gives me the briefest of nods, and *doesn't* launch into a story about his journey. Weird.

I go back to reading an email chain.

Samira comes bustling through the double doors and I raise my hand in greeting, only to have her completely blank me. What on earth is going on? At this rate, Mr Have a Nice Day on reception is the only friendly face I'm going to see all day.

I turn my attention back to my emails. I don't have time to be caught up in any dramas.

Zoe comes in, sees the free seat beside me and keeps walking. Now I am seriously confused, not to mention annoyed. I thought I was supposed to be the unfriendly one?

After about half an hour of sitting at my desk, trying to work but finding myself unable to concentrate, I go over to Zoe. 'Everything all right?'

'Was that on your list of things to ask me today?' Zoe's voice is icy and she doesn't look up from her computer screen.

'I'm sorry?'

Zoe sighs heavily. 'Was it on your list, Loretta? You know, like "ask Zoe about IVF appointment" and "listen to one of Pete's stories" and "sign up for softball" and all the other things you did because they were tasks you had to tick off your list?'

The nausea I thought was gone returns. Zoe has seen my lists. But how?

'We couldn't understand why you would do it at first but then Maddie worked it out. It was all part of your promotion effort, wasn't it? We should have known better than to think you genuinely liked us.'

I should jump in here and say that I do genuinely like her but I am unable to form words and just stand there, going redder and redder with my mouth opening and closing like a guppy.

Zoe shakes her head and lowers her voice. 'Don't you dare tell anyone about this pregnancy before I have my twelve-week scan. At least be decent enough to promise that.' She reaches across her desk, picks up my Moleskine notebook and stuffs it into my hands. 'Oh, and take this back.'

As I walk away from Zoe's desk, it takes all the power in my body not to cry. I don't know why I'm so upset – I'll be out of this place soon – but I am just so humiliated and, as I walk across the office with everyone's eyes on me, I am once again the little girl no one wanted to hang out with in the playground.

I am trembling by the time I sit down, my mind racing. How on earth did Zoe find out about Operation Mesh With The Team? And that's when I look down at the notebook in my hand and I realise. I don't even have to open it to know that it won't be my current notebook, but the one I was using when I embarked on my mission to make myself likeable.

A memory from Saturday afternoon flashes into my mind – Phoebe sitting surrounded by a load of stationery and piles of identical navy Moleskine notebooks. I must have put the wrong one back in my work bag.

A reminder pops up on my computer screen to tell me that I have a client meeting starting in five minutes. I take a deep breath and tell myself that I can get through today. That I am no stranger to shame and humiliation and I can bury it, just as I always do.

Chapter Sixty-One

I wake up before it's light on Saturday morning, my stomach knotted with anticipation. If I was desperate to secure the job at Hola before the whole notebook thing, it's even more non-negotiable now. I have spent years thinking that work is about work and I have neither the time nor the skills for friendships, but there's a huge difference between not feeling like part of the gang and everybody hating you.

Robert's breathing is slow and steady. He is the tidiest sleeper I have ever known, waking in the exact same position he went to sleep in. My guts twist, thinking about how tense things have been between us. I'm sure we can find a way back to each other, though.

Today is my last remaining opportunity to meet Finn before he formally interviews me. It's not just the kids who have goals at Little Seahorses, it seems. I have spent a lot of time this week worrying that word of the notebook thing would reach Chris's ears, scuppering my chances of him introducing me to Finn as his friend or saying good things about me. However, it seems the rumour mill hasn't made it as far as Chris because, every time I've seen him around the office, he has been as friendly as ever. Yesterday, he was teasing me about whether I had spritzed the copy brief I handed him with anti-bacterial spray. After glancing around to check no one else was in earshot, he even asked me if everything was okay with Robert. He said he'd been worrying about me. 'I'm fine,' I said quickly. 'Absolutely fine.'

I ease myself out of bed as quietly as I can and pad into the kitchen. It's 5.30 a.m. now which is nearer to morning than night. I make myself a cup of tea and settle down on the sofa. I prac-tise what I am going to say to Finn in my head. I want to come across as nice but not too 'try hard'. Oh, and the most important thing of all is that I act completely surprised if he mentions Hola. I open Instagram on my phone and have a quick look at his profile to remind me of some 'shared interests' I can casually drop into conversation.

I must drift off to sleep because I wake up to the sound of my mobile ringing. It's Sylvia, of all people.

'Phoebe has a terrible cold. Unfortunately, I think she is going to have to give swimming a miss today.'

'No!' I sit bolt upright, making my head spin a little. If Phoebe doesn't go to Little Seahorses, I will miss my chance of a casual meeting with Finn. I make my tone gentler. 'What I mean is that I think a bit of exercise will do Phoebe good.'

'Well, that's as may be,' Sylvia says. 'But I don't think she should go swimming. She might catch a chill.'

'It's always very hot at the leisure centre, actually, and the pool water is like a bath. Also, did you know that people don't really catch a chill as such—'

'Well, of course they do. Especially if they go out with wet hair.'

I realise that I have taken a wrong turn here. Telling Sylvia you can't catch a chill or worsen a virus by having damp hair is like telling her the world is flat. 'I could make sure her hair is dry before we leave.'

'Well, yes, but I'm still not sure it's a good idea.'

'This is a very critical lesson.'

'Is it? Why?'

Yes, *why*? 'Umm, well, you know Phoebe and her friend are going to be taking part in the inter-school swimming gala soon and she only has a couple of lessons left before that.'

Silence buzzes down the line and I can practically hear the cogs of Sylvia's brain whirring. 'Oh, that. Well, look, I'm sure what Phoebe doesn't know in terms of swimming now, she isn't going to pick up in one lesson.'

Damn it, I can see the meeting with Finn slipping away from me. Think, Loretta, think. 'I bet you could do with a break.'

'Well—'

'I mean, honestly, I love being around Phoebe but when I had her to stay last weekend, it made me realise just how tiring it is.'

'It is tiring,' Sylvia agrees. 'Especially at my age. Do you really think the swimming would do her good?'

'Absolutely. Blow the cobwebs off.'

'Well, okay, then. See you soon.'

I end the call. My meeting with Finn is on track. But I think I may have stooped to a new low.

Chapter Sixty-Two

The universe is paying me back the best it can by handing me the grumpiest, most recalcitrant child. Phoebe does not want to sit where I suggest on the bus, she whines when I try to pull on the swimming cap (despite me having long since mastered the technique) and she makes a full-on scene when we don't get 'her' locker.

And the snot, oh God, the snot! She sneezes constantly, always covering her nose and mouth a fraction too late. I shrink back as fast as I can and resolve to buy industrial quantities of vitamin C and zinc on the way home.

Phoebe's mood brightens when Georgia walks into the changing room and the two of them immediately start chattering about the swimming gala and how they will be much faster than Olivia's team.

My mood is similarly improved when I open the door to the spectator area and see Chris locked in conversation with Finn. Bingo!

'Loretta,' Chris says. 'This is my mate, Finn. I don't think the two of you were properly introduced before.'

I smile, stretch out my hand and try to ignore my heart which is hammering away in my chest. This shouldn't be difficult – all

I have to do is make some polite chit-chat and not say anything strange. However, experience has taught me I am more than capable of screwing this up. My weirdness is always lying in wait and can, like the alien in John Hurt's stomach, burst out at any time.

As it happens, though, I needn't have worried. Chris gives me a glowing introduction, explaining to Finn how Phoebe and I met. He tells him that I was very kind to Phoebe on that awful day and have continued to be good to her ever since. Even though I don't have any kids of my own, I bring her to swimming lessons week in, week out. I am lovely with her.

My skin prickles at all this undeserved praise but it's clear from Finn's face he is impressed.

After that, the chat flows easily, with the three of us discussing everything from 'poncy coffee' to dream holidays to must-see TV.

'I never asked you what you do for a living,' Finn says to me.

'I work in advertising. I'm an Account Director at the same agency as Chris.'

'A very good Account Director,' Chris says, almost as if he is in on my plan. 'Although you know it pains me to say nice things about "suits".'

Finn gives him a mock punch on the arm. 'I've been hearing the "suits" jokes for years. I'm an account man too.'

'You're in advertising?' I say, affecting surprise.

'Yeah.' Finn's brow furrows. 'Wait, you're not the Loretta that's interviewing for a job at Hola, are you?'

I arrange my face to look even more surprised. 'Yes.'

'Oh my God! I've just started working at Hola. You and I have a meeting the week after next.'

'You're that Finn? Small world!'

Finn is laughing and shaking his head. 'It really is.' He glances over at Chris. 'And it was also really indiscreet of me to come out with that in front of Chris. You won't drop Loretta in it at work, will you, buddy?'

I look over at Chris, whose face has changed completely.

He knows.

Chapter Sixty-Three

Chris is waiting for me when I come out of the changing room with Phoebe. 'I've given Zack some money to buy him and Phoebe a hot chocolate.'

Zack looks anything but pleased about this enforced mini playdate but he has clearly been briefed in advance and he and Phoebe head off towards the café.

As soon as they are out of earshot, Chris launches into me. 'So, now I see why you suddenly came up with your "heartfelt" apology.'

'I don't know what you mean.'

Chris shakes his head. 'Skip it, Loretta. You may be able to bullshit clients, but you can't do it to me. It all makes sense now. Why you went from telling me I was a loser you could never be friends with to suddenly wanting to be my pal. Worse still, why you did a massive U-turn about bringing Phoebe to swimming. How could you use a vulnerable child like that? Honestly, is there anyone or anything you actually care about?'

'I do care about Phoebe,' I say, fighting back tears.

'Really? Then decide whether you're in or out of her life.'

The contempt on Chris's face is so palpable I have to look away.

'Do you know what the worst thing is?' Chris says. 'I actually defended you at work. There's some rumour going around that you only started to be friendlier towards people because you thought it would land you a promotion. That you make yourself lists of things you need to do, such as have lunch with someone or ask them how their doctor's appointment went.'

I dig my nails into my palms and stare at the swirly green lino, wishing it would suck me into its pattern.

'And do you know what I said? Okay, so she makes lists but maybe that's because she doesn't find it as easy as some people. That doesn't make her a fake. You should see the way she is with that kid.' He laughs mirthlessly. 'But I was wrong about you, wasn't I?' He turns on his heel and stalks off in the direction of the café. 'You'd better come and collect Phoebe. Unless you're planning on leaving her to go home by herself? I assume even you wouldn't do that?'

Chapter Sixty-Four

I am waiting for the axe to fall. For Lucy the headhunter to phone me to say my interview with Finn has been cancelled. There will be some spurious excuse, but what really will have happened is that Chris will have talked to his friend and warned him about who I really am.

It's Monday morning and I am sitting at my desk, looking at my diary of back-to-back meetings and wondering which one will be interrupted by Lucy. I was so certain I was going to land this job.

So certain I wasn't going to be a failure (again).

All around me, people are easing into the working day, the lines blurred by chat about the weekend. Samira and Tom took their nephews to a theme park and 'nearly vommed' on the rollercoaster, Zoe and her husband went to IKEA and *didn't* fight, Pete had a murderous journey down to the coast. They took the A412...

No one asks me what I did. I am officially persona non grata. Still, what would I say? I watched something I thought was mine slip away from me.

I wonder if Chris will tell people here I was chasing a job at Hola? My body flames with humiliation at the thought of my colleagues whispering and laughing behind my back. You know she didn't get the promotion here, right? Well, she tried to land the exact same role somewhere else and they didn't think she was up to it either. You'd think she'd get the message, wouldn't you?

I open the presentation for this afternoon's client meeting and start marking up changes and moving slides.

Robert mentioned I seemed very quiet on Saturday night and, for a second, I thought about telling him everything. Where to start, though? I never told him what Greg said in my appraisal or about my subsequent attempts to ingratiate myself with my colleagues. I haven't explained the connection between Chris and Hola or admitted that I started taking Phoebe to Little Seahorses again so I could garner a meeting with Finn. Of course, Robert will know soon enough I haven't won the job at Hola. The thought makes my guts twist. I don't want to see disappointment in his eyes when he looks at me.

Greg appears at my side. There is a problem on the Kitkins account. Can I talk to him this morning? He has fifteen minutes at 11.

I am supposed to be in a meeting at 11 but saying no to Greg is not an option. I watch his back as he walks away. Normally, he would tell me what the problem is instead of leaving me to stew on it until our meeting. It's hard to imagine that I was once his golden girl. Things have been off between us for weeks, becoming worse when he promoted Maddie over me. I am sure talk of the whole notebook thing will have reached him too. Greg prides himself on keeping his 'ear to the ground'. It will offer him proof, as if it were needed, that he made the right decision, that, not only have I been off my game recently, but his previous reservations about me were valid – I cannot swim with the dolphins.

Soon, he will find out I have been pursuing a job elsewhere.

This will displease him. He is fond of telling us 'loyalty is everything' (an adage he seems to apply more in his working life than his personal one given the number of extramarital affairs he is rumoured to have had). But the worst thing of all will be me failing to land the job at Hola. If you're going to be a traitor, at least be a successful one.

My mobile vibrates on the desk and my heart sinks.

It's over.

I reach for the phone but am surprised to see it's not Lucy but my mother.

She never calls me at work.

'It's your father,' she says. 'He's in the hospital. They said you should come here as soon as you can.'

Sometimes, it's a different axe than the one you were expecting.

Chapter Sixty-Five

My mother's cheek feels cool and powdery as I brush my lips against it.

She tells me my father had a massive bleed on his brain. He had gone out to buy paint, can I imagine? She told him they should have a decorator in. He collapsed in the street and a passer-by called an ambulance. The doctors have told her they don't know what to expect, that the next few hours and days will be critical.

Her voice is flat and devoid of emotion. It occurs to me, suddenly, that I can count on one hand the number of times I have seen her cry, and three of those times were within a couple of days of each other.

My father doesn't look nearly as bad as I was expecting. He is conscious and there is no visible sign of injury. But then he starts to talk and it's a stream of gibberish. We need to go down into the dugout, he says, we need to go *now*. Did someone take the chicken out of the oven? Whose dog is that?

It isn't clear if he recognises my mother and me.

The machines bleep around us and my mother stares at her shoes.

I take my father's hand. I can't remember the last time I saw him. Christmas, maybe? My parents live less than an hour from me and yet, somehow, months go by without us seeing each other. I have been too busy chasing after jobs I'm not going to get.

We are in the Acute Medical Unit. I guess Kate must have been taken to an Acute Medical Unit? After all this time, I realise I never found out if she regained consciousness between collapsing in the airport toilet and her death. Did she have any sense of what was happening? I hope not.

A round-faced nurse with too much eye make-up comes to tell us my father is being moved to another ward. My father starts retching and the nurse scrabbles to find a cardboard sick basin. 'Don't be sick now, Mr Martinelli. Not just before changeover.'

My father responds by vomiting copious amounts of yellowy green liquid all over himself.

'Shite,' the nurse says, almost inaudibly, trying to smile.

My mother and I stand outside the curtained-off area while my father is cleaned up. I think how immaculate he normally is. He has a weakness for expensive jackets and a proper manicure. His shaving takes a full half an hour.

'I'm sorry to call you at work,' my mother says.

'Don't be silly.'

My father is moved to the Christine Brown ward. I am not a fan of hospital wards being named after people – in my opinion, they should simply be given a number. My mother and I go with my father as two squat-looking hospital porters manoeuvre his bed into the lift. The nurse is there too and this time she has a clean sick basin with her.

I can't remember when I last told my father I loved him. Maybe not since I was a teenager?

There is some confusion over which bay my father should go in and my mother, myself, the sick nurse and the two hospital porters stand around awkwardly. I want to tell the nurse and the porters to go, that we can take it from here, but I expect that's against protocol.

My father is talking about wine. He doesn't know whether to buy red or white. Which would go better with the food?

I look across at my mother as she struggles to find an answer. She looks older than I remember, and smaller.

Finally, my father is 'handed over'. A whey-faced healthcare assistant uses a magic marker to fill in the chart above my father's head. She leaves 'Expected discharge date' blank.

My phone buzzes away in my pocket. I didn't tell anyone at work my dad had been taken into hospital, instead explaining my need to rush away by saying there was a water leak in my flat. I knew if people showed me any sympathy, it would have completely undone me.

A doctor in pale pink ballet pumps comes to look at my father. Afterwards, she talks to us, asking if we have any questions.

'Is he going to live?' my mother asks. She is not one to skirt around things.

The doctor looks younger than me but she meets my mother's eye as she says it's impossible to tell at this stage. I know they must be trained for situations like this, but I can't imagine it ever being easy.

My mother nods. 'And if he does survive, will he be impaired?'

I wince at her choice of word.

'Again, it's impossible to tell at this stage. It was a significant bleed.'

I think about the chart above my dad's head. It says his name and date of birth alongside today's date and the name of his consultant. I suddenly have the urge to add more sections to tell the world that my dad was – *is* – so much more than that. He's

269

a brilliant cameraman who has worked on some of the biggest movies of the last twenty years. He can speak three languages fluently and make gnocchi that is pillowy light. He loves Scandi noir, dark thrillers and good red wine. The wine has to be Italian. My father is the person who had the biggest smiles and the biggest hugs when I was a little girl, the one who made me feel as if I was enough.

I say none of that, instead just standing there mute while my mother cross-examines the doctor. Eventually, she stops because she realises there are no answers.

My father has his eyes closed when my mother and I draw back the curtains. At first, I think he's dead, but then he mumbles something in his sleep. There is only one chair so I make my mother take it and I perch awkwardly on the end of the bed, my legs dangling next to a bag of my father's dark yellow piss.

'How's work?' my mother says.

Really? 'Fine.'

'I told him we should pay a decorator.'

The healthcare assistant comes back and says she'll find another chair for me. She glances from me to my mother. I imagine she is thinking what a weird, robotic pair we are. That we are acting as if we are in a station waiting room and not sitting at the bedside of a dying loved one.

Chapter Sixty-Seven

'Olivia's mummy is having a baby,' Phoebe pipes up on the bus journey back to Sylvia's.

'Oh.'

'I want a baby sister.'

My mind spins. What am I supposed to say to this? There is no sister on the horizon for Phoebe. 'Babies can be annoying.'

Phoebe considers this. 'I like babies. If they're girls.'

I am thinking about the days after Emilia was brought home from the hospital. The crushing disappointment I felt. I had been promised a playmate but this... this... thing didn't play. It just cried and guzzled milk and pooed its nappy.

Once, when she was having yet another feed, I approached my mother with a book.

'Let me finish feeding your sister.' My mother was the colour of the square of muslin that was always hanging off her shoulder nowadays.

I put my hand on the baby's arm, squeezed.

'Careful,' my mother said, her voice reedy. 'You don't want to hurt her.'

I do want to hurt her.

I'm ashamed of that thought now, of course. But then, I'm ashamed of a lot of things.

Chapter Sixty-Eight

No one can say for sure if my father is dying but, from a layperson's point of view, it seems to me his body is shutting down. He sleeps almost constantly – and that is altogether too peaceful a word for what really seems to be going on here – and is barely present when his eyes are open.

Six days ago, my father was fine. He was getting under my mother's feet, drinking espressos so strong you could stand a spoon in them, and shouting at the politicians on the *Today* programme.

My mother and I are at his bedside. We have exhausted our attempts at small talk and are sitting in silence. I say silence – hospital wards are never silent, of course. A volunteer is having a long conversation with the man opposite about the book he wants from the library trolley, a doctor is talking to the man on the other side of the curtain about whether he has had a bowel movement yet today, a nurse's rubber soles squeak across the lino.

I need to find a way to say sorry to my sister. I know my dad would want me to.

But how do you even begin to apologise for something so huge?

I roll the words around my mind. Try to think of where to even begin.

And then I do what I always do.

Nothing.

I place my hand on top of my dad's, being careful not to knock the cannula. His hand feels rough and warm.

My mum has gone to the toilet.

A memory floats into my consciousness. I would have been about twelve or thirteen at the time. An age that's universally accepted as being awkward but is especially tricky to navigate when you're already something of an oddball. It was a Sunday in the middle of summer and we'd had a huge group of extended family for lunch. The day brought one excruciating thing after another. The cheek pinches I was too old for, the remarks about how much I'd grown (did they mean I was fat?), the endless questions about what I wanted to do when I grew up. But the worst moment loomed. Having to kiss everyone goodbye – even Uncle Ricardo with his big, bristly moustache.

When I sensed it was coming, I hid in the airing cupboard with my book. I knew my mother would be mad at me. Good manners were non-negotiable. It was worth it, though, and I would just pretend I hadn't heard her call me.

My dad opened the airing cupboard door. 'Lorri?'

I burst into tears. I wanted to explain to my dad, but how could I? What kind of freak works themself into such a state at the idea of having to say goodbye to people?

My dad pulled me towards him, told me to 'shh', that it was okay. He said to enjoy my book and that he would tell Mum he couldn't find me.

He understood.

*

Ballet pumps doctor appears and asks my mother about my father's DNAR instruction. Do not attempt to resuscitate. My mother confirms this as impassively as if she is confirming his choice of sandwich for lunch.

Not that my father will be eating lunch. He hasn't eaten anything since he came in here, and ballet pumps doctor now raises the topic of whether he should be given an NG tube. She explains that, in his confused state, my father will almost certainly try to pull it out. She shows us what look like white nylon boxing gloves and explains my father could wear these if that proved to be the case.

The boxing gloves don't look like something that would be part of modern hospital care. Nor are they something I want to see on my dad. 'Isn't there a better way?'

'Loretta,' my mother says admonishingly. 'I'm sure if there was, the doctor would suggest that.'

'It's okay,' ballet pumps says. 'These things are very difficult. We don't have to decide now, anyway. I just wanted to start the conversation with you.' She spritzes her hands with the anti-bac hand foam at the end of my father's bed and says she's going to look him over quickly, if that's okay.

My mother and I step outside the curtained area. The man in the opposite bed is moaning in pain.

'Let's grab a quick coffee,' my mother says.

The hospital café is loud and overlit. My mother stares at her nails, her cappuccino untouched beside her.

'Hospitals always remind me of Emilia,' I say.

My mother doesn't look up but I see her fingers curl into a ball. She does not want to talk about this. But I knew that already. She never wants to talk about it. Normally, I defer. No, that's not even accurate. I am as reluctant as she is. Today, though, something makes me press on. 'I am so sorry about what happened.'

My mother raises her head, her eyes flashing. 'Not now, Loretta.'

'It's always "not now". But I need to tell you that I am sorry.'

My mother is silent. I reach for my coffee but my hands are trembling too much to pick it up. I leave it where it is. 'We can't keep pretending it didn't happen.'

Chapter Sixty-Nine

I haven't been here for years.

I have always told myself that's because I'm too busy.

That's not the real reason, of course.

Not coming here has allowed me to pretend it never happened. To continually push it to the dark recesses of my mind. To squash down any memory of it.

My legs feel unsteady beneath me as I walk past the church and towards the graveyard. I am clutching the cellophane-wrapped carnations I bought in the hospital gift shop. They are horrible but I wanted to bring something, and I knew if I allowed myself to search farther afield I would chicken out of coming at all.

I reach the burial spot. *Emilia Flora Martinelli 1991–2007. A shining light. Taken from us too soon.*

My sister.

Chapter Seventy

Thirteen years earlier

I am furious Emilia has been invited to James Blair's party. James is in my class and it beggars belief that someone two years below has scored an official invitation from the host himself. What makes this especially painful is that I had no such thing and am only going because Rose, my one friend at school, is confident James's parents are in Manchester for the weekend and no one will be turned away. She says we have to start doing things like going to parties, we're eighteen now and everyone does.

Emilia comes into my room, looking impossibly pretty in a red silky top that falls off her shoulders. 'Will you give me a lift to the party?'

'I might not have room in the car. I'm taking some friends.'

My mum bustles in, carrying a big basket of washing. 'Don't be ridiculous, Loretta. By "friends" I assume you mean Rose?'

The comment stings. I'm actually not even taking Rose because her mum is dropping her there on the way back from visiting her grandma.

My mum puts a pile of washing on the end of my bed. 'Of course you will take your sister.'

In the car, I turn the music up loud and ignore Emilia's attempts at conversation. I know it's not fair to be annoyed with her. It's not her fault she is invited to this party. Any more than it's her fault that people always seem to gravitate towards her. She has always been the same. Aged three, she seemed to cast the whole of her class at nursery school under her spell and she has always made friends easily. She is a sunny bunch of daffodils and I am an ornery cactus.

I concentrate on the dark, winding roads. I thought when I passed my test it would be my passport to freedom. I didn't imagine it would mean I would be saddled with my baby sister.

I turn up the music, my mind drifting to James Blair. I haven't even admitted this to Rose but I like him and, astonishingly, I think he likes me too. We have bumped into each other several times in the library and chatted and I feel as if he is coming to know the me that others don't bother to find. The other day, he even laughed at one of my jokes. It did worry me a bit that he hadn't formally invited me to the party but I figure that's just because it's assumed our whole class will go.

We pull up outside the large red-brick house, the sounds of music and laughter spilling from open windows.

'Sorry I've been a bit of a grump,' I say to Emilia. 'I don't really mind giving you a lift.'

'S'okay,' she says, giving me her trademark sunny smile. She is so easy and uncomplicated. No wonder Mum and Dad are besotted by her. I might be the one who gets the grades and wins the prizes, but Emilia has scored in the life lottery.

I look in the rearview mirror and wipe away the smudges of mascara from under my eyes. I don't normally wear make-up and I suddenly feel overdressed in my minidress. 'Do I look okay?'

'You look great,' Emilia says, stepping out of the car.

The house is heaving with people and, judging by the look of things, many of them have already enjoyed a little too much of what James described as his 'special recipe' punch. He came over to say hello the second Emilia and I walked through the door and my heart squeezed with pleasure. I haven't been imagining it, he does like me.

Emilia is immediately absorbed by a throng of her mates and I head off to try to find Rose. She is in the kitchen, washing up some glasses. 'Thank God you're here,' she hisses.

'Why are you washing up?'

'For something to do. It's awful out there. Everybody is pissed or snogging or both and no one wants to talk to me. I wish I was at home watching telly.'

I know exactly what she means but nothing is going to get in the way of my mission tonight. 'C'mon. Let's go and talk to people.'

Rose and I go back into the living room and I spy a gaggle of girls from our class who are not part of the in-crowd. 'C'mon,' I say, clutching her arm. 'We'll talk to them.'

Twenty minutes later, although Rose and I are standing with this group of other girls, it still feels as if we are very much on the outside.

'Shall we go?' Rose whispers to me.

'No. You were the one who said we had to do this.'

'But I didn't know it would be this awful.'

The next thing I know, Rose excuses herself to go to the toilet and comes back telling me she has phoned her mum and asked her to pick her up.

'I would have taken you home,' I hiss.

'Yes, but I want to get out of here *now*.'

So do I, of course, and, in any normal circumstances, Rose and I would already be in my battered old Renault buckling our seatbelts, but I am not going to waste this opportunity with James.

The party feels even scarier when Rose leaves and I wish I could at least steady my nerves with the punch but, as I am driving, I stick to water.

The music is becoming louder and I can barely hear what anyone is saying so I just laugh and nod in what I hope are the right places. I suddenly realise that I have lost sight of James, who I have been trying to keep track of all evening.

'Excuse me,' I say to the people I am standing with. 'I'm just going to get some air.'

The group look at me, nonplussed. They weren't really talking to me, anyway. I burst out of the back door, the cold air welcome on my hot cheeks. I don't think I'm very good at parties. They are not like exams. You can't prep for them. When James and I are boyfriend and girlfriend, I will tell him that I prefer smaller, more intimate gatherings.

I pass a group of boys smoking and sit down on the back step. At the end of the garden, a couple are snogging.

Save for my aborted kiss with Richard Duffy in year nine, I have never kissed anyone, and Richard and I did not kiss each other with anything like the intensity that these two are going at it with.

My eyes are adjusting to the darkness now and I realise, in a sickening moment of clarity, that the boy is James Blair.

No, I feel like screaming, this is not the plan. Who is James kissing?

And then the couple break away from each other and I see a flash of red top.

The girl James was kissing is my sister.

Chapter Seventy-One

I sink to my haunches and lay the cellophane-wrapped carnations on my sister's grave.

'I'm sorry,' I say.

The words feel woefully inadequate. Emilia will never graduate, or get married or hold her child in her arms. Unlike me, she was always sure she wanted to be a mother.

Memories crowd into my mind. Me marching down the garden and telling Emilia that we had to go. She protested and so did James. It was still early, the party had hardly started. I said I had a headache and we had to leave *now*.

In the car, Emilia babbled about how she couldn't believe she had kissed James Blair. He was going to take her out next week on a proper date, wasn't that something?

Rage pumped through my veins as I threw the car round the winding dark roads. It wasn't fair. She got everything. Didn't James see that prickly pears are sweet once you're past the tough outer layers?

On and on Emilia went. She was normally sensitive to my mood but, that night, she must have interpreted my silence as interest. Or been too giddy to care.

There is some lichen on the gravestone and it suddenly seems very important that I remove it. I owe my sister that much, at least. I scrabble in my handbag for a tissue, daub it with anti-bac hand gel and start rubbing furiously. My face is wet with tears now and I am vaguely aware that an older couple a few feet away are staring at me.

Emilia's sing-songy voice was impossible to drown out. I gripped the steering wheel so hard my fingers turned white. 'SHUT UP!' I suddenly heard myself screaming. 'I wish you had never been born.'

Emilia looked as if I had slapped her. I turned my eyes back to the road and there, right in front of me, was a deer.

I rub harder and harder at the lichen and, when the tissue dissolves into muddied shreds, start using my bare hands. 'I'm sorry, I'm sorry, I'm sorry.'

My fingers are bleeding now but I cannot rub away the pale green fungus, cannot even do this for my sister. I sink to my knees, howling like a wounded animal. 'I'm sorry.'

It starts to rain, slowly at first but then more insistently. I don't move, though.

I have spent too long running away from the grief and the shame.

Too long running away from what I did to my sister.

Chapter Seventy-Two

'My God,' Robert says, when I walk through the door, soaked through and covered in mud. 'What happened to you?'

'I got caught in the rain.' I feel a strange sense of calm which is odd given both what I have been doing and what I am about to do. 'We need to talk.' I stare at my bloodied knuckles and tell Robert that I don't think we should get married.

'You're not thinking straight,' Robert says, when I stop talking. 'You're upset because of your dad.'

I look at his face which I know almost as well as my own. The tiny scar on his chin he got when he was three, the little crease that appears between his brows when he is concentrating, his long, dark lashes.

'I am upset, but I am thinking straight.' I don't add that what happened to Emilia and Kate and my dad is part of this. We don't always have all the time in the world.

Robert is shaking his head. I know this has come as a total shock to him because it's a shock to me and I am the one who is instigating it. I hate that I am hurting him.

'You've been different ever since you started seeing that child.'

'I know.'

Robert stares at me. 'Right,' he says, moving to his feet. 'I'll go to stay with my parents.'

'You don't have to do that.'

'I don't want to be here,' he says simply. 'I'll call you in a few days to discuss the practicalities.'

I stay on the sofa while Robert packs his bags. I thought I'd used up every tear in my body at Emilia's graveside but it seems like the reserves have arrived.

I almost want Robert to scream and shout but we are not that sort of couple.

We are not any sort of couple.

The thought brings me up short and it's all I can do not to rush into the bedroom and beg Robert to stay. What am I doing breaking things off with a good man, a man who would never break my heart?

But then I steel myself not to move. Because, if someone can't break your heart, then maybe you never really gave it to them in the first place?

Chapter Seventy-Three

My mother's back stiffens when I tell her I went to Emilia's graveside.

'Aren't you hot in that jacket?' she says eventually. 'It's roasting in here.'

'Did you hear what I said?'

She sighs.

I pick at the skin around my cuticle. I shouldn't be pushing this right now. So far today, I've visited my sister's graveside for the first time in years, told my fiancé I don't want to marry him and then rushed here to the hospital where my father is probably dying.

'Why do we never talk about her?' The words spill from my mouth before I can stop them.

My mother stares at her shoes. Bright red blotches have risen on her long pale neck. 'Not now, Loretta.'

Fury courses through my body. It's always not bloody now. 'I know you and Dad blame me.'

My mother's head snaps up. 'What? We don't blame you.'

'I was driving the car, wasn't I?'

My mother's face is ashen. She tugs at the collar of her shirt. 'You were just a kid. You hadn't been drinking. You weren't speeding. We never blamed you. *Never.*'

Hot tears prick the back of my eyes. 'Dad was so different with me – after it happened. Sometimes I felt as if he couldn't even bear to look at me.'

'Oh, Lorri.'

It's been a very long time since my mother has called me Lorri.

'Your dad *was* different after it happened. We all were. But it wasn't about being different with you. It changes you, losing a child. It's not right, not how things are meant to be. No parent wants to outlive their child.' She glances towards the hospital bed where my father lies under the thin green blanket, seemingly oblivious. 'He never blamed you. Neither of us did.'

'Did you wish it was me and not her?'

My mother looks as if I have slapped her. 'No! How can you even ask that?'

Because you always preferred her.

It seems too cruel to say that but it's as if my mother can read my thoughts. 'I wasn't always the best mother to you, Lorri.' Her voice cracks. 'I had a terrible time giving birth to you. The labour lasted twenty-six hours and then, right at the end, they had to get you out in a hurry and one of my arteries was cut—' She stops, takes a breath. 'Look, it doesn't matter about the detail, but it wasn't easy. And then, when we were home, that wasn't easy either. You cried all the time and nothing I could do seemed to make it right. The only person who could calm you down was your father. He spent hours walking the floor with you, all night long. I just sat around feeling helpless and inadequate. I was Italian, for God's sake, being a mamma was supposed to be in my blood. Looking back, I think I had post-natal depression.'

'And then I became a difficult child.'

'No.'

I raise my eyebrows.

'I didn't always understand you,' my mother concedes. 'I just wanted you to be happy. And sometimes I wasn't sure you were.'

Tears roll down my cheeks.

My mother rises from her seat and moves towards me. She puts her hand on my shoulder and pats it roughly. 'We never blamed you for what happened to your sister and we never wished it was you.'

Chapter Seventy-Four

My conversation with my mother, while not exactly a Hallmark moment, has left me feeling lighter. As if forgiving myself for what happened is now at least a possibility.

That said, it has not been an easy few days and, for someone who prides herself on having laser-sharp focus, I'm not sure why I chose to address so many huge things the weekend before the most important interview I've ever had.

The flat seems empty without Robert, and his belongings stare reproachfully at me wherever I look. *What were you thinking?* say his immaculately pressed shirts when I reach into the wardrobe. *You'll probably die alone,* goads his favourite thin-cut marmalade. *You've pushed away the only person who said they loved you,* chimes in a half-used tub of hair wax.

Work is as busy as ever but, rather than finding it a comfort as I normally would, I feel as if I am drowning. I have a perpetual sense of not keeping up and, yesterday, I forgot I was supposed to be in a pre-production meeting because I was hiding in the toilets crying.

I rush straight from work to the hospital every evening. My interview prep, which would normally dominate my attention, is reduced to snatched moments on the train or on the bus. I only hope that Lucy the headhunter is right when she says she thinks the job is already as good as mine.

Weirdly, given how many of my own problems I have right now, I constantly find myself obsessing over Phoebe. How is she feeling about the swimming gala? Is her friendship with Georgia solid? Is the imaginary friend really a harmless thing?

For all my concerns about Phoebe's imaginary friend, I may soon have to find one for myself. If I felt isolated from my colleagues before, now I may as well be on a different planet. It's weird none of them knows about my break-up with Robert or about my father (not to mention me finally facing up to my sister's death).

Perhaps that's why, when Zoe and I are locked away in a meeting room preparing for a Kitkins meeting, I suddenly find myself blurting out a rather inelegant apology. 'I'm sorry about how I have behaved but, for what it's worth, you should know that I genuinely like you.'

Zoe fiddles with a blob of Blu-Tack she is using to put up the presentation boards. 'You were the very first person who knew I was pregnant apart from David.'

'I know.'

Zoe looks at me, her expression unreadable. 'We need to prepare for this meeting. The client will be here any minute.'

After this less than fulsome success, I can't imagine what propels me to Chris's side but, as he gets into the lift to go home, I squeeze in next to him and ask if he has time for a very quick drink.

'I'm sorry,' Chris says. 'I have to collect Zack from the child-minder.' His tone is bemused but not harsh.

'Okay, just give me a couple of minutes,' I say, as we walk out onto the street.

'Sure.'

'I wanted to tell you that I'm sorry – genuinely sorry for the things I said to you before and for the underhanded way I used you to get to Finn. I still can't believe you decided not to rat me out to him. That was very decent of you.'

Chris chews on his lower lip. 'Thank you for your apology.' He turns to go.

'There's something else,' I say, calling after him. He turns around. 'I do genuinely care about Phoebe. I know why you think I don't but I do. And I'm rubbish with her – really rubbish and out of my depth – but that's not because I don't care and, I swear to God, I've spent more time worrying about her bloody swimming gala tomorrow than my interview.'

The corners of Chris's mouth twitch. 'Spoken like a true parent. Night, Loretta.'

I watch his back as he disappears into the throng of commuters.

Chapter Seventy-Five

I am at the hospital. My mother has gone for a walk and my dad is sleeping. It is all I can do not to lie down next to him. I am overcome with the sort of exhaustion you feel in your bones. As soon as I arrive home, I am going to have a hot bath and prepare for bed. I need to be a lot sharper than I am now when I go to that interview tomorrow.

A nurse comes to check my father's obs. I squash down the urge to ask her if he is slipping away. They say they don't know but I feel like they must.

The man in the bed opposite has a crowd of visitors ranging in ages from about two to about ninety. They are all arguing loudly and eating the food they have brought him. A grape skitters across the floor and I watch in fascinated horror as the toddler dives to collect it.

The inter-school swimming gala is also tomorrow, of course. I wonder if Phoebe is nervous or just excited. I wish I could be there to watch her. She still struggles to put on her swimming cap properly by herself. I expect Sylvia will be able to do it, even though she did look rather uninterested when I talked her through my technique. I reach for my phone. It won't hurt to give Sylvia a little reminder and I can speak to Phoebe and wish her luck at the same time.

'7359, hello,' Sylvia says.

'You sound awful.'

A sigh that could make a building shake comes down the line. 'I think I am coming down with something. Plus, today has been the most horrendous day – I was called into the school because Phoebe hit a boy in her class.'

'Really? I've never known her to hit. Well, except for that time at the summer fun day.'

'Apparently, she told him that her mum was coming to watch her in the inter-school swimming gala and he said she was a liar because her mum is dead.'

I sit down on the hard plastic armchair, Sylvia's words swirling around my brain but not making very much sense. 'Her mum?'

'Yes,' Sylvia says, sniffing. 'You know we thought she had an imaginary friend? Well, it turns out that was Kate.'

'That's why she talks about her in the present tense so much.'

'I guess so. I blame the RS lessons at school. I think it was learning about Jesus coming back to life that put the idea in her head. Anyway, it's all a bit of a mess. The headmistress said she knows Phoebe has had an awful lot to deal with recently but the school has a strict zero tolerance policy towards violence and there was no choice but to tell Alfie's parents.'

My mother walks in, smelling of the outside, her cheeks slightly pink from the cold.

'How is Phoebe?' I say to Sylvia.

'Terrible. She hasn't stopped crying since. And she's so angry too. She keeps saying it isn't fair because she's not a liar and she does see Kate every day. She says she is glad she hit Alfie and he's a horrible boy, that she will hit him again as soon as she can. Apparently, he told her Kate is just a pile of bones now.'

'Eurgh, he does sound like a horrible boy.'

'Well, yes,' Sylvia says. 'But we can't all just go around hitting people who are horrible. It would be bedlam.'

I rise and stand next to the window, pressing my thumb and forefinger into the bridge of my nose. I think about Chris accusing me of teaching Phoebe to suppress her emotions and not deal with them and wonder if this is a direct result of that. All her feelings have been pushed down and pushed down and now, bam, they're exploding.

'The headmistress says she worries that Phoebe is very isolated now,' Sylvia says. 'I mean, you can imagine, can't you? Who wants to hang out with a kid and her dead mother, particularly when it might land them a thump into the bargain? Phoebe told me that even Georgia has said she doesn't want to be friends with her anymore.'

My heart hurts at the thought of Georgia saying this to Phoebe. Given Georgia's mother, I shouldn't be surprised she'd have a nasty streak. I have spent weeks squashing the urge to grab her by the shoulders and tell her she must never hurt Phoebe, that she is very vulnerable right now and she needs a proper friend. I've never actually done this, of course, what with Georgia being six years old. Now, I kind of wish I had, though.

'She's refusing to come out of her room, won't eat any supper and is saying she won't go to the swimming gala.'

'Right,' I say, 'I'm coming over.'

'Really?'

I picture my hot bath and my early night that I so badly need before my interview. 'Yeah, I'd like to see her.' I end the call and turn to my mum. 'I have to leave.'

'Okay, I'll see you tomorrow evening.'

I pick up my coat and bag. 'Yes, call me in the meantime if anything changes, won't you?'

'Of course,' my mother says, sounding slightly exasperated.

I am just about to head out of the double doors to the ward when I turn and run back to my father's bay.

My mother looks up from her book. 'Did you forget something?'

'I wanted to tell you that I love you.'

'Oh, okay.' She smoothes a non-existent crease on her skirt. 'Umm… you too.'

I turn to my dad and take his hand in mine, being careful not to dislodge the cannula again. I lean down and put my face close to his ear. 'I love you, Dad.'

My father's eyes flicker open and my heart squeezes.

'Cancel the newspapers,' he bellows and shuts his eyes again.

Chapter Seventy-Six

Sylvia's eyes are red and puffy. 'Thank you for coming. She has locked herself in her room.'

'Her room has a lock?'

'Yes, look, it was never intended as a bedroom for a child.'

'I suppose not,' I say, heading up the stairs. I don't know why I'm giving Sylvia a hard time. If anyone is responsible for this terrible mess, it's me. I'm the one who has spent months teaching Phoebe to bury all her sadness and anger. I now see this has been damaging, maybe catastrophically so. It's dangerous to be a person I care about – just look at my sister.

'Phoebe,' I say, knocking on the door. 'It's Loretta. Can you let me in, please?'

Nothing.

'Grandma told me what happened at school, and I know you must be very upset. Can you let me in?'

'No.'

Phoebe's voice sounds small and sad.

'Okay, well, can we talk to each other like this?'

Silence.

The cat slinks past, stopping briefly to glare at me. *You did this*, say its narrowed eyes.

'Phoebe?'

'Okay,' she says, almost inaudibly.

I let out the breath I didn't know I was holding and sink down to sit on the floor with my back against the door. 'Grandma said you hit someone at school.'

'Alfie. And I'm *not* sorry.'

Despite the gravity of the situation, I can't help but smile at this. I know I can't let Phoebe think I condone her behaviour, though. 'Hitting is wrong.'

'Not when it's Alfie.'

'Even when it's Alfie.'

'He said Mummy wasn't going to watch me in the swimming gala. He said I was a liar. I'm not a liar. I do see Mummy every day. I didn't at first but now I do. She cuddles me and asks me about my day and tells me stories.'

My head spins. I feel out of my depth (as per usual). It scares the hell out of me that Phoebe is seeing her dead mother, but I don't feel right to just squash something like that either.

'Do you believe me about Mummy?' Phoebe says.

My heart hammers against my chest. 'I… I… well—'

There's a thump from the other side of the door that sounds very much like a kick. 'YOU DON'T BELIEVE ME. YOU THINK I'M A LIAR JUST LIKE EVERYONE ELSE.'

Oh, crap. 'I don't think you're a liar.'

'Yes, you do.' She starts to cry.

'Phoebe,' I say. 'Please let me in.'

'Go away.'

I let my head fall into my hands. Maybe I should go away; maybe I should never have come here in the first place. If Sylvia can't calm Phoebe down, why would I think I can?

I press my thumbs into my temples. The sound of Phoebe's

hiccupy sobbing on the other side of the door is almost unbearable. I know I have made her feel even worse by not believing her, and have this sudden visceral memory of what it was like to be a kid and have my feelings dismissed by adults.

You're not scared of something on TV, are you, you know it's all made up.

I know you're not going to cry. Big girls don't cry, do they?

You're not angry about a silly girl taking your pencil case.

I clear my throat. 'I believe that, when you love someone very much and they die, they will always be with you.'

'So, you do think Mummy is with me?'

'Kind of.'

The door suddenly swings open, and I fall backwards into the bedroom.

'Oops,' Phoebe says. 'I didn't know you were leaning on it.'

She looks terrible, her small face grey and her eyes red and swollen. I reach out and stroke her slightly matted hair. 'I had a little sister called Emilia and she died.'

'You never told me that before.'

'No. For a long time, I couldn't even bear to mention her name or think about her at all.'

'Why?' Phoebe says, rubbing the edge of her toy penguin's ear.

'I think, sometimes, when we lose someone we love very much, we have such big feelings we don't know what to do with them all.'

Phoebe carries on rubbing the penguin's ear, her eyes downcast. 'Did your sister have something wrong with her heart?'

'No, she died in a car crash.' *I was driving the car.*

'What was she like?'

I smile. 'She was happy and funny and sometimes very annoying and she always wanted whatever I had, right from when we were tiny. She hated bananas and loved apples and she could stay in a handstand for what seemed like hours.'

'I can see Mummy now,' Phoebe says, tears brimming. 'Over there by the wardrobe.'

'Why don't you tell me about her?'

There's a pause and then Phoebe starts speaking. 'Well, she has brown hair like me, only hers is a bit darker and she always says she has some grey hairs but I can never see them. And she has freckles all over her face. Lots and lots and lots of freckles, so you can't count them all…'

By the time she has finished talking about her mum, Phoebe is sobbing hard and I wonder if I made a dreadful mistake. I put my hand on her heaving back.

The tiny touch is enough to make Phoebe hurl herself at me and I put my arms around her as she sobs into my chest. 'Shh,' I say, patting her on the back. 'Shh.'

And then, suddenly, just as abruptly as she started crying, Phoebe stops and declares herself so thirsty she could drink a pint of water. She pronounces 'pint' as if it rhymes with 'mint' and it breaks my heart a little to realise it's a word she must have learned from reading. She is still so little.

She grabs her pink plastic water bottle from the bedside table and drinks noisily.

'Phoebe,' I say. 'You know it's okay to feel sad or angry some-times, don't you?'

'Even if it makes you hit people?'

'Well, it's the hitting that's the problem, not the feelings. It's normal that you feel sad about your mum.'

We sit in silence, Phoebe working at the ear of the little cloth penguin. It's a couple of minutes before she speaks again. 'I'm not going to go to the swimming gala tomorrow.'

'But you were so excited about it.'

'I'm not excited about it anymore.'

'But you've worked so hard at all your swimming lessons.'

Phoebe shrugs. 'I'd go if you could come to watch. And if Georgia would sit next to me on the coach.'

My stomach knots. 'I can't come but I'll be thinking about you and cheering you on in my head. And I will be feeling so proud of you. Just like your mummy would have done.'

Phoebe seems to turn this over in her mind. 'And what about Georgia?'

'I'll see what I can do.'

Chapter Seventy-Seven

I would never do karaoke, I don't like fancy dress and I avoid anything I'm not good at. In other words, I don't like making a fool of myself. So throwing myself on the mercies of a woman who is far from keen on me isn't how I'd pick to spend my Wednesday evening.

Georgia's mother's face falls when she opens her front door and sees it's me.

'I found your address in the class contact list that Phoebe's grandma had,' I say, by way of explanation. 'I would have called but then I saw you were only a five-minute walk away, so I thought I'd come in person.'

'Riiiiight. Listen, I'm in the middle of trying to put the kids to bed.'

As if on cue, Georgia and her little brother appear at the top of the stairs, both in their pyjamas.

'Why is Phoebe's nanny here?' Georgia says.

'I'm not her nanny. I just look after her sometimes.' Not sure why I felt the need to establish that; it's hardly what matters here.

'Georgia, James, go back to bed and Mummy will be with you in a minute.'

She turns to me. 'What can I do for you?' Her tone is glacial.

'I need you to make Georgia sit next to Phoebe on the coach tomorrow on the way to the inter-school swimming gala and I need you to make her be nice to Phoebe.' I see her eyes flash and realise I had the tone of that completely wrong. 'Sorry, that sounded a bit—'

'Rude? Bossy? Imperious?'

'Yes, all those things. I'm sorry. Let me start again. Phoebe could really use a friend right now and I was wondering if maybe you could have a word with Georgia and see if she could look after Phoebe a bit tomorrow?'

'Georgia is six years old. It's not her job to look after anyone.'

It takes all the strength in my body not to roll my eyes. 'Of course not. But she's obviously a very kind little girl.' I wonder if I might have gone too far with this blatant lie. Georgia displays all the empathy of a serial killer or a Tory cabinet minister.

'She is very kind,' Georgia's mother says.

Un-bloody-believable! I've said it before and I'll say it again: people are utterly deluded when it comes to their children.

'I know that, as a mother, you'll be very sympathetic towards Phoebe.' Again, I wonder if I have gone too far. I hate the 'as a mother' schtick. Like only mothers can possibly understand that a child would be sad about their parent suddenly dropping dead.

Once again, Georgia's mother buys it, though. 'Of course.'

'So, if you could work your magic that would be wonderful.' Work your magic? I'm making myself feel queasy.

'I'll see what I can do.'

'Thanks.' Right, one humiliating conversation down, one to go.

Chapter Seventy-Eight

I need some advice and there is only one person who has witnessed recent events closely enough to give it to me.

Unfortunately, that person pretty much hates me. And is surrounded by lots of other hostile faces right now.

I board the tube. It's that quiet lull between the commuters and the pissed people, so there are only a few other people in my carriage. The girl opposite is fiddling with her Eiffel Tower keyring. It's funny how people are drawn to miniature versions of things – three sliders instead of one big, tedious burger, doll's houses, micro pigs (*micro pigs!*). Perhaps that's why they lose their heads over children? Until I got to know Phoebe, the appeal of kids eluded me, and my affection for her has crept up on me and totally surprised me. That said, I'd argue she isn't like other children, more like an old soul trapped in a small body.

The pub is on a chi-chi road near Primrose Hill. It's cold and I pull my coat tighter. I should be at home now, psyching myself up for the interview tomorrow, but I can't get Phoebe out of my head or relax until I have resolved what I'm going to do. Anyway, if I'm honest, I hate being in the flat at the moment. It seems so cold and empty without Robert, and it's weird because I know for sure that breaking things off with him was the right thing to do – in fact, I think I should have done it a long time ago – but that doesn't mean to say it's easy.

It seems almost half the agency must have gone to softball this evening because there are two long tables of people. Everyone looks very surprised to see me, of course. I mumble something about needing to talk to Chris, and Samira says, 'Uh oh, mate, sounds like there are problems with your copy!'

'It's nothing to do with work,' I say tightly, across the titters of laughter. I don't know why I'm offended – chasing someone down in the pub at 8.30 at night to talk about work is far from beyond me.

Chris tells Pete to budge up a bit and gestures for me to sit next to him on the bench. 'Fire away.'

'Actually, can we talk outside?'

Chris groans. 'Do we have to? I've only just warmed up.'

I look up. Almost everyone is here – Zoe, Samira, Pete, Maddie, Kathleen, even Greg. I could do without an audience, but I suppose the people here already hate me so I have little to lose. Anyway, they're all taken up with their own conversations.

'I wanted to ask your advice about Phoebe. I've just been with her now and I'm worried about her. You know I told you that she had an imaginary friend? Well, it turns out it's her mum.'

'Poor kid.'

'I know,' I say, picking at my cuticle. 'And the thing is, I want to try to help, but I'm worried I'm going to do more harm than good. Do you remember a while back, you said I had to decide whether I was in or out of her life?'

Chris takes a sip of his pint. 'Umm, yeah.'

'Well, I think I want to be in but I'm worried that's not what's best for Phoebe, because I'm not very good with kids at the best of times and this isn't the best of times – not for Phoebe, obviously, but not for me either. I've split up with my fiancé, my father is dying and I am only just facing up to the death of my little sister in a car crash thirteen years ago when I was driving the car.'

I look up to see that not only is Chris staring at me but so is everyone else at the table. It seems they weren't all so caught up in their own conversations after all.

Chapter Seventy-Nine

'My God,' Chris says, as we sit down at a table in the deserted pub garden. 'I would have come outside before if I'd known what sort of conversation you wanted to have. It's not that cold.'

'It bloody is,' I say, scrabbling in my pocket for my beanie hat. 'Anyway, I don't care about the public humiliation. They all hate me anyway.'

'They don't hate you.' Chris shoves his hands deeper into his pockets. 'I'm sorry you've had such a tough time of it lately. I had no idea about you and...'

'Robert.'

'Robert. Or about your father. Or your sister. Do you want to talk about it?'

'No thanks. I want to talk about Phoebe and my relationship with her.'

'Okay,' Chris says, giving me a very strange look.

'What?'

'It's just that I used to think of you as someone who suppressed all your emotions but now it seems you've decided to have *all the feelings* at once.'

I laugh. 'I never do things by halves.'

'So it seems,' he says, laughing with me. 'Tell me about Phoebe.'

I bring him up to speed about Phoebe hitting the boy at school and how she is adamant she sees her mother every day. I admit that I now think some of the strategies I've been teaching Phoebe may have actually been counterproductive.

'Don't be too hard on yourself,' Chris says, in response to this. 'It's very difficult to get things "right" with a grieving child – in fact, I'm not sure you ever can. Zack had to have heaps of grief counselling before he even began to process Lara's death.'

'Do you think Phoebe would benefit from grief counselling?'

'Probably.'

I make a mental note to chat to Sylvia about it and wonder if it's something I should consider for myself as well. I have always been dismissive of the idea of therapy. Let those worms stay firmly in their cans. Now, I wonder if sometimes it's better to tackle things head on, however hard that feels.

I rub my hands together, trying to get some feeling back in my fingers. 'So, like I started to say inside, I've been thinking about that thing you said to me ages ago about me having to decide whether I'm in or out of Phoebe's life, and I think I want to be in but I'm not sure what I'd be to her exactly.'

'I think there are lots of people who touch a child's life. It takes a village, as the old adage goes. So, I'm not sure you need a formal title, but I guess you could think of yourself as a sort of unofficial godmother?'

'Hmm. The world's crappest godmother.'

Chris smiles. 'I didn't say that.'

'Would that actually be a good thing for Phoebe, though? Would it be in her best interests?'

'Of course,' Chris says, laughing. 'Unless, of course, you're planning on being an arsehole?'

'But that's just it. I'm not planning on it but maybe I just am an arsehole? Maybe I'll do more harm than good? I don't know what I'm doing with kids.'

'Firstly, you're not an arsehole, Loretta, and, secondly, none of us knows what we're doing. We're all just making it up as we go along.'

'Really?'

'Really. Anyone ever tell you that you're way too hard on yourself?'

'Maybe,' I say, smiling.

'Can we go back inside now? I think I have lost all sensation in my toes.'

'You big softy,' I say, rising from the table.

We walk back towards the noisy pub. 'Chris,' I say suddenly, just before we reach the door. 'You know you said you thought I am having all the feelings at once? Well, I think some of those feelings might be towards you.'

My words come as a total surprise to me – indeed, I hadn't even consciously registered the thought until this very moment. It has obviously come as a total shock to Chris too – in fact, judging by the look on his face, he is horrified.

'Forget I said that,' I say quickly. 'I didn't mean it. I don't think I have any feelings towards you. I certainly didn't until about five seconds ago. I didn't even like you for the longest time.' My heart feels as if it's about to hammer its way out of my chest. 'I've only just split up with Robert. And, anyway, you probably think I'm weird.'

'I don't th—'

'Please don't say anything else,' I say.

'Listen, I know you have your interview with Finn tomorrow. This isn't about that, is it? Because I've only said good things about you to him.'

Hurt blooms in my chest, sharp and jagged. 'It's nothing to do with that. But thanks for thinking so highly of me.'

'Sorry,' Chris says. 'It's just it was so out of the blue.'

'Thanks for the advice about Phoebe,' I say coldly. 'It was really useful.'

'Loretta—'

'*Please* don't say anything more.'

We go back into the noisy pub and sit back down. I'm glad the lights are low in here because, despite how cold it was outside, it feels like my whole face is on fire. What the hell was I thinking?

'Crisp?' Maddie says to me, proffering the bowl towards me.

'No, thank you.' I can do without germ-laden crisps on top of all tonight's other horrors.

Chapter Eighty

L ater, there will be time to bathe in the humiliation of last night. The shocked faces in the pub as I spilled my deepest, darkest secrets, the way the table fell totally silent and, of course, worse than any of that, me blurting out to Chris that I have feelings for him. Feelings (and even the word sounds teenage) that were as much of a shock to me as they were to him.

Right now, though, I have to push all those excruciating moments to the back of my mind. It is just over two hours until my interview with Finn and I have to focus on that and that alone.

I put a pod in the coffee machine. If I wanted the job at Hola before, I am desperate for it now. The idea of continuing to work in the same building as Chris is unthinkable. It would be bad enough being around the others now, but I could probably just about survive the pity.

I take a sip of my coffee, open up my notebook and start making a list of questions to ask Finn. I am good at interviews, I remind myself. Nerves bubble in my stomach, though. I hope Phoebe isn't feeling the same about the swimming gala. She sounded pleased when I called her after leaving Georgia's house last night to reassure her about her friend's support, but I have worried ever since that I overpromised. Can I trust Georgia's mum to have done what she said she would? There's a real chance the woman would have said anything to get me out of her house. And even if she did talk to her daughter, does that mean that Georgia will follow instructions?

I reach for my phone. I can at least wish Phoebe luck for the day and tell her I will be thinking about her.

'7359, hello.' If anything, Sylvia sounds even worse than yesterday. She tells me she now has full-blown flu and feels deadly.

'So, you can't go to the swimming gala?' It's not the most sympathetic response I could have come up with, but I can't help myself. I hate the thought of Phoebe being there alone.

'No,' Sylvia says. 'Oh, get off me, Atticus.'

I picture the world's largest and most unpleasant cat. You certainly wouldn't want it climbing on you if you were feeling below par. Or ever, really.

'Please can I have a quick word with Phoebe,' I say. 'I'd like to wish her luck.'

'Oh, you've missed her. I dropped her off about half an hour ago.'

'But it's only 8 o'clock?'

'You know how slow school coaches are. And the gala is at some school in the depths of Surrey. Atticus, stop making that terrible noise. I will feed you in a minute. Atticus, down from there…'

Sylvia carries on her dialogue with the cat, but I have tuned it out because all I can think about is how Phoebe is going to be at that swimming gala by herself. I bet most of the other kids will have their mums or dads there, or maybe both – and they won't be dealing with people sniggering and whispering behind their backs. *Phoebe hit Alfie. Phoebe thinks her dead mummy talks to her. Phoebe told Alfie her mummy was going to watch her swimming.*

'Which school is the gala at?' I say, cutting in as Sylvia implores Atticus to stop yowling.

'St Dunstan's, Claygate,' Sylvia says. 'Why?'

Surely, I can't do this?

I have my interview with Finn. The most important interview of my life.

It's just a school swimming gala.

An image appears in my mind: Phoebe in her yellow swimming cap and goggles, a tiny alien lost and alone.

'Because I'm going to go there.'

Chapter Eighty-One

If you're going to make a heroic gesture and cancel an important interview, my advice would be to make sure you check Citymapper first.

St Dunstan's, it turns out, is in the middle of bloody nowhere. Two trains away and then half an hour from the station by bus. The buses run every two hours. *Every two hours!* What use is that to anyone? People bang on about how idyllic it is to live in the countryside but at least in London we have public transport.

I pace around my flat, sweating. I will take a taxi from the station. It will be fine. I check the app again. If I hurry I can make the 8.41 from Waterloo, which should mean I can catch the connecting train at Esher at… damn it, I would be too late for Phoebe's race.

I have to reach St Dunstan's by car. Unless I can manage to teleport, there's no other way to be there in time. I scrabble in my handbag to find the class address list I took from Sylvia last night.

'Hi,' I say to Georgia's mother. 'It's Loretta. Phoebe's…' This is what I meant when I said I need to know what I am to Phoebe. Crappy pretend godmother doesn't really cut it here. 'Phoebe's person. I came to see you—'

'I know who you are,' Georgia's mother says.

I steel myself to ignore the iciness in her tone. 'I was just wondering if I might be able to beg a lift to the swimming gala. I don't drive and it's a nightmare to get there by public transport.'

'I'm sorry, but my husband and I are already on the motorway.'

I end the call feeling slightly sick because there is only one other person who I know that is going to the swimming gala. The last person in the world I want to speak to right now or ask for help.

Chris picks up his phone almost straightaway.

'I've decided I'm going to go to the swimming gala. Sylvia is ill and I don't want Phoebe to be there with no support, not after the last couple of days, or, well, everything.'

'But don't you have your interview with Finn this morning?'

'I've rescheduled it. Well, tried to reschedule. The headhunter left me under no illusions that I may as well have cancelled. Apparently, I should have pretended I was ill or something instead of just telling Finn's PA I couldn't make it.'

'Riiiiiight,' Chris says.

'Anyway, I was wondering if you could give me a lift there?'

'I'm already on the coach with the kids. I'm one of the parent helpers.'

Of course he is. 'Is Phoebe sitting next to Georgia?'

'I don't know, there are two coaches and I'm on a different one to Phoebe. How are you going to get there?'

I sink down on the edge of the bed. 'I have no idea.'

That's not entirely true, though. I do have an idea. It's just not one I like very much.

Chapter Eighty-Two

My hand shakes violently as I press the clicker to open Sylvia's car. I cannot believe I am doing this. It's thirteen years since I was behind the wheel of a car and we all know how that ended.

I get in and open the window, desperately gulping air into my lungs. It's an icy, grey morning but I am bathed in sweat.

Sylvia was breezy when I asked her if I could borrow her car. 'Of course. It's insured for anybody I permit to use it.'

I go to put the key in the ignition but, instead, open the car door just in time to vomit into the gutter.

For so long, I thought I could ignore that night. That the grief and sadness and shame could be squashed down forever. After all, hadn't I spent years teaching myself never to be vulnerable – developing a shell no one could penetrate? This was just another thing to stay locked inside me.

Except…

Now is not the time. I have to get to Phoebe.

I scrabble in my bag for a tissue, wipe my mouth and take a deep breath.

I turn the key in the ignition.

I inch out of the parking space. I can do this. I *am* doing this.

318

A junction looms and I slow to a stop. I go to indicate but, instead, turn on the windscreen wipers.

A car flashes its lights to say they are letting me out but I stay put, my hands white on the steering wheel. The other driver shoots me a furious look.

I can't do this. Not even for Phoebe.

I have to.

Another gap appears in the traffic and, this time, I put my foot gently on the accelerator. I am on the main road. I am going.

The pavements are flooded with small children walking to school, book bags and sports kits and musical instruments hanging off them as they skip and bounce, their breath making clouds in the icy air. An image forces its way into my consciousness: me losing control of the car, mounting the pavement and ploughing into the children. Screams of terror and agony.

I hear Emilia's scream as she saw the deer.

Stop it, I tell myself. I am not going to lose control. Driving is not difficult. People do it every day.

The woman in the car behind toots her horn and flashes her lights. Her face in the rearview mirror is twisted and angry.

I ignore her and focus on the road and my breathing.

Traffic lights turn red in front of me. Thank God. You can't hurt anyone when you're stationary. A teenage girl crosses the road, chatting on her mobile. She looks exactly like my sister. I blink and she is gone.

All too soon the lights turn green. Angry woman overtakes me, gesticulating wildly.

I come to a roundabout and, for a fleeting moment, I can't remember who has right of way. I shouldn't be doing this. I could kill someone.

Another person.

Breathe, Loretta, breathe.

I force myself to keep going, following the directions from the satnav and thinking of nothing but the road ahead. And then I start seeing the signs for the motorway.

The motorway.

You can't do twenty miles an hour on the motorway.

Once more, I am covered in sweat.

A motorway is just a big straight road. I can stay in the slow lane.

There are more and more signs now. The countdown is on. I swerve suddenly into a parking space and the man behind me leans on his horn.

I turn off the ignition and start to sob. I cannot do this. Not even for Phoebe.

My hand trembles as I jab at the satnav, looking for another route that avoids the motorway. The journey time doubles. I will miss not only Phoebe's race, but maybe even the whole swimming gala.

A picture of her sad and alone by the side of the pool crashes into my mind. I lay my head on the steering wheel and howl. I'm sorry, Phoebe. I'm sorry, Emilia.

Phoebe has been through so much. The shock of her mother's death, the life-changing grief, and then, just when the world surely could not dish out any more cruelty, the rejection at the hands of her peers. We don't want you. Phoebe has faced all of these blows with a bravery that puts me to shame. Look at me now – too scared even to drive a car.

A scent fills my nostrils. It is achingly familiar and yet I can't immediately place it.

Lemony body spray, clean washing and cherry lip balm.

The smell of my sister.

I open my eyes and sit up with a jolt. The passenger seat is empty. Of course it is. The smell is definitely there, though.

'*Emilia?*' I say.

Nothing.

'*Emilia?*' I stare at the empty space beside me, my nostrils twitching, my brain struggling to process.

And then I hear Emilia's voice inside my head, loud and clear.

You need to get to Phoebe.

'I can't,' I say out loud.

You can.

Chapter Eighty-Three

I pull into the St Dunstan's school car park seven minutes before the swimming gala is due to start.

'You made it,' Chris says.

I nod. He has no idea what that entailed. I scan the poolside looking for the familiar bright yellow cap. And then I see her. She is completely alone, her skin almost blue under the harsh fluorescent light. A few feet from her is a gaggle of little girls, chatting and laughing. Georgia is one of them, the treacherous little cow.

'Phoebe,' I shout, waving. 'Phoebe.'

Her eyes stay fixed on the floor.

'I don't suppose she can hear you over all this noise,' Chris says.

'I want her to know I'm here.' I pull off my shoes and then realise, because I didn't have time to change out of my smart interview outfit, I am wearing bloody tights. There is no way to remove tights from under a pencil skirt elegantly, of course. Still, no matter. It's not as if I'm going to be taking my clothes off in front of Chris in any other context.

I stuff the balled-up tights into my bag and run towards the pool.

'Phoebe,' I shout, as I move closer towards her. She doesn't hear me but a woman with a tight bun and a stance like a bulldog bustles towards me, telling me the gala is about to start and mummies and daddies aren't allowed poolside now.

'Please,' I say. 'I just want to tell her I'm here.'

'If you could take your seat.'

I'm aware of people staring at me. Out of the corner of my eye, I can see Georgia's mother and a group of her mates, looking aghast. A few feet in front of them is Chris.

'I only need a minute,' I say to Ms Bulldog.

'I'm sorry,' she says, sounding anything but.

I don't know if it's the pent-up stress from the drive here but, suddenly, my whole body fills with rage. 'A few months ago, the mother of that little girl over there suddenly dropped dead. An apparently healthy woman of just thirty-one. So, the kid is sad and frightened and alone and I, God help her, am the only person she has today, so I will thank you to step aside right now.'

The woman's pinched face registers several emotions all at once but she takes the smallest of steps aside to let me pass.

'Phoebe,' I say, getting up close to her.

She turns to look at me. 'You came.'

'I came,' I say, sinking down to my knees and pulling her towards me.

Chapter Eighty-Four

Phoebe comes second to last in her race but I clap and cheer as wildly as if she has just won gold at the Olympics. Afterwards, I wait until she has changed so I can see her onto the coach. I'd like to take her back to London in the car but I know that will be against the rules and, anyway, I want to do a lot more driving practice before I take Phoebe anywhere.

Chris catches up with me in the car park and I feel my heart plummet. The stress of the missed interview, the drive, and then seeing Phoebe so isolated and unhappy achieved the seemingly impossible by pushing last night's events to the back of my mind.

But now, they are here in the car park with Chris and me, like assassins who were crouched behind the bushes all along.

'Loretta,' he says, slightly out of breath. 'You were amazing to ditch your interview to come here today and amazing to take on that teacher. I'm sorry I ever questioned your commitment to Phoebe. It's clear you care about her very much indeed.'

'Thanks,' I mumble.

'Also, about last night—'

'Please,' I say, interrupting him. 'Let's not do this. Like I said, I was very overemotional. I wasn't thinking straight.'

'Okay,' Chris says slowly. 'But I am thinking straight, and I have something I want to say to you.'

I stare at the cracked tarmac.

'I don't think you're weird.'

I raise my eyebrows.

Chris smiles. 'Okay, I do, but I think you're weird and rather wonderful.'

I kick at the ground with my shoe in a way that surely portrays an image of a sleek, sophisticated woman.

'And actually, I realised that I have had feelings for you for quite a while now.'

'*Really?*'

'Yes, really. You're a one-off, Loretta.'

'I've been called that before, but it's never been a compliment.'

'Well, I mean it as a compliment,' Chris replies, laughing.

I laugh too and then there's a beat of loaded, awkward silence.

'Listen,' Chris says eventually. 'You obviously have a lot going on in your life right now.'

'Just a bit.'

'So, maybe we could take things really slowly. Starting with a non-date date tonight?'

'Sounds like a plan,' I say, just as Phoebe and a group of kids are led towards their coach. 'But I'm afraid I already have a date for tonight.'

Chris looks confused but then I nod towards Phoebe and he smiles, and, while I'm all for taking things slowly, I have to admit it's a smile that makes my tummy flip.

Chapter Eighty-Five

I am up in my parents' loft, the glow of the camping lantern illuminating the dust motes. The air smells musty and stale. The loft is stuffed full but, as is my mother's way, it's rigorously ordered, with everything from the Christmas decorations to tools in their own neatly labelled clear plastic boxes.

My mother asked no questions when, earlier at the hospital, I told her I needed to collect something from the loft; she just handed over the spare house key. I know her head is full right now.

I move aside a couple of suitcases, my mind serving me up an image of Phoebe's small ride-on tiger suitcase that tripped me up all those months ago. So much has changed since then.

My breath catches in my throat as I see a box that is labelled simply 'Emilia'. This is not what I came for and I am not sure I can cope with it right now. Ditching the interview, that horrible drive, Phoebe being so upset, the conversation with Chris, going to the hospital and wondering as I was buzzed into the ward if today might be the last time I will see my dad – today has been *a lot*. It seems the rational part of my brain isn't talking to my fingers, though, because they are fumbling to unclasp the box. Inside is a jumble of school books, heartbreakingly young clothing and the sort of make-up you wear before you start wearing proper make-up. I pore over the photos, ticket stubs and postcards – memories of a life cut short. I hold a fluffy blue jumper close to my cheek and smell the same scent that filled the car earlier. How weird that was. Rationally, I know it must have been in my imagination, but it was so sudden and so intense. It wasn't just the smell either, but the sense my sister was right there with me.

For months after the accident, no one touched anything in Emilia's room. Dust gathered on half-used tubes of lip gloss and tops discarded on the floor. Then one day I came home from school and it was all gone and the room had freshly painted magnolia walls and new white bedding. It had been transformed into the blandest of spare bedrooms, even though no one ever came to stay.

I look at one of the photos of Emilia holding Auntie Emmanuela's new baby. I remember Emilia feeding him his bottle, her face aglow as she enthused about his pudgy little toes. I could never understand it. Still can't, really. I like Phoebe a very great deal but I have no desire to 'squeeze those little toe toes'.

The thought of Phoebe reminds me why I'm here and I put the fluffy jumper in my bag and close the box.

I carry on with my search, wondering vaguely if what I'm looking for is even here. Maybe my mother gave it away?

Surely, she wouldn't have done that, though, not without asking me.

Suddenly, I spy it stuffed into a dark corner. It's underneath a dust sheet but the shape is distinctive.

I have what I came for.

Chapter Eighty-Six

Phoebe and I return to the flat and, without me even asking, she immediately goes to the bathroom to wash her hands. I feel a small swell of pride and suddenly realised that there is more narcissism involved than people might care to admit, when it comes to the love of a child.

'I thought after all those swimming lessons I might do better in my race,' Phoebe says.

'Hey, you did brilliantly. And even if you hadn't, it wouldn't matter. Your achievements are not you.'

Your achievements are not you? Who even am I? I have spent the best part of thirty-one years chasing things to prove my worth.

'I am very proud of you,' I say. 'And your mum would be too.'

Phoebe looks at me, her eyes dark and serious, and I worry that I've upset her by mentioning her mum, but then she asks me if we can have extra pepperoni on the pizza and if we're going to order it now.

'Yes, and in a bit. I have something I want to give you, actually.'

We go into the bedroom. Rain batters against the dark windows and I close the blinds, grateful to be warm and dry inside. Phoebe, meanwhile, is hopping from foot to foot as she tries to decipher the shape draped under a sheet. 'Go on.'

Phoebe pulls at the edge of the sheet and unveils the doll's house, a small gasp escaping from her lips.

'It was mine,' I say. 'And now, I would like you to have it.'

'Thank you!' Phoebe says, sinking down to her knees. 'I love it!'

The doll's house is smaller than I remembered it, just two rooms downstairs and two rooms upstairs, but it's in pretty good condition considering the years it has been in my parents' loft. Just seeing it takes me back to all those hours spent making up stories in my head about the family who lived in it. Unlike my actual family, they were pleasingly biddable. I blew every penny of my pocket money on buying furniture and still have a visceral memory of the joy when I ripped off the packaging on the miniature green sofa and armchairs. Once, my mother accidentally stood on a tiny kettle and I cried for two days.

I hand Phoebe the clear plastic box that contains the handleless kettle and all my other doll's house paraphernalia.

'A cot!' Phoebe says, pulling it out of the newspaper it is wrapped up in.

'There's a baby for it somewhere,' I say, wondering if I was more maternal than I gave myself credit for. Then, I remember the baby has a slightly chewed leg because I left it in the dog basket.

'It's more fun here without Robert,' Phoebe says.

'*Phoebe!*' I laugh. I have to admit she has a point, though. I miss Robert at times, but it's more that I miss having another living, breathing thing around than missing him per se. Sometimes, the very idea of the two of us planning to get married feels like a fever dream.

'Is Zack's daddy going to be your boyfriend now?'

'No,' I say, feeling myself blush. It amazes me how a child I have to ask to put her shoes on at least three times can somehow have heard some tiny clue to make her ask this question.

Phoebe keeps unwrapping miniature furniture, and each piece brings back a flood of memories. I see my grandma's expectant face as she handed me the parcel containing the four-poster bed, I remember collecting matchboxes to make a chest of drawers like the one on *Blue Peter*, and I recall my fury when Emilia snapped the shade off one of the lamps because I had annoyed her (she wasn't always perfect).

'Do you have any godparents?' I say.

Phoebe's button noses wrinkles. 'What are godparents?'

'Well…' I pause, not quite sure how to explain this. I certainly don't imagine myself taking on any duties in terms of Phoebe's almost non-existent religious education. 'I guess they're people, adults, who promise they're going to be connected with a child throughout their life.'

Phoebe puts down the small wooden dining chair she was examining. 'Connected?'

'Yes, it just means they're not going anywhere. That they are going to be part of their godchild's life. I was thinking I could be your unofficial godmother? If you'd like that?'

'I'd like that,' Phoebe says, putting the dining chair at the dining table.

I smile. Sylvia's reaction was equally low-key. 'Sounds great,' she'd said vaguely. Frankly, I think she is so grateful for any kind of support, I could give myself any title I like.

Phoebe finds the toilet, marvels at how you can depress the teeny flush and then places it carefully in the bathroom.

'Would you like pizza now?' I say.

'Can I play for a bit longer?'

'Sure,' I say, sinking down on my knees next to Phoebe. 'But only if I can play too.' I start unwrapping more of the buried treasure and placing it inside the house. Normally, I struggle to play with kids, even Phoebe, finding the games tedious, but this I could do all day long. It's like having your own perfect little world.

Phoebe peels the newspaper off a small blonde doll with a red and white checked dress.

'The mummy,' Phoebe says, sitting the doll on the couch.

'You okay?' I say, noticing the change in her body language.

'I miss my mummy.' A fat tear rolls down her cheek and sploshes onto the newspaper-clad package she has just picked up.

'I know you do.' I am about to tell Phoebe not to upset her-self – or try to distract her in some way – but it has dawned on me recently that isn't the right thing to do at all. That Phoebe needs to cry and needs to know that's okay, and that my role is just to be here.

The tears stop as quickly as they came, and Phoebe wipes her nose on her sleeve.

'I chatted to your grandma about this, and we wondered if maybe you'd like to go see a grief counsellor?'

'What's a grief counsellor?'

'It's someone who is trained who you can talk to about your mum dying.'

Phoebe stares at the floor and I wonder if the tears are going to start up again. 'I do want to talk about Mummy, even if some-times it makes me sad.'

'Grief counsellors have lots of practice in helping people.' I fiddle with a jug the size of my fingernail. 'Have a think about it. I might talk to one myself, actually – about my sister.'

Phoebe nods. 'If I do talk to a grief counsellor, does that mean I can't talk to you?'

'No,' I say, taking her small warm hand in mine. 'Of course it doesn't. You can always talk to me about your mummy or anything else. That's what godmothers are for.'

Phoebe nods approvingly and places a small roast chicken in the middle of the dining room table.

'There's a bowl of roast potatoes in here somewhere,' I say, scrabbling around in the box and eventually finding it and handing it to Phoebe.

She places it on the table right next to the chicken and rocks back on her heels. 'Good.'

Chapter Eighty-Seven

Phoebe and I are halfway through an unfeasibly large pizza when my mobile rings and an unknown number flashes up.

'Loretta, it's Finn from Hola.'

'*Finn?*' I say, through a large mouthful of half-chewed pizza.

'Listen, Chris phoned me to explain what really happened today and why you had to miss the interview—'

'I didn't ask him to do that. I didn't even know he was going to.'

'Don't worry,' Finn says. 'He made that very clear. Look, he told me today was all about reaching the little girl whose mum died and making sure she wasn't alone at her school swimming gala. That was a very nice thing to do.'

I look across the room at Phoebe. Her small legs are dangling far from the floor and she's munching on a slice of pizza while talking earnestly to the doll's house family, whose dining table, complete with roast chicken and roast potatoes, has been moved to our table so they can have dinner with us.

'I wish you had told my secretary the full story,' Finn says. 'Or asked to talk to me. When she said you just told her "something had come up" and you couldn't make the interview, we both assumed you'd decided you didn't want the job, especially when

Heather asked you if you were ill and you said you were perfectly well.'

'Oh. No.'

Finn clears his throat. 'The thing is, Loretta, this is so awkward, but I've already offered the role to our second-choice candidate. He came in to see me a couple of hours after I was supposed to see you. I wanted to phone you so I could explain properly, but he has accepted the job, and there is no way I can take the offer back. It just wouldn't be fair. I'm sorry.'

'It doesn't matter.' As the words come out of my mouth, I'm surprised to realise I actually mean them. There will be other jobs.

I look over at Phoebe. She has a tiny splodge of tomato sauce on her cheek and is bent over the doll's house family.

I chose the thing that matters.

Chapter Eighty-Eight

'Are godmothers only for people who don't have mummies anymore?'

Phoebe's voice is small in the darkness. My hand is on the doorknob. I have just tucked her into the small fold-out bed I bought this afternoon and turned off the light.

'No,' I say, sitting back down on the bed.

'But I think children without mummies need them more than other children.' Phoebe's voice is thick with tears.

A lump rises in my throat. 'Yes, I think they do.' I reach out and pull her small, warm body towards me. She smells of chlorine and toothpaste. She is too little for all this. She doesn't deserve to have been robbed of her mum. Or her childhood.

We hold each other and cry. Big, messy, hiccupy sobs. I make no attempt to stop her or me.

Eventually, we both judder to a halt and Phoebe pulls back and asks me if I can put the light back on so she can find her water bottle. She takes a big drink and looks at me with the eyes of a sixty-year-old woman. 'Were you crying about your sister?'

'Yes. And your mummy and my dad. I was crying about lots of things.'

Phoebe nods. 'Grandma says it's good to cry sometimes. I

don't know why, though – I think it's horrible.' She wipes her nose on the sleeve of her pyjamas. 'We need to buy a new kettle for the doll's house.'

'Yes,' I say, smiling. It seems like a lifetime ago that I met Phoebe and Kate at the airport and, even though I would do almost anything to undo the dreadful events of that day and bring Kate back, I can't help but acknowledge that my life is so much richer for having this funny, unique little person in it. It's not just that she has wormed her way into my heart – more that she has made me open my heart in a way I thought I didn't know how to.

I stroke Phoebe's hair. 'How come you have bedhead when you only just went to bed?'

Phoebe shrugs. 'Do godmothers take children to swimming lessons?'

'Yes.'

'Do they have them for sleepovers?'

'Yes. I bought you your own bed, didn't I?'

Phoebe gives me a gap-toothed smile. 'What about to the Science Museum?'

I laugh. 'Do you want to go to the Science Museum?' She nods. 'Then I'll take you.'

'Do godmothers see you at Christmas?'

I smile. Phoebe's need to nail things down reminds me of myself when a creative team talk to me about some vague idea. But how many times are you going to mention the product? What does it say about the brand? How exactly will you execute this? 'Godmothers definitely see you at Christmastime.'

'Do godmothers leave you?'

'N—' I stop, thinking of Kate. She didn't want to leave Phoebe. 'Not if they can help it.' I hold my breath, wondering if this answer will be upsetting to Phoebe, but she doesn't seem fazed.

'Tomorrow, I'm going to make a list of more things we need for the doll's house.'

I smile. 'A new kettle.'

'Yes, and more food. They can't have roast chicken every day.'

'No, I don't suppose they can.'

Phoebe yawns. 'But most of all, I want another doll's house person.'

'Oh?'

Phoebe nods. 'Yes, we need to get a godmother.'

* * *

Acknowledgements

It's hard to write acknowledgements without gushing. Especially when you owe so many people so much.

The first thank you has to go to the brilliant Ger Nichol. I feel extremely lucky that you're my agent, always there to offer feedback, advice and unwavering support.

I am equally fortunate to work with Bedford Square publishers. I will go to my grave banging on about *Swimming for Beginners* being one of the first books you acquired! Thank you to Carolyn Mays, who is everything I could wish for in an editor, and Laura Fletcher for believing in Loretta and Phoebe from the get-go. Thanks also to Polly Halsey, Stephen Mair and Sharona Selby and to Henry Steadman for his fantastic cover.

A massive thank you to the D20 Authors. We met during lockdown, and since then we have pulled each other out of plot holes, brainstormed ideas and unravelled the mysteries of the publishing world (some of them!). I am particularly grateful to Frances Quinn for the title and so much more besides. I could not have written this book without you. Gillian Harvey and Louise Fein have also done more than their fair share of cheerleading.

Thanks are owed to Anstey Harris and Sophie Hannah, both of whom have offered lots of support and sage advice.

I'm also in awe of the book bloggers and booksellers whose energy and love of books is so inspiring. I am especially indebted to Hazel Broadfoot and her team at Village Books in Dulwich – it's the best bookshop in the world and that's just a fact.

Thank you to my mates whose stories I steal and who constantly put up with me saying 'No, I'm writing': Hedy-Anne Freedman, Debra Davies, Caroline Donn, Steve Clinton, Sally Bargman, Sara Nair, Katia Hadidian, Carol Deacon, John O'Sullivan, Gemma Champ, Frani Heyns, Nicky Peters, Alex Judge and Georgina Hayward.

My family are just as supportive. My brother, Patrick Crichton-Stuart and my sister, Sophie Crichton-Stuart. And not forgetting the rest of the crew: Jenny Crichton-Stuart, Kit Crichton-Stuart, Harry Crichton-Stuart, Freddie Crichton-Stuart, Toby Green, Lex Green, Saskia Green, Jo Dangerfield and Uncle Bill. And never forgetting Mum and Dad. I wish I could share this with you both.

Thank you to my husband, Stuart, and my sons, Charlie and Max. I'm sure there are more articulate ways of saying this, but I love you more than anything in the world.

Finally, a huge thank you to all the readers who review and recommend my books, especially everyone who takes the time to contact me. Your messages never fail to make my day.

Photo credit: Stuart Gill

Nicola Gill lives in London with her husband and two sons. At the age of five, when all the other little girls wanted to be ballet dancers, she decided she wanted to be an author. Her ballet teacher was very relieved.

When she's not at her desk, you can usually find Nicola reading, cooking up vast vats of food for friends and family or watching box sets. Occasionally, she even leaves the house…

@Nicola_J_Gill

Nicolagill.com

Bedford Square Publishers

Bedford Square Publishers is an independent publisher of fiction and non-fiction, founded in 2022 in the historic streets of Bedford Square London and the sea mist shrouded green of Bedford Square Brighton.

Our goal is to discover irresistible stories and voices that illuminate our world.

We are passionate about connecting our authors to readers across the globe and our independence allows us to do this in original and nimble ways.

The team at Bedford Square Publishers has years of experience and we aim to use that knowledge and creative insight, alongside evolving technology, to reach the right readers for our books. From the ones who read a lot, to the ones who don't consider themselves readers, we aim to find those who will love our books and talk about them as much as we do.

We are hunting for vital new voices from all backgrounds – with books that take the reader to new places and transform perceptions of the world we live in.

Follow us on social media for the latest Bedford Square Publishers news.

🐦 @bedsqpublishers
facebook.com/bedfordsq.publishers/
@bedfordsq.publishers

https://bedfordsquarepublishers.co.uk/